TWO COMPLETE WESTERN NOVELS
IN ONE LOW-COST VOLUME!

HELL TO HALLELUJAH

An unparalleled figure in American legend, Confederate Ranger John Singleton Mosby made history with his strength and courage. In *Hell to Hallelujah*, Mosby leads a Confederate guerilla force into a desperate battle against Union troops and murdering renegades.

RIDE TO THE GUN

Turley "The Butcher" Jaffick and his outlaw gang were the greediest bunch of killers to roam the West. While they were getting rich on stolen cattle, a nearby Army post was starving for meat, and things looked pretty grim. But Dave Stanbuck had an old score to settle with Jaffick, and he wouldn't ride off until "The Butcher" was cut down to size.

RIP-ROARING WESTERN ACTION BY
RAY HOGAN
One of American's Classic Western Writers

HELL TO HALLELUJAH
AND
RIDE TO THE GUN

RAY HOGAN

LEISURE BOOKS   NEW YORK CITY

For my wife—Lois

A LEISURE BOOK®

January 1990

Published by

Dorchester Publishing Co., Inc.
276 Fifth Avenue
New York, NY 10001

HELL TO HALLELUJAH

Foreword

SO NUMEROUS are the legends pertaining to the life of the fabulous Confederate Ranger, John Singleton Mosby, that it is difficult to determine where fact ends and fiction begins. It is indisputable, however, that he was a bold, courageous leader and that he executed feats of such spectacular and daring nature that both the North and the South of a hundred years ago, applauded and admired him and his reckless followers.

There is no historical basis for the events narrated in this book and it, therefore, must be considered fiction. Many of the names, places, dates and incidents mentioned herein will be recognized as actual. It is done so for the purpose of clarity.

Ray Hogan

1

JOHN MOSBY, crouched low in the shallow depression, felt the earth heave and tremble beneath him as the huge artillery shell exploded. Trash, leaves, brush and rock plumed upward in a milling geyser, hung momentarily and then showered down in a pelting rain of litter. He grinned tightly. That had been a close one—only yards away.

He brushed impatiently at the dust that began to settle on his face. Four days . . . four horrible, frightful days filled with din and destruction and violent death. Even Gettysburg with its Little Round Top, Devil's Den, Pickett and Cemetery Ridge, all the other terrible engagements, seemed pale in the shadow of the battle that now raged in the fifteen square miles of tangled Virginia known as the Wilderness.

Smoke, like a thick, smothering blanket, enveloped the area. Fires billowed and raced unheeded, unchecked, through the maze of tinder-dry brush and twisted, sunlight-starved trees. All about him the screaming of cannon shells, the vicious snap of muskets, the cries of wounded and dying men blended in a cacophony of horror. Riderless horses charged back and forth, eyes rolling white with terror: friend fired upon friend and foe alike, unable to determine accurately at whom he discharged his weapon in the hideous, unearthly encounter.

Mosby, dispatched by General Jeb Stuart to observe and report on the left flank movements of Grant's mighty Army of the Potomac, lay quietly in his brushy concealment and waited. Four times that day blue-clad, grim-faced Union soldiers had surged by him: four times men and boys in gray hammered them back. No one seemed to know just where the lines were. It appeared to be more of a sortie involving small parties than a huge contest in which sixty thousand Confederates struggled against almost double their number of Yankees.

Mosby saw now why General Lee had chosen not to strike, that midnight four days before. On scout duty that night with four of his men from the 43rd Battalion, Partisan Rangers, Mosby had witnessed the exodus of the vast Union force, under newly commissioned Lieutenant General U.S. Grant, from its winter quarters north of the Rapidan River. He had realized immediately that this was the beginning of the spring offensive and invasion of the Wilderness, along the western edge of which Lee, with the Army of Northern Virginia, lay encamped. He had watched the horde of blue uniformed men, backed by five thousand wagons of supplies and almost limitless artillery, break down to the shoreline of the two hundred foot broad Rapidan at Germanna Ford, and start across on the pontoon bridge the Yankee engineers had constructed. Within minutes Mosby had had a similar report from one of his men stationed at Ely's Ford, a short distance away. When he was certain it was no false, diversionary tactic on the part of the wily Grant, he had reported to Lee.

The tall, solemn-faced commander of the southern forces, with Stuart and a half a dozen other officers at his side, had listened carefully to the information. After a few moments consideration, he thanked Mosby and turned to his secondary leaders.

"Gentlemen, it has begun. And all is in our favor."

"Do we move at once, sir?" bushy-haired J. M. Jones asked eagerly.

Lee shook his head. "No, General. That is exactly what Grant expects us to do—attack during the crossing. Consequently he is ready for us. We wait. We fight on our own terms, in our own good time.

"Let Grant lead his army into the Wilderness. His artillery will be almost useless there. So also will be Sheridan and his cavalry. Meanwhile we shall take the positions I discussed with you earlier in the evening. Our reception for General Grant will be most warm."

It worked out just as Lee had prophesied. The Union force, encouraged in that it faced no opposition during the crossing of the Rapidan, rolled forward confidently into the wild tangle of the Wilderness. Lee had then struck swift and hard. Grant's Army of the Potomac reeled, recoiled. But there was no place where a retreat and regrouping could be effected. Confusion swept through the Yankees and the invasion bogged down into a desperate, bloody stalemate.

8

Lee had met and countered every move Grant devised, giving thrust for thrust, parry for parry. By the skillful maneuvering of his brigades he had evened the tremendous odds—but the cost was high. J. M. Jones was among those killed early in the engagement. Longstreet met almost the same fate as his brother officer, Thomas J. Jackson, had met at Chancellorsville a year prior: he was shot from the saddle by his own men in the gloomy, smoke-ridden depths of the forest. But fortunately his wounds were only disabling and not fatal as were those of the great Stonewall.

Grant's advance stalled completely. What next would he do? Lee called in his officers to discuss probabilities.

"Grant has said the one way to crush the Confederacy is to defeat the Army of Northern Virginia and occupy Richmond. We can assume that such is what he has in mind. Now, halted here, and with that purpose still paramount, he has one logical move."

"By-pass us, get between us and Richmond," the red-bearded Stuart said at once. "If he could draw us out into the open, he could pound us into the ground with his artillery and superiority of numbers."

"I believe it is what he will attempt," Lee said. He had turned then to John Mosby. "Major, I want you to take a number of your scouts and scatter yourselves along the Chancellorsville road. Advise me of any movements on the part of the Union army along that route."

Stuart, thinking aloud, said, "It's the only thing Grant can do now. Failing to break through here, he will have to swing around us and drive southward, otherwise his campaign has ended practically before it has begun."

"Such is only supposition, of course, but any concerted shift of Union forces on the left flank would indicate that we are correct," Lee had said. "General Stuart, you and your cavalry will stand ready to drop back and bar the road south. Anderson will combine with Longstreet's corps, and, if it becomes necessary, he will make a forced march to Spottsylvania Court House and there oppose any advance by the Union army at that point. However, General, you will not wait for my order but upon being convinced that Grant has such a purpose in mind, you will act."

9

"What about reinforcements, sir?" Anderson, now commanding the wounded Longstreet's men, asked.

"As quickly as I am informed of the Federals' intentions, I shall dispatch both Ewell's and Hill's corps to join you. Fitz Lee's cavalry is already in that area." The commander of the Confederate army had then paused, looked from one man to another. "Is everything understood, gentlemen?"

The officers nodded. Mosby had saluted, hurried off to set up his observation posts fronting Grant's left flank. Now, with the afternoon beginning to wear on, he wondered if Lee had overestimated Grant, if the Union leader had decided to fall back to the Rapidan after all instead of endeavoring to swing wide of the southern forces and striking south for Richmond. There appeared to be little cessation in the fierce fighting. Indeed, the tempo had stepped up on the part of the Yankees.

Grant's big artillery pieces were booming with greater frequency, lobbing their monstrous shells with seeming abandon. Smoke had thickened through the brush and trees and while visibility was restricted, Mosby could hear the shouts and cries of soldiers above the crackle of muskets and pistols as they raced about searching either for the enemy or for their own lines.

"Major—"

Mosby twisted around at the urgent summons. It was Ben Frost, one of the sergeants he had detailed to a post a half mile west.

"Over here," he called. "Careful, there's a company of Yankees off to your left."

"I see them," the Tennessean replied. "Had to work my way around them."

A few moments later the Ranger crawled down into the shell crater where Mosby was hiding.

"Wagons are on the move," he said. "Just like the General expected. Right now they're lined out on the road to Chancellorsville."

Lee had guessed accurately. Grant had elected to skirt the Confederate forces, was sending his supplies on ahead while he covered their departure with sharp fighting. Once they were under way, the main body of the Union army would begin to shift westward and eventually swing south.

"Let's get to the General," Mosby said.

They crawled from the crater on hands and knees, keeping well in the brush until they had circled the company of Federal soldiers. When it was safe, they rose to their feet and started for Lee's command post at a steady trot. The battle appeared to be more to their right now, Mosby noted as they hurried along. That would indicate that the Union forces were already in the process of fading back. It would be a part of Grant's plan.

Lee was not at the post, was somewhere forward with Stuart and Ewell, Mosby learned when they reached the cabin the Confederate general had improvised into a headquarters. The two Rangers immediately struck off in the direction the adjutant indicated and soon located the officers at the edge of a small clearing.

"Grant is on the way," Mosby said, after saluting. "His wagon train is on the road and the brigades seem to be falling back."

Lee, a sheaf of dispatches in his hand, nodded slowly. In the murky gloom his silver hair appeared dull and lifeless.

"It is as we suspected," he said, his voice reflecting his satisfaction. He half turned, looked off toward the south. Standing thus, his profile etched a grim and craggy outline upon the smoky, gray-green of the background. Watching him, John Mosby thought he had never seen such sadness as he beheld in the Confederate commander's eyes during those brief moments. It was as if he looked beyond the apparent victory in the Wilderness, saw nothing but heartbreak and defeat in the days that were to come.

"Gentlemen," he said, his voice scarcely audible above the dull booming of the cannons, the irregular crackling of muskets. "We shall follow the plan outlined. General Stuart, you will proceed in all haste toward Richmond and counter any thrust made upon the capital. General Ewell, issue the necessary orders and advise the other commanders of what is to be done."

Both officers nodded. Only Ewell saluted. Stuart threw his sharp glance at Mosby. "Major, call in your men. We've got quite a chore ahead of us—"

"I regret, General," Lee broke in quietly in that gentle but firm way of his, "Major Mosby's services are required elsewhere. You are, of course, at liberty to make use of the men from his battalion that he has no need for."

11

Mosby studied Lee's features more closely. Stuart said, "Of course, sir."

"These dispatches," Lee said, waving the packet of papers he held in his hand, "were taken off a captured Union courier only a few hours ago. They advise General Grant that steam trains loaded with ammunition and supplies necessary for the continuation of his offensive, are en route from Washington. There is also information that reinforcements are marching to join him.

"There is little we can do about the reinforcements as we must keep our brigades concentrated. They won't matter too greatly in any event. But the ammunition and supplies are something else. By tomorrow Grant will be needing them—particularly the ammunition. If we can prevent the train's arrival, we can enhance our position and likely hold our own against any Union attack.

"The advantage is ours insofar as the country is concerned. Actually, the arrival of reinforcements for Grant will be a factor in our favor since an increase in soldiers means a corresponding increase in demands upon supplies and ammunition. You can therefore see how vitally important the arrival of that train is to General Grant and how advantageous it would be to us if it did not arrive."

Mosby, a slight, slender man alongside the tall Lee and burly Stuart, said, "Yes, sir. I fully understand."

"That's the chore I have for you, Major," Lee said, folding the dispatches and thrusting them into his coat pocket. "Cut Grant's life line from Washington and we shall be able to handle the rest. Now, I have given the matter considerable thought since these reports fell into my hands. I believe the most effective point where you could strike, where the greatest damage could be done— is the Mogatawny Bridge."

2

The Mogatawny Bridge!

JOHN MOSBY had a quick, mental vision of the structure; a towering, two hundred foot long wooden trestle spanning a gorge that split a mountain of the same name. It was a full day's ride north of the Wilderness. Its destruction would, indeed, be a blow to Grant since it would end all rail shipments of men and supplies from the Union capital.

But, because it was of such prime importance, it was one of the most heavily guarded bridges on the railroad. At one time Mosby, himself, with a number of Rangers had patrolled it for the sake of Confederate supply lines. That was when the fortunes of the South were at a higher plane. Now, having pushed back the gray armies, Federal soldiers were performing an identical function.

"I realize such a task involves great risk and presents almost insurmountable odds," Lee said, "but the importance of such a disaster to the Union cannot be minimized. It could very well be the weapon with which we can turn back Grant, for, without supplies and ammunition, an army flounders and soon becomes helpless."

"But the Mogatawny Bridge!" Stuart said, his voice heavy with doubt. "Your pardon, sir, but that is almost like telling a man he is to capture the Yankee capitol building in Washington singlehanded. Now, I have the utmost confidence in the abilities of—"

"As I have said, I am aware of the enormous risks involved," Lee interrupted. "And, of course, Major Mosby has the right to decline. But because of the importance I attach to the mission, I hope he will accept. I place as many men and as much equipment as he deems necessary at his disposal."

John Mosby was only half listening. Already his quick mind was at work, planning, calculating the possibilities. He said, "Two men will be all I'll need. Sergeant Frost here and one more—Private Rutledge. He is expert with explosives. The fewer in the party, the better." The Ran-

13

ger chief paused, looked directly at Lee. "How much time do I have?"

Lee tapped the papers in his pocket. "Not much, according to these. This is Saturday. I expect the train will reach the bridge sometime Monday afternoon, barring delays en route. Two days . . ."

"Enough," Mosby said. "We can leave in the morning, reach the bridge by dark, or shortly thereafter. That will give us the night and part of a day to devise and put a plan into effect."

"Provided you yourself are not held back," Lee said. "It will be slicing matters most thin, Major."

Mosby smiled, his young, black beard bristling in the half light. "We shall make it, sir, never fear. I promise you Mogatawny Bridge and, if possible, the destruction of the train with its supplies, as well."

Lee's eyes lit with a prideful glow. "And I promise you, Major, if you accomplish this, Richmond will never fall into the hands of the northern army!"

Again Mosby smiled. "It appears we have a pact," he said, and extended his hand.

Lee accepted it solemnly. Stuart, silent through it all said, "John, I'll warn you against Sheridan. His cavalry is reported to be prowling the surrounding country, doing what it can to disrupt our communications and supply lines. Have care and be on the watch for him."

"Thank you, General," Mosby said. "Another reason why a small party will be better than a large one. Easier for us to move about."

"Agreed," Stuart said. "And now, I best be about my own duties. I shall miss having you with me, John—and I hope we meet again."

"We shall, Jeb," Mosby replied, taking the cavalry officer's hand. The hidden meaning in Stuart's words had not escaped him and he looked more closely into the eyes of the man he had come to know and respect so greatly. But Stuart only smiled as if dismissing all dark thoughts that had entered his mind, and turned away.

"Good luck," he said as he moved off.

"The same to you," Mosby answered. He watched the cavalryman's departing figure thoughtfully for a moment and then swung back to Lee "With your permission, sir. I'll start making preparations."

14

"By all means, Major. And my own blessings and best wishes ride with you. When your mission is completed report to the usual rendezvous at Dumfries. Orders will be awaiting you there. Goodbye and good luck."

"Thank you, sir," Mosby said. He saluted smartly, spun about and, with Ben Frost at his side, hurried off toward the command post.

Shortly after five o'clock that following morning, Mosby with the tall Ben Frost and Jess Rutledge, a squat, powerfully built Virginian with an uncanny knack for handling gunpowder, rode out of the now almost deserted Confederate camp in the heart of the Wilderness and struck a course due north.

Lee had put the army into motion during the night hours and it was now shifting sluggishly toward the south. Orders had gone out earlier to Anderson but he was already on the move, having acted as instructed, on his own initiative. Stuart, too, had departed into the strangely hushed darkness.

Distributed among the saddle pouches of the three Rangers were eight measures of explosive, cleverly contrived lethal packets with lengthy fuses that had been assembled by Private Rutledge. They needed only to be attached to Mogatawny Bridge and ignited to work their destructive power.

Mosby, having on previous occasions seen proof of the Virginian's skill with his artfully arranged devices, had no doubt in his mind that the bridge could be destroyed completely, once the explosive charges were in place. The problem that faced them was how they might get to the trestle and affix the bombs, as Rutledge termed his brain children.

But Mosby gave it little thought at that moment. It was a question that would be met and answered once they reached Mogatawny Mountain. It would be no simple chore, he knew, but he had encountered difficult, seemingly impossible tasks before and somehow mastered them: he would do so again.

They rode in silence for the first hour, each occupied with his own deep thoughts. When they crossed the Rapidan and pressed on through the low hills, white-spattered now with late blooming dogwood, the sounds of the war dropped further behind them. The muskets had stilled

15

and there was only an occasional sullen boom of a cannon.

But the evidence of the frightful battle was not to be denied. A thick smoke pall hung over the once prosperous mining area, long abandoned and now termed the Wilderness. The breeze was rank with the smell of burning wood, scorched earth, gunpowder—and death. Nowhere could be seen any living man, bird or animal. It was a world abandoned by all.

"Like ridin' out of hell into hallelujah," Ben Frost said in a low voice when they paused to look back. "Reckon any man that went through that fuss has got a right to say he'd been to purgatory."

"Never saw the like of it," Jess Rutledge added. "And I've seen a smattering of skirmishes since the trouble started. Man never knew who was standing alongside him, a southern boy or a bluebelly. Things were that mixed up."

"You figure we won that fight, Major?" Frost wondered.

Mosby, his pale blue eyes focused on smoke far to the west, shrugged. He removed his plumed hat, ran fingers through his brown hair. He was not a big man but a slender one, all muscle and bone and steel wire nerves. A lawyer by profession and enjoying a good practice in Bristol, Virginia, at the time of the war's outbreak, it was paradoxical that he should emerge as the feared leader of one of the most able fighting groups in the struggle. As a guerrilla he had no peer in either Confederate or Union ranks.

"How do you determine who won or lost?" he said. "We stopped Grant, but the war goes on. When it ends, once and for all time, then we can say who won or lost— if there is such a thing of winning at war."

"Reckon this ruckus in the Wilderness might better be called a standoff. Was like two bulls meetin' head on and neither one givin' a inch," Ben Frost said as they resumed the trail.

"Except you'll have to admit Grant gave ground," Rutledge pointed out. "He backed up and cut for another direction."

"He still wasn't hurt much," the sergeant said. "Sure, he lost a lot of men and equipment but he could afford to with them standin' two to one against us. We should've kept after them, kept hittin' them while it hurt."

"Well, they didn't push us out of the Wilderness and

that's what they was hoping to do. Bet that's a heap of satisfaction to you, Major, knowing how you feel about old Sam."

Grant and Mosby were long time enemies. It had been the Union general who branded Mosby and the Rangers as renegades and outlaws, and had issued a directive to all Federal commanders that any Ranger, particularly John Mosby, captured, was to be hanged on the spot. This despite the fact that Richmond and the Confederate States' Congress had officially recognized Mosby's Rangers as a legitimate division of the regular army and given them status as the 43rd Battalion.

"Grant's a good officer—and an able one," Mosby said. "Regardless of my personal feelings I think that, for the first time, the Army of the Potomac has a man at its head that knows how to fight. He'll push hard this summer and we can expect a tough campaign. Big reason why it's so important we knock down Mogatawny Bridge. He'll be desperate for those supplies in another day or two and if we can keep them from reaching him, we will be hurting him where it counts most."

"We'll take care of that bridge sure enough," Rutledge said. "When we get through with it, the Yankees won't figure it's worth fixing up."

"If we can get close enough to it," Ben Frost added. "Ain't that what you say, Major?"

Mosby turned his lean face toward the sergeant. "We'll get to it," he said quietly.

Near mid-morning, with the warm May sun beaming down upon them, they halted at a small creek to rest the horses. They had been riding steadily and had covered the miles much faster than the Ranger chief had expected. They would arrive at Mogatawny Mountain well ahead of the supply train if they maintained their present pace.

"What do we do when we get finished with that bridge?" Rutledge asked as they sprawled out beside the stream. "If there's nothing special, I got a little work around my farm that I ought to be doing, Major."

The Rangers, although attached to Jeb Stuart's cavalry, operated in a different manner from regular soldiers. While the Battalion consisted of as many as two hundred men at times, Mosby generally kept only a few with him on active duty, and permitted the others to follow their

17

ordinary routine of life. When a need for them arose, such as a raid or a special mission, a courier was sent to summon them. After the occasion was over, they returned again to their homes, there to work at farming, or shop-keeping, or whatever their trade or profession might be until once again needed.

It was an independent mode of fighting that all men appreciated and there was seldom anyone who failed his duty or ignored Mosby's call, the penalty for which was an immediate reassignment to the regular army. Nor was there ever a lack of applicants to fill the few vacancies that arose. As a result Mosby commanded, by careful choice, a select band of expertly trained fighters who were the equal of several times their number in warfare.

"No reason why you can't go home when we're finished with this," Mosby said. "General Lee gave me no specific instructions except to report to Dumfries. Same applies to you, Sergeant," he added to Frost. "Seems to me you're due some leave if you want to go home. Don't think you've taken any time off since you enlisted with me."

"Guess my home's right here with you, Major," Frost replied. "The bluebellies burned my place in Tennessee. No call to go back there now."

"No folks left?" Rutledge asked.

"Nope. I'm the last of the Frosts. Yankees saw to that, too."

That explained much to John Mosby. He had wondered about the lanky, drawling Tennessee man. He had joined the 43rd and moved up quickly through the ranks by sheer will and ability. He had learned well and seemed to make a point of always being in the thick of fighting, or of becoming a part of the most dangerous missions. It was easier now to understand why he was so intent on doing more than his share.

The war had disrupted many families, John Mosby realized, thinking of his own. His wife, with their two small children, now lived with his father-in-law, Jim Hathaway. They were not far distant, as actual miles went, but as remote as Inverness insofar as his being able to see and talk to them was concerned. The Yankees kept a constant watch over the Hathaway place, hoping the man they would most like to lay by the heels would one day risk a visit to his family.

"Major!"

Ben Frost's voice was low, urgent. Mosby rolled to his stomach, crawled quickly to where the sergeant lay. "What is it?"

"Cavalry!" Frost muttered. "Blasted bluebelly cavalry —comin' straight for us. Must be some of Sheridan's bunch."

3

IT WAS too late to move, at least for the moment. Better to lie quiet and hope the Yankee horsemen would ride on by. John Mosby stared hard at the captain riding at the head of his company. He was a wide shouldered, florid faced man whose red hair shone brightly beneath his forage cap.

Tom Underwood!

With a start, he recognized the officer. They had been classmates at the University of Virginia and once fairly close friends. When the clouds of war had begun to gather and the inevitable opposing lines to form, they had drifted apart. Both had upheld the solidarity of the Union, believing it unwise to split. But on the matter of State's Rights they could find no common ground. Mosby had championed the cause: Underwood, a Marylander, had unalterably stood against it. Then, when the first gun was fired at Fort Sumter, Underwood had enlisted immediately on the Union side while John Mosby had been true to his native Virginia. This was the first time he had seen the tall redhead since that last day at the University when they had shaken hands, wished each other luck, and gone their separate ways.

"What's our move, Major?" Ben Frost whispered. "They'll be passin' no more'n fifty feet of us, if they keep on comin'."

"Stay low," Mosby said. "No chance to reach our horses now. Let them go by. Then we'll make a run for it."

"If our horses don't give us away," Rutledge murmured.

That was the point of greatest danger. Any one of their mounts, hearing the passing cavalry, or smelling it, could move, nicker and reveal the hiding men. The animals were not likely to be noticed otherwise. Mosby had seen to it that dark colored horses were chosen for the mission. He had exchanged his own favored white for a bay. Rutledge was on a dull, dappled gray and Frost rode a black. All three blended well with the shadows.

"If they do—then do we fight?" Frost asked, a thread of eagerness in his voice. "Could get me that captain and four, five more of them bluebellies with my pistol before they knew what hit them..."

Mosby said, "No fight, Sergeant. If they spot us, we get away best we can. Our job is to destroy that bridge, not to try and wipe out some of Sheridan's cavalry."

The riders drew nearer. Mosby could feel the faint vibration of the horses' hoofs on the soft ground, hear the jingle of bridle metal, the low run of conversation between the soldiers. He watched Underwood closely. The officer rode a few yards forward of his men, his face still and severe. Back of him followed a young lieutenant and a thick bodied sergeant major whose lower jaw thrust outward aggressively. Then came the regulars. They looked efficient, compact and ready for any eventuality.

"Going to pass us by," Rutledge said. "Good break of luck for us."

"Don't move!" Mosby warned. "Give them plenty of margin."

The three men watched the company ride by slowly. Frost said, "Where you figure they're headed, Major? Ain't none of our boys in that direction."

"Probably just a patrol. Would be Grant's idea to keep all our force penned up within the Wilderness area."

"Would mean there's more cavalry scattered around us, then," Rutledge said.

"Expect so," Mosby answered. "General Stuart cautioned me about Sheridan, said he was running loose around the country. Appears he was right." The Confederate officer paused, studied the Yankee cavalry for a few moments. Then, "Be ready to move out. When we do, crawl. Don't stand up. If any of those soldiers happened to look back over his shoulder, he'd see you sure."

They lay quietly for another length of time. Tom Underwood and his men trotted by slowly, began to pull away. Fifty yards.... Seventy-five...A hundred...

"Now," Mosby said.

He twisted about, began to work his way through the low brush toward the waiting horses. Behind him he could hear Frost and Jess Rutledge following.

"Keep low," he warned again.

He raised his head slightly, looked forward. Their hor-

21

ses were a long fifty feet away, standing in a shallow depression. Mosby continued on. When they reached the edge of the small clearing he halted, glanced back toward the departing cavalrymen. They were gone from sight, cut off by a jut of trees.

"Let's get out of here," he said, pulling himself upright and starting for the bay.

Frost and Rutledge were at his heels. They gained the open ground, swung to their saddles. Frost asked, "Which way, Major?"

"Straight ahead. Keep to the brush for the next mile or so—don't want to take any chances on Underwood seeing us. If we get separated, bear north."

"Yankees!" Rutledge suddenly yelled.

Mosby wheeled his horse sharp left. Half a dozen blue-uniformed riders had appeared abruptly before them. A squad flung out by Underwood to comb through the brush. Their appearance had startled the Yankee buck sergeant and his men as much as the unexpected contact had jolted Mosby and his two Rangers.

"Run for it!" Mosby yelled, taking advantage of the surprise. He dug his heels into the flanks of the bay.

The horse bolted forward, plunged head-on at the gaping cavalrymen. Frost sent up a wild, keening yell that echoed eerily, and followed instantly. To his left Mosby could hear the hard driving pounding of Rutledge's gray.

They broke out of the trees onto smooth, open land. A half mile straight away Mosby saw another thick grove similar to the one in which they had hidden. It was their only hope. He bent lower over the bay's extended neck, urged the horse to greater speed.

Gunshots crackled across the hushed, warm air. The Yankees had recovered, were now giving chase. Frost dragged out his pistol, began to throw an answering fire. Mosby looked to his left, to the point where they had last seen Underwood and the rest of his troop. The captain had heard the gunshots and was at the moment swinging his command about and returning at full charge.

Mosby added his own weapon to those of Rutledge and Ben Frost. But neither their bullets nor those of the Yankees were doing any harm at such distance. The danger lay, he realized, in Underwood's ability to slice

22

across the wide, pasture-like flat and intercept them before they could gain the safety of the wood.

"Save your powder!" he shouted at the two men flanking him. "We've got to make that brush before we're cut off." He pointed toward Underwood. The officer and his men, like a swift arrow, were racing in, determined to block their way.

Frost and Rutledge immediately holstered their weapons, concentrated on getting the utmost speed from their mounts. Mosby watched Underwood, out in front of his men by a dozen yards. He estimated their point of meeting. It would be close.

The dark green of the forest was not too far ahead. Mosby glanced over his shoulder. They had left the buck sergeant and his squad well behind. The initial surprise had afforded the Rangers a good start. It was Tom Underwood and the yelling cavalrymen streamed out behind him they must fear.

Mosby began to veer slightly to the right, thus broadening the angle that lay between themselves and the Yankees. In so doing he was increasing the distance Tom Underwood must cover while affecting very little the distance he and the two men with him must cross.

"They're splittin' up!" Frost announced.

Mosby looked again. Underwood and a half a dozen riders were maintaining their direct approach. The remainder of the company was swinging further north. The captain's strategy was evident; his cavalrymen would now reach the wood at three different points. The main body would likely scatter when it reached the grove and begin an encircling action. Underwood, with his squad, would press the Rangers hard from the rear. The sergeant and his men very probably would now slant further to the right. Thus Underwood could hope to trap Mosby and his men somewhere in the center. The Ranger leader turned his attention toward the buck sergeant. As expected, the non-com was drawing off, pointing for an entry farther to the right.

Mosby grinned at Frost and Rutledge. "Going to be a tight squeeze! Keep up close!"

Both men nodded. They had but one chance, Mosby knew; gain the brush, swing off to the side and trust that Underwood and his squad would over-ride them. It was an old trick used many times before but it usually worked well if the brush and trees were dense enough to afford good cover. And if it failed—it meant a fight. But tangling with only a half dozen Yankees would be better than facing the entire company. Unwittingly, Tom Underwood had done them that much of a favor if it came down to a clash.

They reached the first outthrust of growth, plunged recklessly into it. The horses were beginning to tire from the long sprint and Mosby was glad there was not much farther to go. Bending low over the saddle to avoid the branches, he rushed on. He kept a close watch on the edge of the grove, estimating the point at which Underwood would enter.

A long stand of boxwood suddenly shut off his view. Instantly he swerved in behind the dense tangle. He slowed the bay, waited for Frost and Rutledge to draw in beside him.

"Fan out and double back," he said. "Let them go by. Meet you at the edge of the clearing—where we came in."

The two Rangers understood instantly. They wheeled away, Frost cutting off to the left, Rutledge the right. Mosby brought the heaving bay into the depths of the thicket and halted. He could hear shouting over on the north edge of the grove and guessed the lieutenant, with the balance of Underwood's command, had reached the trees and was now voicing his instructions.

At that moment he heard the redheaded captain break into the grove. He had slowed his pace to a fast walk, had his men flung out on either side, like a line of foraging soldiers searching for food. Mosby watched them narrowly. Underwood was expecting just such a trick as the Rangers were hoping to pull off—was taking all possible precautions to not by-pass his intended captives.

But he would. Both Frost and Jess Rutledge were beyond the ends of Underwood's line and Mosby, now out of the saddle and leading his horse deeper into the thicket, was passing through it. When he was exactly abreast the half a dozen riders, he stopped. He could not see either of the two cavalrymen who were to his right and left, or any of the others farther along, but he could hear them distinctly as they moved through the brush.

He waited, immobile as a granite statue, until they were

24

beyond him, and had continued on. He broke out of the thicket a few moments later, and now, with the dense green band between Underwood and himself, he mounted up and rode back to the edge of the grove. Frost and Rutledge were there ahead of him. They greeted him with wide grins.

"We sure suckered that Yankee captain into a tow sack!" the tall sergeant said. "Sure wish we had time to draw up the strings."

"Won't take him long to figure out what happened and come back," Mosby replied. "Let's move on."

"Which way?"

"Straight north. And keep along the edge of the woods, in the brush. Not likely anybody will spot us there."

They rode off at once, Mosby in the lead, followed by Rutledge and then Sergeant Frost

"One thing I'm mighty grateful for," Rutledge said after they had traveled a short distance in silence, "is that one of those Yankee bullets didn't smack into one of our bombs. We'd be sailing yet . . ."

"For sure," Frost said, "but I never did see a bluebelly cavalryman that could hit a barn with a handful of rocks. Major, you figure that Yankee captain will keep on chasin' us? He's bound to pick up our trail once he cuts back and takes a look around."

"Depends on what orders Sheridan gave him," Mosby said. "My guess is that he will—or at least he'll send a squad after us."

"Been watchin' our back trail but ain't seen nobody."

"Keep at it," Mosby replied. "I know Underwood—that captain. He won't give up easy."

They pressed on, always staying in the brush and trees and carefully avoiding the occasional farmhouses they encountered. Likely the families living in them would be friendly, Mosby knew, but he would take no chances. There was always the possibility they would ride straight into the hands of Union soldiers who had been quartered at some strategic point and he was unwilling to risk any uncalled-for delays.

Early in the afternoon they reached the rougher, higher hill country. They were not far from Mogatawny Mountain and the bridge. At the rate they were traveling they would arrive well before sundown—and that, too, held its peril. Yankee soldiers could be expected to be numerous in the area immediately adjacent to the bridge and it would be wise to approach with care, preferably under cover of darkness.

Mosby pulled to a halt. He raised himself in his stirrups, looked ahead to the green crowned hills as he sought to determine the exact location of Mogatawny Mountain. If it were near, they would dismount and wait for night.

The shrill, piercing scream of a woman gripped by mortal fear suddenly ripped through the warm hush.

4

THE SHATTERING cry, arising somewhere off to the left, brought the Rangers around sharply. The sound had been throttled quickly, as though a hand had been clamped abruptly over the woman's lips.

"Where'd that come from?" Jess Rutledge asked, his voice low and strained.

"Back up the slope a piece, seemed like," Frost replied. "Now, what would a woman be doin'—"

Again the cry broke the silence, lifting wild and forlorn and then ceasing in mid-sound. Mosby was off the saddle instantly. Rutledge and Frost dropped beside him.

"Hide the horses, Ben," he whispered. He waited until the sergeant had led their mounts into the deep brush and returned, "Quiet now," he said and began to work his way through the thickets toward the cry.

Fifty yards up the slope of the mountain they again heard noises, this time the dry rustling of leaves, the thick, husky breathing of a violent struggle. Mosby motioned for Frost and Rutledge to fan out, to circle around and move in from different points on what appeared to be a small clearing. When they had disappeared, he counted to ten slowly and then moved on. He heard a voice before he saw a speaker.

"Just you hush yourself, honey. We don't want the rest of the folks down here now, do we? Take yourself a swaller from this here bottle. It'll make you feel right good all over—"

John Mosby parted the thick screen of brush. There were two roughly dressed, bearded men. Between them they were holding a young, blond girl of perhaps eighteen or twenty. One held her arms pinned behind her back while the other attempted to force the neck of a bottle between her lips and compel her to drink. The girl's face was chalk white. Her eyes rolled with terror.

Mosby's hand dropped to one of his pistols—as quickly came away. A shot would attract Underwood and his cavalrymen, if he still happened to be in the area. He reached then into his boot, drew the long, slim bladed knife he carried. He hoped Rutledge and Ben Frost would remember the presence of the redheaded Yankee captain and observe the same precaution. In a single, lengthy stride, he stepped into the open.

"Get away from that girl!"

The two men sprang to their feet, their dark, glistening faces slack with surprise. The girl, free, screamed once more, a shocking, piercing wail, and fainted.

"Who're you?" the heavier of the pair demanded, his stocky shape settling into a threatening crouch. His filth-encrusted hand slid slowly toward the knife thrust in his waistband. "Where'd you come from?"

Before Mosby could reply, the second man, thin and wiry and with a narrow, evil face and close-set eyes, spat noisily and said, "Don't see as it makes no difference. Let's get him, Tobe!"

Both lunged for Mosby. The Ranger chief stepped lightly aside, avoided their clawing hands. At that instant Ben Frost exploded from the brush. Beyond him Rutledge also appeared. There was a brief glitter of metal as the four men came together. The one called Tobe wrestled his pistol into view. Frost batted it out of his hand. The two went over and down, now blade against blade. A few paces away Jess Rutledge got slowly to his feet, his gaze on the quiet figure of the man who had attempted to match his skill against that of the Ranger.

"Scavenger," the stocky Virginian muttered in disgust as he sheathed his knife.

Mosby wheeled to Ben Frost. The sergeant was rising, pulling himself off the body of the man with whom he had fought. A streak of blood lay across his neck where the outlaw's knife had drawn a sharp trace. But it was no more than a scratch. Mosby dropped to his knees beside the girl. He slid one arm under her shoulders, raised her to a sitting position.

"Where you figure she came from, Major?" Rutledge asked.

"Probably kidnapped in a raid around here somewhere," Mosby replied, trying to arouse the girl. "Could mean there are more of their kind close by."

The girl opened her eyes slowly. When they beheld Mosby they flared wide with fright. Her full lips shaped

28

themselves into another scream. Mosby quickly pressed his hand over her mouth, smiled reassuringly at her.

"Don't be afraid. We won't hurt you. Who are you and where are you from?"

The girl stared at him wonderingly. Her glance moved to Rutledge, to Frost and back again to the Ranger chief. The uniform he wore seemed to dispel some of the terrible fear that had seized her. The bright anxiety in her eyes dwindled and she nodded slightly. Mosby removed his fingers. She looked at the still figures on the ground nearby, shuddered uncontrollably.

"They can't hurt you now, ma'am," Rutledge said quietly. "You or anybody else . . ."

The girl was pretty in a doll-like way. She had a round, softly contoured face, light eyes and hair yellow as spring flowers. She glanced down at her dress, ripped and torn by the two men, began to pull it into place.

"I'm Nell Messner," she said haltingly. "We—my folks and I—and a friend, we were captured by these men. And some others. There are more of them . . ."

"Where?" Mosby asked.

"Up on the side of the mountain. In a cave. They're holding us for ransom. My father is Colonel Stephen Messner, of the Federal army . . . We were on our way to my wedding . . ."

"Who are these men who are holding you? Do you know their names?"

The girl moved her shoulders slightly. "No. Only the leader. He calls himself a general. His name is Jackman."

Jackman!

Mosby felt anger rise swiftly within him. Kidd Jackman—one of the most vicious outlaws and cutthroats the war had produced. The man ranged far and wide across the country with a ruthless band of followers, sometimes wearing the uniform of the Confederacy, other times in Union blue—whichever suited his needs. A hundred tales of pillage, murder, rape and kidnapping were charged to him and his band of lawless renegades.

"How many men does Jackman have with him?" Mosby asked after a time.

"At least a dozen. They murdered the escort that was with us. We were going to my wedding. I was to marry Orville Cole—he's a lieutenant and he's with us. We were supposed to be married . . . and then they stopped us and killed those soldiers. . ."

Nell Messner's voice rambled on, became faintly hysterical. Mosby comforted her gently. "Don't worry. You're safe now. We'll do what we can for the others. Who besides your parents and Lieutenant Cole is in your party?"

"That's all . . . Just four of us. They killed all the soldiers. And Orville is hurt. One of them hit him with a pistol when he tried to help me . . ."

"How long have they been holding you?"

"Since early this morning. We've been in that cave ever since they brought us here . . . I just happened to wander away. I needed to walk a bit . . . I was so upset. Those two men must have followed. I didn't see them. They slipped up behind me, caught me . . They carried me here. I tried to fight but—"

"It's all right," Mosby said soothingly. "You're out of danger now. Can you take us to where the others are?"

Nell Messner nodded. "It's not far. Just on the other side of that rise. Will you—can you help us?"

"We'll sure try," Rutledge said. "We'd like to get our hands on this General Jackman, as he calls himself."

Mosby glanced toward the sun. The afternoon was wearing on. They had little time to spare—but he could not abandon the Messner party to the mercies of Kidd Jackman and his renegades, even if it did involve the rescuing of two Union officers.

"We had better start now," he said and then hushed abruptly. The faintest sound off to their left had caught his attention. It could have been a bird, a small animal, or it might have been the scrape of clothing against dry brush. Frost and Rutledge had heard it also. Both stood motionless, listening and waiting.

"What is it?" Nell Messner asked, fear again rising to her eyes. "What's wrong—"

The clearing was suddenly ringed with men. Mosby's hands darted for the pistols at his hips, halted. A huge, grim-faced individual, dressed in a faded Confederate officer's uniform, swaggered into the open. His small, black eyes were hard and his thick lips, buried deep in a matted beard, pulled down to a cruel grin.

"Go ahead, soldier," he said. "It'll be a sudden way to die."

30

Mosby recognized Jackman from previous descriptions. He remained motionless, his gaze on the outlaw. Jackman grunted, touched Rutledge and Frost with his icy glance. "Looks like we've gone and got us three of old Jeff Davis's boys."

One or two of his men laughed dutifully. They all crowded into the clearing. Nell Messner began to sob again. Jackman placed his attention on her.

"Told you not to go meanderin' off, didn't I, girl? Told you some of my boys might take a fancy to you. Next time maybe you'll mind old Kidd."

"Tobe's dead. So's Enoch," one of the outlaws said, crouching over the two men on the ground. He started at once going through the dead renegades' pockets, removing everything, valuable or not. Their pistols and knives he handed to Jackman.

"Dead, eh?" the outlaw leader echoed unfeelingly. "Well, they wasn't much count nohow."

"Cavalry comin'!" a voice warned from the edge of the clearing. "Yankees!"

Jackman knelt swiftly. He seized Nell Messner, spread one huge hand over her lips. With the other he pressed the point of a knife against her white throat. He glared at Mosby.

"One sound out of you Rebs and she's a dead gal!" he warned. "Get down—all of you!"

There was nothing to do but comply. Mosby nodded to Frost and Rutledge, dropped to a crouch. Jackman's men followed their leader's order. The cavalry was likely a part of Underwood's company, Mosby realized. Being in the area they too, had heard Nell Messner's screams, just as had Jackman.

"Keep an eye on them, Andy," the outlaw chief murmured to one of his followers. "And somebody get the guns off these here Rebs. Quiet now."

Mosby felt his belt lighten as the two revolvers were removed. No further search of his person was made. He watched Frost and Rutledge as they also were relieved of their weapons. He smiled inwardly. They still had their knives, carried inside their boots as all Rangers were taught to do.

"They've gone on," the man called Andy announced, crawling back into the clearing. "Headed straight out

31

across the valley. Reckon they must have heard the gal yellin'."

Jackman grunted. "Maybe they've gone and maybe they're only foolin'. Go back and take another look. Got to be sure."

"Hell, Kidd, they done rode off!" Andy protested. "Seen them with my own eyes—"

"Take another look, damn you!" Jackman snarled.

Andy scurried off. The clearing lay in silence, broken only by the smothered sobs that came from Nell Messner. Mosby studied the waiting men. Seven, including Jackman. The possibilities for escape were slim, although they might pull it off successfully. But to attempt anything at that moment would imperil the girl's life. Kidd Jackman was a man who would do exactly as he promised. Mosby glanced toward the sun again. There was still a little time left. Better to wait until Nell Messner was out of Jackman's reach before they made their try.

Andy returned to the clearing, walking upright. "They're for certain gone now, Gen'ral," he said carefully. "Standin', you can see them on the yonder side of the valley."

Jackman released the girl, rose to his feet. The others followed his example. Mosby looked out across the long swale. Six blue uniformed riders were just disappearing into the trees.

"Good," Jackman said. "Now we'll be gettin' back to camp. Any of these Johnny Rebs takes a notion to cut and run for it, blow his head off. Them Yankees won't be hearin' us this far off."

He reached down, seized Nell Messner by the arm and jerked her violently to her feet. "Come on, girl. Get back to your mama. But next time you go traipsin' off into the woods, I won't be comin' to help when you holler. I'll just let my boys go ahead and have themselves a time with you."

5

THEY STARTED up the mountain, Jackman in the lead dragging the unwilling girl along behind him. Mosby and the two Rangers came next with the rest of the outlaws bringing up the rear. They traveled a short distance, reached the crest of a low ridge, and dropped off into a sharp ravine. Mosby saw the cave then. It appeared to be the mouth of an abandoned mine shaft.

At their appearance three men, evidently left by Jackman to guard the remaining prisoners, came to their feet and moved out a few paces. At the same time Nell Messner's mother, a cry breaking from her lips, rushed by them and hurried to her daughter. The girl wrenched free of Jackman and the two women met, clinging to one another.

"She's all right, madam," Jackman said, "but this sure better be a lesson to her—and to you. After this you keep an eye on her."

Mrs. Messner, an older edition of Nell, swept Jackman with a hate-filled glance. She seemed about to say something, paused when she saw Mosby and his men. Abruptly she turned away and started back for the cave with her daughter.

The two captive officers appeared in the mine's entrance at that moment. One, a tall, lean, sharp-faced man with piercing, dark eyes, wore the uniform of a full colonel of the Union army. The other, a lieutenant, much younger, had a blood stained bandage about his head. He would be the fiancé of Nell Messner, Orville Cole.

Messner took a step toward the women. "Amanda, is she all right?"

One of the guards wheeled quickly about, lifted the musket he held and made as if to strike the officer.

"She's all right," Amanda Messner replied.

The Yankee colonel fell back a step before the renegade's threatening pose. Mosby saw Cole's shoulders go down in relief when he heard the older woman's words.

33

Messner glared at Jackman. "A good thing for you she's not harmed," he said. "I would have—"

Jackman halted in front of the officer. "You would have what?" he said with a broad smirk. "Just what would you do about it, Colonel?"

The officer waited until the two women had passed and were inside the cave. His eyes never wavered from those of the outlaw. "I would kill you, Jackman. With my bare hands if need be."

The renegade chief made a slight motion with his hand. The man standing next to Messner with the upraised rifle swung quickly, drove the butt into the officer's belly. Messner gasped, buckled forward. An oath exploded from Orville Cole's lips. He lunged at the outlaw. Another man standing near him extended his foot. The lieutenant tripped, went sprawling to the ground. Messner slowly straightened, pain contorting his face. He reached down stiffly, grasped Cole's arm and helped the young officer to his feet. His gaze came back to Jackman.

"I say it again," he said, speaking slowly and with great effort. "I would kill you."

The outlaw with the musket moved to deliver a second blow. Jackman shrugged, turned away. "Get him inside, out of my sight," he said, and swaggered to where Mosby and his men watched and waited in silence. "Now, just who the hell are you buckos? Deserters?"

Mosby seized the cue thrust at him. "Might call us that. Who are you?"

"Me? I'm General Kidd Jackman. These boys are some of my private little army. We kind of operate on our own."

A ripple of laughter ran through the men gathered around. Messner and Cole were back in the cave with the two women. Mosby glanced about, escape once again a paramount item in his mind.

"That's a might fancy uniform you're wearin'," Jackman said, looking more closely at Mosby. "You take it off'n some Reb officer?"

Mosby shrugged. He was proceeding cautiously, allowing matters to take their course. Until he had a workable plan, it was better to go along with Jackman and his band of outlaws.

"Plenty more around," he said. "Especially over Wilderness way."

Jackman's bushy brows lifted. "That where you come from? Heard there was quite a fuss goin' on. Who come out on top?"

Mosby shook his head. "Not finished yet. Last we heard Grant was moving toward Richmond."

"He'll get there, too," Jackman said, confidently. "He's a regular bulldog when it comes to fightin'. But it ain't nothin' to us. Point now is what am I goin' to do with you?"

Mosby said, "You could let us join your outfit. We know this country better than most men."

Jackman was again examining Mosby's uniform, seemingly fascinated by it. "Sure do wish them duds was a bigger size. Mighty fancy and I'm needin' a change. You figure you'd like to join up with me, eh? What they call you?"

"John. John Singleton. My tall friend there is Ben. Other one is Jess."

"Well, John Singleton, I just don't take on recruits because they've a mind to join up. Ain't so easy to get in my army. Anyway, I don't know nothin' about you. Maybe you're who you are and maybe you ain't. Few things I got to know first. Somehow I got a feelin' I know you from somewhere. We ever met before?"

"Don't remember it if we did," Mosby replied. "Of course, I've been around this part of the country a long time. Could be our paths crossed. Way I see it, you're two men short now. Leaves room for my friends and me."

Jackman spat. "Reckon I didn't lose much when you killed Tobe and Enoch. All they thought about was likker and women."

"Could be they're part of that there bluebelly cavalry we seen," the outlaw called Andy said. "Could be they've been sent here to do some spyin' on us—"

"Was Union cavalry," another man pointed out. "These here potlickers is wearin' Reb clothes."

"Could still be bluebellies, couldn't they? Just dressed that way to fool us."

"I don't figure we need no more men, Gen'ral," a third man, much older than the others, observed. "We gets too big, makes it hard for us to move around easy. On top of

35

that the divvyin' up is thin already. Ain't hardly worth a man's time no more—"

"I'll do the decidin'," Jackman cut in harshly. "I'll say what we do and what we don't. Just don't you go forgettin' who's runnin' this army, Rufe!"

"I ain't forgettin'! Was just thinkin as how we—"

"Don't do no thinkin' either! Could get you in a heap of trouble."

Rufe moved in a step. His face worked angrily. "Now, wait a minute here, Kidd! We started out in this here thing together. Reckon I got a right to speak my piece—"

Jackman took a long stride forward. He lashed out with his ham-like hand. It caught Rufe squarely in the face, sent him reeling backwards. His heel caught against a rock. He went down, cursing volubly. Jackman spun, glared at the others. His thick shoulders were hunched, his coarse, bearded face out-thrust.

"Any more you privates got a question about who's headin' up this army?"

There was a long minute of silence. A tall, young-faced boy finally answered. "No, sir, General. Reckon there sure ain't."

Jackman's huge frame relaxed. "Then don't let me hear no more of the kind of talkin' Rufe just done. Maybe we'll be takin' these Rebs in and maybe we won't. I'll make up my mind when I'm good and ready. And when I do, there ain't goin' to be no bellyachin' about it. That understood?"

"Sure, Gen'ral, sure."

The outlaw chief returned to Mosby. "And you better pack that in your head, too, Mister John Singleton. You got the looks of a man who might want to run things his way. Well, around here I say what goes. I'm the general. You got that straight?"

Mosby nodded. "Only one man gives the orders in any army. I know that. And you're the general here."

Jackman moved his head with satisfaction. "Right. Just don't be forgettin' it."

Mosby, playing it all the way, said, "Yes, sir. Now, can we have our pistols back, General? We feel kind of undressed without them."

"Not so fast," Jackman said. "I ain't said you was with

36

us yet. Got to mull it around for a bit. I keep thinkin'
I've seen you somewheres."

"Gen'ral," one of the outlaws cut in, speaking in a
respectful voice, "If'n you don't jine them to us and we
got to kill them, can I have one of them pistols? This
old musket I'm carryin' sure ain't much good no more."

"That there uniform would sure fit me good," another
added hastily. "I'm askin' for it first, Gen'ral."

Mosby saw Ben Frost stiffen. The Tennessean had
listened to about all he could stand. He caught the sergeant's eye, shook his head slightly. It was hard to anti-
cipate Kidd Jackman's decision but, regardless, the time
to act was not yet at hand. He again gauged the sun. They
could not wait much longer, however. That was a definite
fact.

"Throw them in the cave with the others," Jackman
said. "Ain't nobody takin' nothin' until I decides what I
want to do and have my own first pick of things. Joe,
you and Tombo stand guard. Don't let none of them come
out unless'n I say so."

The outlaw turned away. "Andy, you and Shakespeare
trot over there to the ridge. Take a good look around and
see if there's any sign of that cavalry. Rest of you start
stirrin' up some vittles. Most time to eat."

"Why don't we make them women do the cookin',
Kidd?"

"Main reason is I don't figure you'd leave them be long
enough to get it done. Besides, I got some other plans
for them. Now, get movin'..."

Mosby felt the hard, round muzzle of a pistol jab into
his back. "You heard the Gen'ral. March yourself up to
that there cave and get inside. And don't poke your head
out 'til he hollers for you, less'n you want it blowed off."

6

THERE WAS little light in the cave, only the reflected rays of the sun breaking the darkness. Mosby, flanked by Rutledge and Frost, halted just within the entrance and allowed his eyes to adjust to the sudden change. He could hear Nell Messner somewhere over to his right, still sobbing softly.

Gradually the surroundings became more distinct; the rough walls of the mine's entrance, the rotting timbers overhead, the shaft itself fully blocked by a cave-in. He made out the two women crouched in a far corner. Near them, distrust strong in his attitude, stood Stephen Messner. Cole, his back resting against the opposite wall, squatted on his heels, head between his hands. He looked up, his face mirroring the pain that flogged him and the hopelessness that possessed his mind.

"Nell has told us what you did," he said. "We want to thank you—"

"Don't waste words on this trash!" Messner snapped. "I doubt if she would have been any better off, had Jackman not come onto the scene when he did. You heard them talking out there. They're no better than the others."

Mosby stared at the officer while anger ripped through him. He heard Ben Frost mutter something under his breath. But it would be only natural for the Yankee officer to think such of them, he realized in the next moment. The conversation he had carried on with Jackman would have given anyone listening that impression.

"Think what you will, Colonel," he said quietly, "but we're not renegades."

"We're not deaf, Singleton," Messner replied. "Given the opportunity I'll wager you would follow exactly in the footsteps of Jackman."

Mosby turned to Rutledge and Frost. "Stand by the entrance. Warn me if anyone comes this way." He waited while the two Rangers took up positions on either side of the opening, then he again faced Messner.

"My understanding from your daughter is that you

are being held for ransom. Do you have any plans for escape or are you under the impression that you can deal with Jackman?"

At the mention of escape Orville Cole came off the floor. "Is that what you have in mind—escape?"

Mosby moved deeper into the cave. "We don't intend to remain here and let them murder us," he said.

"Have you a plan?" the young lieutenant asked in an anxious voice.

"Not at the moment."

Messner wheeled angrily to Cole. "Hold your tongue, Lieutenant! Can't you see this is some kind of a trick—that he's hand in glove with Jackman?"

"Major—" Jess Rutledge warned softly. "Man coming."

Mosby moved to the wall of the cave, leaned against it. A figure darkened the entrance, paused there momentarily, and then passed on.

"All clear," Rutledge said after a time.

Messner's hot eyes were on Mosby. "That man called you major. That mean you are a secessionist officer?"

"I am an officer in the Confederate army."

"Rebel traitor!" Messner spat. "That's what you mean. Name?"

Mosby shrugged. "It's of no concern to you and it doesn't matter here."

"The name you gave Jackman is false?"

"Perhaps."

Messner drew himself up. "Well, officer or not, I can't see that it matters. We are still in the hands of brigands —freebooters—"

"It does matter!" Orville Cole exclaimed. He wheeled to Mosby. "Major, if you plan to escape, get us out of here, too. Please! If you can't manage for the colonel and me, at least take the women. You know what's ahead for them!"

"Lieutenant Cole!" Messner shouted. "Remember your position! You are an officer of the United States army. You will not beg this rabble for our lives!"

Cole faced the colonel. "I'll get down on my hands and knees, if necessary," he said. "Anything to get Nell and Mrs. Messner out of here."

"You're a fool!" the officer barked. "A blind, stupid fool! And you're a disgrace to the uniform you are wearing. You heard what was said out there."

"That was a matter of prudence," Mosby said. "If you weren't so overburdened with pride and dignity you would have realized what I was trying to do—simply gain Jackman's confidence. Then we would have a chance." The Ranger chief spun about, walked quickly to the mouth of the cave and looked out. Anger brightened his eyes, shot color into his cheeks and his lips were a pale, firm line. Men like Stephen Messner were fools to begin with; putting an officer's uniform on them multiplied their short-comings, amplified their egos.

He watched Jackman's men, scattered about in the small clearing, while the heat within him died slowly. Several of the outlaws worked over the fire, above which a soot blackened kettle simmered. The pair Jackman had sent to look for Underwood's cavalry had returned and were talking with the outlaw leader. Apparently all was well. He could almost wish the Yankee captain and his men would show up. At least the odds against the renegades would be more even. And he would as soon take his chances on escape from the cavalrymen as he would from the outlaws.

"Major," Jess Rutledge said, "what are we planning to do? Sure can't stay here long if we're going to get to that bridge in time. You got any ideas?"

"Only one—escape soon as possible. Jackman's worrying me some. There's something he's trying to remember and it could mean trouble for us, if he thinks of it."

"Maybe he'll wait until mornin'," Frost said. "Sort of sleep on it. What about these Yankees? I heard what that lieutenant said about taking them with us. We sure can't be bothered with them. Goin' to be hard enough gettin' away."

"That's part of our problem, Sergeant."

"Then I reckon we better just forget them. That stiff necked colonel don't figure us for much anyway. Let them get out of this mess they're in best way they can."

"But the women!" Jess Rutledge protested. "Like that lieutenant said, we can't leave them to Jackman and his bunch of scavengers."

"Why not? Been a lot of fine southern women who got the same treatment from bluebelly soldiers. They ain't no better than them. I figure it's that colonel's worry. We got a real important chore to be doin'. You said so

40

yourself, Major. Ain't nothin' should keep us from doin' it—and that includes Yankee soldiers and their women."

Frost's bitterness was not difficult to understand. Mosby recalled the sergeant's words spoken earlier when they had talked of home.

"Everything you say is true, Ben" he said softly, "but we've got to keep this in mind. They're people, just like us—just like our own folks. Maybe they are on the other side of the fence in this war but right now we're lined up against a common enemy—Kidd Jackman and his renegades. Makes a difference."

"Expect you're right," Frost said, unconvinced, "but I don't figure we ought to let them get in the way of us blowin' that bridge to hell. To my way of thinkin', it's a sight more important than they are."

"No question about it," Mosby said and lapsed into silence.

Their position was growing critical, there was no denying that. They must get free and reach the Mogatawny Bridge. The very life of the Army of Northern Virginia could depend upon Grant's failure to receive the supplies and ammunition being shipped to him. But to escape, to flee and leave the Messner party—Yankees or not—in the hands of Kidd Jackman, was a decision John Mosby found hard to make.

"I figure we can get out of here without much trouble," Frost said. "Soon as it's dark. Won't be no chore slippin' by Jackman's guards and reachin' our horses. And we can get back our pistols. Saw right where they put them. But if we go tryin' to take them Yankees with us, we got us a big problem. First off, what'll they do for horses? Ain't seen none around here."

The sergeant was right on that point. Mounts would have to be provided for the Messner party. That Jackman had horses hidden somewhere in the area was probable but it might take time to locate them, get them ready. And every minute would count. Under such circumstances—did he dare to help? With the importance of the Mogatawny Bridge and its destruction facing him, did he have the right to jeopardize their chances for escape?

Rutledge, quiet through most of the hushed discussion, said, "I leave it up to you, Major. Whatever you decide is

41

good for me, but if it comes to a vote, I say we got to at least take the women with us."

"And I say we better be thinkin' about that bridge and General Lee and the army. Let them Yanks look out for themselves," said Frost.

"Vittles is ready!" a voice near the fire sang out.

Jackman and his men began to gather. Each carried a plate or a small tin can that was to hold his portion of the stew or whatever it was the blackened kettle contained. Mosby counted the outlaws. Thirteen in all, including Jackman. Each received his share of the food, then backed off to the side to eat.

"Smells good," Rutledge commented. "Hope they got enough to go around."

The sun was down. Darkness was beginning to close in. Mosby, staring out across the hills, was endeavoring to fix landmarks and directions in his mind before all were hidden by the night. Once they escaped, if they managed to, there would be no time for indecision. He must head directly for Mogatawny Mountain without delay. Straight up the valley that lay ahead, he saw, was the course they must follow. Beyond its far rim should lie the mountain—and the bridge.

He touched Rutledge and Ben Frost on the arm, gave that information to them. "In case we all don't get through and you have to go it alone," he said. "We each have enough explosive to do the job."

"Hope they haven't found our horses," Rutledge said, voicing a new possibility.

Mosby considered that for a few moments. "Don't think they have. Otherwise they would have brought them into camp."

"Here comes our supper," Frost said, pointing at two of the renegades moving toward the cave. Between them they carried several cans of the stew. "Might be a good time to get ourselves some weapons."

"Be eleven of them left out there," Mosby said. "They'd have us trapped like rabbits in a snare. We'll have a better chance later."

"Sure, Major, reckon I know that," Frost said. "Guess I'm gettin' a mite jumpy."

Mosby smiled at the lean Tennessean. "Don't fret, Ben. The time will come."

7

THE OUTLAWS halted at the mouth of the cave. They placed the cans of stew on the ground, hastily drew back a few paces as though fearing to get too close. In the half darkness Ben Frost chuckled.

"Looks like we got them walkin' soft, Major. Even when they got all the guns."

Mosby nodded. But it meant something else to him. It was an indication that their chances for escape might be smaller than he had anticipated. Apparently Kidd Jackman had given orders to use extreme care and take no risks with the Rangers.

Rutledge stepped forward, picked up two tins of the food. He carried them to Nell Messner and her mother. Mosby listened to their exhausted refusal. He glanced to Messner.

"I suggest you persuade your wife and daughter to eat a bit, Colonel. Going to be cold tonight and they will need all their strength."

Messner's face stiffened. "I'll not force my family to eat that swill, not if they're unwilling.

Cole moved by Mosby, took up his portion of the food. There were no spoons or forks and it was a matter of sipping the steaming liquid from its container. After a swallow or two, he said, "Little more than water but it is hot."

Mosby and the Rangers ate their shares, finding Cole's comments to be accurate. Messner refused, as had his wife and daughter. While they ate, Mosby watched the activities of the outlaws. The two men who had brought their food, had returned to the fire and now, with the others, were squatted around it.

Jackman sat on a log and stared into the flames. The fire was purposely small, Mosby realized, so that no glow would be noticeable from the valley beyond the ridge. The outlaws came and went periodically, slipping off into the darkness to return a short time later. Each was making the trip to the top of the hill, apparently, where he spent a time

43

observing the valley. Evidently Jackman was not convinced that all danger from the Yankee cavalry was past.

It grew completely dark within the cave. Night began to set in, chill and damp. A fire inside was, of course, out of the question since there was no chimney for the smoke. One just outside the entrance might prove of some benefit and Mosby considered it for a time. He discarded the idea. It was better to suffer the cold and keep the area entirely in darkness. A fire would light up the mouth of the cave and make it impossible for them to do any moving about without being observed.

They must act soon. Time was running out. Mosby throttled the impatience and urgency that pushed at him. They could do nothing until the renegades fell asleep; then would come the moment to make their move.

He crossed to where Orville Cole was again hunched, back to the wall. He knelt beside the young officer. "Didn't notice any horses when we came in. They have them hid out somewhere close by?"

Cole said, "About fifty yards on down the ravine. There's another abandoned mine shaft. They've thrown up a rail fence across the front of it. Horses are in there." He paused, looked more closely at the Confederate leader. "You getting ready to make a break for it?"

Mosby nodded. "Nothing we can do until Jackman and his bunch quiet down."

Cole laid his hand on Mosby's wrist. "I'm asking you again, as one man to another—take the women with you when you go. Leave the colonel and me, if you have to, but, for God's sake, get Nell and her mother out of here!"

John Mosby glanced toward the fire in the clearing. At that moment two of the outlaws were looking in the direction of the cave, their dark faces thoughtful, hopeful. The Confederate turned to the young officer. "Might as well take all of you as half. What about the colonel? Will he do as he's told?"

"He will!" Cole said quickly, his voice alive with eagerness. "Maybe he won't show it but he will be grateful. And he won't give you any trouble. Does this mean you'll help us—all of us?"

Mosby studied Cole for a long minute. "Lieutenant, we may be on opposite sides in this war but that doesn't mean I'm not a human being. I'll tell you frankly, it's not

44

convenient for us to aid you in any way. We have an important job to do and this could delay us dangerously in the completion of it. But I can't leave you here in Jackman's hands. In return, I expect you to give us no trouble. Do I have your word on that?"

"You have," Cole said, solemnly. "As an officer and a gentleman."

"Good. Now, keep this to yourself. Don't say anything to the others just yet."

Mosby moved back to the mouth of the cave where Rutledge and Frost maintained their watch. "Horses are below us," he said. "Fifty yards or so, according to the lieutenant. They've built a yard in front of another mine shaft."

Frost did not look around. "That means we'll be takin' them Yankees with us. Well, I'm all for it, Major. Wasn't thinkin' straight when I said what I did. I'm sorry."

Mosby said, "It's all right, Ben. I understand how you feel. But war or no war, a man has to do the decent thing."

"I know that but sometimes the past just sort of crowds up in front of a man and keeps him from seein' things straight."

"When do we make the break?" Rutledge asked. "Don't like the way some of those cutthroats keep looking this way."

"I think looking is all they're doing. There's too many of them for us to rush. All we can do is wait for Jackman and most of them to go to sleep. Then we'll know what we're up against in the way of guards."

"Looks like they're startin' to turn in now," Frost said.

Mosby swung his attention to the men sprawled around the fire. "Can't be too soon," he murmured. "Every minute that goes by hurts our chances so far as that bridge is concerned."

"Major," Rutledge said, "supposing we get hung up here and don't make it in time. What about wrecking that train somewhere along the line?"

"That's our second choice. We can blow it up, destroy the supplies and tear up the tracks some but it would be only a temporary set-back for them. They would soon have repairs made and another train on the way."

"We just got to get to that bridge," Frost said. "Once it's down, they're out of business for months. It's the only sure way to put a crimp in Grant. We've got to make it, Major."

"We're going to try," Mosby said quietly. "Careful. Here comes Jackman."

The outlaw leader had risen to his feet. He glanced toward the cave, walked closer to the dwindling fire. He halted there, gazed down at the men lying about. After a few minutes he strolled on in the direction of the mine shaft opening.

"If he's onto you, Major, we better grab him," Ben Frost murmured. "Maybe we could use him as a hostage to get by the others."

Mosby nodded. "Be ready. I'll give you the signal if it comes down to that."

But Kidd Jackman was no less careful than his men. He halted a full dozen paces in front of the cave's entrance, well out of reach. "Singleton! You awake in there?"

Mosby said, "I'm awake."

"Want to ask you a question. Still can't keep from thinkin' I've seen you somewheres. Was you ever in Springfield, down Missouri way? Seems I recollect somethin' there."

"Wasn't me, General. Never been in that town."

"You sure? I'd a swore it was Springfield."

"Have to be somebody else. Maybe if you'd sleep on it, it would come to you."

"Reckon that's right. You say you'd never heard of me, either?"

"No. I've heard of you. Expect everybody has."

"Reckon that's a gospel fact," Jackman said, pride filling his voice. "Where'd you say you got that uniform you're wearin'?"

If Jackman was attempting to trip him up, Mosby thought, he's making a poor job of it. He said, "Over around the Wilderness. Find plenty of them there, both kinds, if you head out in that direction."

"Just might do that."

The outlaw wheeled about, walked back to the fire. He nudged two of the now sleeping men to wakefulness with his toe. "Claude, you and Tombo stand watch on them prisoners. Better set yourself right up there at the mouth of the cave. You get sleepy, roust out Dever and

Corbett and trade off with them. I want somebody watchin' the whole night."

The two men struggled to a sitting position. One rubbed at his whiskered jaw, said, "You sure there's a need for it, Kidd? They ain't goin' no place. We'd ketch them afore they got a half mile. And I'm mighty well tuckered—"

Jackman drove his boot into the man's rump. "Get up there like I told you!" he roared. "Damn it! It's got so I can't give an order without gettin' back a lot of lip. I'm tellin' you I'm sure gettin' fed up with it!"

The pair scrambled to their feet, trotted off for the cave. Jackman turned away, still muttering, and settled down beneath the overhanging branches of a small tree.

"Dang it all!" the man called Claude exclaimed as he took up a position beside the entrance to the shaft. "Old Kidd sure is touchy nowadays. Just can't say nothin' to him without he jumps down your throat."

"Somethin's sure come over him," Tombo agreed, leaning back against the opposite side. "Reckon we'll be in for a hard time of it if Durham don't show up with some good news about that there ransom."

"You think the Yankees will fork over all that money he askin' them for?"

Mosby, with Rutledge and Ben Frost close by, listened to the conversation. They made no noise, kept well in the shadows.

"Kidd sure thinks so. Says that colonel we got is real high up and mighty important. And him havin' his womenfolk with him makes it all the better. Claude, you got any that drinkin' likker left?"

"Not a drop. Sure could use a swaller or two myself."

Jackman was asleep. Mosby could see the regular rise and fall of the man's barrel-like chest. The remainder of the men had also dropped off. Mosby counted the number of figures. Ten . . . twelve including Claude and Tombo. One was missing There should be thirteen. Where was the absent outlaw? A frown creased Mosby's brow. Was he standing guard at the edge of the camp, a precaution Mosby had not expected Jackman would take? Was he with the horses, or possibly on the ridge where he could watch the valley?

47

"How about it, Major?" Rutledge whispered. "We move out?"

"One man missing," Mosby answered. "Ought to know where he is before we do."

"Sure didn't see anybody leave."

Finding out would take time—and there was none to spare. They would have to risk it. To Frost and Rutledge he said, "Take care of the two guards. Then prop them up so they will look natural. I'll get the Messners and Cole."

The two Rangers glided silently through the cave's entrance. Mosby turned, crawled to the rear. Cole and the colonel were awake.

"We're leaving," he said. "You're welcome to come along if you wish. But if you do, you take orders from me."

"And become your prisoners," Messner said, his voice heavy with sarcasm.

"No loud talk!" Mosby said harshly. "It makes no difference to me whether you come or not, Colonel, but if you have any consideration for your wife and daughter, you will. I leave it up to you."

"We'll go, Major," Cole said quickly. "Just tell us what to do. What about horses? We'll never make it on foot."

"We'll get them," Mosby said. "Are you ready?"

"Ready," the young lieutenant answered through the darkness.

"Then move up close to the entrance of the cave. . We wait there until my men return. If it is all clear, we move out, one at a time. Go fast but don't run. Watch where you step so you won't fall down."

"Which way do we turn when we leave the cave?"

"To the right, toward the horses. There may be a guard there. Or he may be posted somewhere else. Don't do any talking. Once we get to the horses, we've got a good chance. Is everything understood?"

"We understand." It was Amanda Messner's voice. She sounded strong and unafraid. "We want to thank you, Major, for helping us. Even if we fail, I want you to know I—we are grateful."

"Major!" Ben Frost's summons came from the shadows outside the cave.

"Here."

There was a faint rustling and then the sergeant was

by his side. He felt the cold steel of his revolvers as they were pressed into his hands.

"Got these while I was out," the Ranger said. "Everybody's sleepin' like a baby. Safe to go."

"Where's Jess?"

"Waitin' outside."

Mosby said, "Lead off. We pick up horses first, then swing over and get our own."

Frost, crouched low, faded into the night. Mosby halted by the opening. "All right," he whispered. "Go out, one by one. Keep down low."

Mrs. Messner was the first. She crept outside, halted abruptly. Mosby saw her hand fling up to her lips, heard a gasp escape her. "Those men!" she murmured. "Won't they see us?"

Mosby glanced at the propped up shapes of Tombo and Claude. Jess and Ben Frost had done a good job of making them appear on duty—and alive.

"No," he said quietly. "They can't see anything. Move along, Mrs. Messner."

8

ONE BY one they left the cave, turned sharp right and made their way across the open ground to the protective screen of brush beyond the clearing. Jackman and his outlaws slept soundly, sprawled about the slowly dying fire.

When they were away from the cave and out of the renegade's range of vision, John Mosby breathed easier. The extreme nervousness and near-hysteria of the women, especially Nell, had worried him considerably. He feared the slightest move on the part of any one of the outlaws would evoke a scream from the girl and bring the renegade chief and his men to their feet.

But that danger passed and, when they were well hidden, he called a halt. Frost and Jess Rutledge, who had scouted ahead, reappeared.

"One man at the other mine," the sergeant reported. "He won't trouble us."

"How about the horses?" Mosby asked.

"Ready. Never had been unsaddled. All we got to do is climb aboard."

They moved on at once, reached the makeshift corral in a few short minutes. Rutledge led out three of the mounts for temporary use of Mosby, Frost and himself. Lieutenant Cole, probing among the animals, selected the four horses that bore the mark of the U.S. Army on their hips.

"These are the ones we had to ride," he said. "Belonged to our escort—the men Jackman murdered when we were attacked."

They mounted up quickly, rode off into the brush. Their own horses were waiting on the far side of the ridge and Mosby headed on a direct line for them. They continued for a good half hour, finally reached the thicket where their horses waited.

Mosby and the two Rangers exchanged mounts. The Confederate leader felt better after that; now they once again were free and in possession of the explosives with which they could carry out their mission.

50

"What about these people?" Frost asked. "We can't turn them loose. They'll go trottin' straight to the nearest bluebelly camp. And we sure ain't got no time to waste fiddlin' around with prisoners."

"Don't worry about us," Cole said, overhearing. "You helped us escape from Jackman and we're grateful for that. We'll look after ourselves now. And, as for reporting you to—"

"Lieutenant Cole!" Messner broke in sharply. "You will remember your station as an officer! We make no bargains with this rabble."

"Stephen!" Amanda Messner exclaimed in a shocked voice. "We owe these men our lives! You can't—"

"I believe I am better qualified to decide what we can and cannot do," the officer said. "These men are Rebel soldiers—traitors. Worse, I believe I know now who they are." Messner paused, placed his attention on Mosby. "You are John Mosby, the guerrilla. Is that not so?"

"I am Mosby."

"See? Just as I suspected. Out of the hands of one bloodthirsty outlaw into the hands of another! Where were you going, Mosby, when you ran into Jackman? To raid some quiet little town and murder the inhabitants?"

Color flushed into John Mosby's face. "I see you believe the false reports your northern newspaper writers print. You might look deeper for the facts, Colonel. I am a soldier fighting for what I believe is right. And right now you are in my way. I'll ask you for your word—"

"My word!" Messner echoed scornfully. "I'll not honor any guerrilla blackguard with my word!"

"Stephen!" Amanda Messner cried again.

"You are a traitor to your country!" the colonel continued, ignoring his wife's protests. "You are a renegade, the worst kind of outlaw—a heartless cutthroat. I am duty bound to turn you over to the first Union soldier I can find."

Mosby's lips had drawn into a tight line. "You forget —you are my prisoners. We are not yours. And since you refuse to give me your word as an officer not to interfere, I am obliged to take measures to see that you do not. Sergeant," he added, nodding to Frost, "tie the colonel's hands to his saddle. The same for the lieutenant.

51

I don't think it will be necessary where the ladies are concerned."

"Nor for me," Cole said. "You have my word, Major."

"I would accept it, Lieutenant, were we alone. But the colonel's attitude changes everything. I would not want you placed in a position of being forced to ignore a direct order from a superior."

"I understand," Cole said, and placed his crossed wrists in position for Frost to bind.

"What do you intend doing with us?" Amanda Messner asked.

Mosby watched Frost complete the binding of the two officers. "I will have to decide later," he said. "Right now we must get as far from here as possible. Jackman or one of his men could awaken at any moment and set up an alarm."

"We keep headin' north?" Ben Frost asked, going back onto his saddle.

"Due north, just as planned," Mosby replied.

The tall sergeant hesitated. "But what about these here Yankees, Major? Won't they get in the way?"

"We'll take care of that problem when we come to it. First thing is to reach our objective—and we have no time to lose."

"North," Messner repeated, his face a deep study. "I'd guess this objective you speak of to be the bridge at Mogatawny Mountain. You know how valuable it is to General Grant and the spring offensive, so you are out to destroy it."

"Move out, Sergeant," Mosby said, ignoring the officer. "Set as fast a pace as possible."

"Well, am I right?" Messner demanded. "Is that what you have in mind?"

"Colonel," Mosby said, facing the officer. "I suggest you save your breath and keep your voice low. I don't intend to answer your questions and we don't want Jackman snapping at our heels."

"I'll speak as I please!" Messner shouted. "I warn you, Mosby! At the first opportunity I shall escape and find help. I'll keep you from getting near that bridge—"

"And I warn you, Colonel. Unless you quiet down and do as you're told, I'm going to take you off that horse,

52

bind and gag you, and leave you behind. I don't intend to fool with you."

Cole moved up beside the older officer. "Sir, I suggest we do as the major says. For the sake of the women."

Frost pulled away, muttering under his breath. Mosby motioned for Nell Messner and her mother to follow next in line, after which would come the colonel and the lieutenant. He and Jess Rutledge brought up the rear, each riding a few yards to either side in flanking position.

The early morning hour was chill and Mosby knew the women were feeling the cold despite the capes they wore. But there was nothing he could do about it. Even if they were not pressed for time, it would be foolhardy to halt and build a fire. Jackman or one of his men would certainly notice it. Likely, at that very moment, the search for them was beginning.

And, if the renegades overtook them—what would he do? Should he stay and fight, protect the Messner party? It was the right thing to do, the human thing, but could he, in fairness to his trust and to the Confederacy, afford to do so?

As they rode on through the cold morning hours, he pondered the problem. Always a man who knew exactly where he was going, and one with a clear cut conception of his duty, John Mosby found himself undecided, wondering what course he should pursue in event the problem materialized. Just where should a man draw a line between duty—

"Major!"

Mosby hauled up quickly, waited as Jess Rutledge swung in beside him. "What is it?"

"Somebody's on our trail!"

MOSBY GAVE a low-voiced command to halt. Ben Frost instantly dropped back to his side. "Somethin' wrong, Major?"

"Horses behind us," Rutledge said. "Could be Jackman and his bunch."

Nell Messner immediately began to sob. Cole and Amanda Messner began to soothe and comfort her. The Union officer, alone, showed no reaction. He sat ramrod straight on his saddle, eyes to the east now graying with the first promise of dawn.

Mosby said, "Take a look. See if you can locate them exactly."

The two Rangers dropped from their horses, faded off into the shadows. Mosby glanced to the Messner party. "Stay mounted. We may have to run for it."

The colonel looked down at his bound wrists. He seemed about to make some remark, apparently thought better of it. Amanda Messner said, "Is it Jackman, you think?" Her face was a chalky oval in the half darkness.

"Most likely," Mosby replied. "But it could also be that Union cavalry that was around here yesterday."

Stephen Messner nodded. "That will be who it is. They're out searching for us by now." He raised his eyes to meet those of his wife. "Don't worry. We'll soon be out of this. When they're close enough I'll call out."

Mosby made no comment. He supposed he should expect nothing else from the man. He was a soldier and, as such, it would be his duty to make every attempt to escape.

Rutledge and Frost reappeared at that moment. They swung immediately onto their saddles, wheeled up beside their commander.

"Jackman all right," Frost reported. "Him and his whole kit and kaboodle. They found their horses."

"How far?"

"No more than a quarter mile."

"You think they know we're ahead of them?"

"Bound to. Must have heard us or else got a look

at us when we were in the open back there. Don't figure they're trackin' us. Too dark yet."

Mosby came to a swift decision. "Cut off to the right. Let's pull out from under them. No point in making it easy."

Frost wagged his head. "Major, that'll cost us time. We got these Yankees free, why don't we just turn them loose and let them run for it? Maybe we can keep Jackman lookin' our way while they skedaddle."

Mosby said, "Doubt if it would work, Ben. Jackman will have his men scattered wide and watching sharp. And we don't dare turn them loose until we know they'll be safe."

"But, Major, we got that bridge to—"

"Right flank, Sergeant!" Mosby said, his tone suddenly stern. "Go a half mile then swing north again."

Frost obediently swung about, struck off to the west. Mosby waved the balance of the party into motion. He beckoned to Jess Rutledge.

"Fall back a ways and keep your eye on the trail. I want to know what Jackman does."

Rutledge turned away. Mosby pulled forward to a position behind Cole. The shadows of night were fading fast now, he noticed. Soon they no longer would have the cover of the darkness to mask their movements.

"Are they—will they catch us again?" Nell Messner's quavering, fearful voice floated to him. "Oh—I don't think I can stand any more!"

Cole pushed to the girl's side. "Don't cry, dear," he said, placing his hand upon hers. "Trust Major Mosby. If anyone can get us out of this mess, it will be him—"

"You talk like a ninny, Lieutenant!" Stephen Messner broke in impatiently. "You know what Mosby is! I would not be surprised to find the rest of his guerrilla cutthroats are camped around here close by and that he is taking us to them. We're up against the same thing as we were when Jackman had us!"

"Lower your voice, Colonel!" Mosby snapped, swinging in next to the officer. "You want them to hear you?"

Messner jerked his horse to a stop. He twisted about in the saddle. "See here! I'm fed up with being talked to in that manner. I am an officer in the United States

Army. I'll not listen to orders from a traitor such as you, Mosby!"

"You'll be quiet—or you'll find yourself trussed up in the brush there," Mosby said coldly. "Either you keep still or get down off that horse. Make a choice, Colonel."

"Stephen—please," Amanda Messner said imploringly.

Messner squared himself around reluctantly and resumed the trail. "I'm not forgetting this, Mosby," he said. "Once we're out of this—"

"If we get out," Mosby murmured, and dropped back to the end of the line. He looked over his shoulder. Rutledge should be reporting in. They were entering a dense grove, he saw. That was welcome. In the growing daylight they would need better cover. He saw movements off to the left at that moment. It was Jess Rutledge.

"They've spread out," the Ranger said. "Jackman's got them prowling through the brush in pairs."

"How close now?"

"Two, maybe three hundred yards."

Their cutting off at a right angle had not fooled the outlaws at all. "Must be reading our tracks now," he said. Then, "Stay here and keep a sharp watch. I'm going up ahead to see what it looks like."

He trotted forward, past the Messners and Orville Cole until he was abreast Ben Frost. They were riding into wilder, more tangled country. While it would be more difficult for any of Jackman's men to see them, it would also slow their pace considerably.

"They're closing in on us from behind," he said to the sergeant. "Sooner we can lose ourselves in this brush, the better."

"Was about to call you," Frost replied. "Thought I heard something over there on the left."

"The left?" Mosby repeated, his face drawing into a frown. "Didn't think any of Jackman's bunch had gotten that near."

"Well, I sure heard somethin', Major. Want me to scout it?"

"Go ahead, but keep in the saddle."

Frost swung off into the trees, was lost quickly in the dense undergrowth. Cole moved up from his place in the line.

"Something wrong here, Major?"

Mosby smiled grimly at the young officer. "Could be. The sergeant has gone to see about it. We know Jackman is back of us and coming up fast but I didn't think he was able to get abreast of us."

"You sound doubtful. You think it may be someone else?"

"Seems more logical."

There was a minute of silence. Cole said, "Major, I'd like you to know I appreciate all you're doing for us. And I don't hold the color of your uniform against you. I figure at a time like this it's not important."

"I agree. But we're not in the clear yet."

"I realize that, and that's why I'm saying this. If it comes down to a fight with Jackman and his crowd, I'd like a gun. You have my promise it won't be used against you or your men. If we come through the skirmish alive, I'll return it to you."

"Thanks," Mosby said. "We'll need all the help we can get. What about the colonel? Could I depend on him the same way?"

Cole shrugged. "He'll fight Jackman all right, only, once it was over, he'd feel it was his duty to capture you. It's not that he doesn't realize that you and your men have saved us from probable death but he's one of those straight-down-the-middle soldiers. To him black is black and white is white. The enemy is the enemy and there are no mitigating circumstances."

"Just the way I had him figured," Mosby said. "So, if we have to make a stand, it will be the four of us against Jackman."

"Poor odds," Cole said. "Must be a dozen of them, at least."

"Been the history of this war, Lieutenant, far as the Confederacy is concerned," Mosby said drily. "Odds have been against us all the way—but we make out."

Cole grinned. "No disputing that. Here comes your sergeant."

Frost approached at a fast trot. He glanced at Cole, frowned.

"It's all right, Ben," Mosby assured the man. "The lieutenant is with us if we have to fight."

Frost eyed the young officer skeptically. "Maybe. Could

57

be he'll change his mind. It ain't none of Jackman's bunch over there, Major."

"Underwood?" Mosby asked, hazarding a guess.

"Right. Him and a dozen or more cavalrymen. They ain't far off and comin' this way."

"Union cavalry, eh?" Stephen Messner spoke up triumphantly. "I've been expecting them."

He wheeled sharply about. Bending forward in the saddle, he drove his heels into the flanks of his horse, sent the animal plunging off into the brush.

"Cavalry!" Messner's deep voice boomed loud in the early morning hush. "Union cavalry—over here! Help!"

FOR A fraction of time John Mosby and the others sat in wordless astonishment. Then Ben Frost yanked his horse around savagely.

"The damned fool!" he muttered. "Don't he know Jackman can hear him, too?"

"Let him go!" Mosby shouted. "Too late to stop him now."

He spun to the Messner women. "Ride on," he ordered. "Keep to the foot of the mountain. Going to be trouble here and best place for you is in the brush."

A pistol cracked sharply along their back trail. A moment later Jess Rutledge burst into view.

"What was that yelling?" he cried. "Jackman heard it and got our location. Then he spotted me. Now they're coming up fast."

Mosby reached forward, slapped Nell Messner's horse smartly on the rump, sent it bolting toward the slope. Amanda Messner needed no encouragement. She followed immediately.

"Go with them, Lieutenant," Mosby said to Cole. "Keep them out of sight."

"I thought I was going to help you fight—" the officer protested.

"Change of plans. Your job is to look out for them."

"Better get out of here!" Ben Frost warned. "First thing you know we'll be caught between Jackman and that Yankee cavalry."

Mosby nodded. "What I'm counting on." He wheeled around, rode toward the oncoming outlaws. He could hear the crackling of brush, the dull thud of their running horses.

Frost spurred to Mosby's side. "What've you got in mind, Major?"

"Jackman," Mosby said with a tight grin. "We'll make Underwood a present of him."

The tall sergeant's face broke into a smile. "Now, I couldn't think of nothin' better for both of them!"

"Here they come!" Jess Rutledge sang out.

A hundred yards away Kidd Jackman and his renegade soldiers burst into view. The outlaw leader was a length ahead of his men. When he saw the Rangers he yelled, brought up his revolver and began to shoot.

As the bullets whined overhead, clipped into the brush beyond, Mosby spun about. "Let's go!" he shouted and rushed across the clearing.

He drove straight for the point where he expected Underwood and his detail would be. Frost and Rutledge swung in behind him, their pistols now out and answering Jackman. There was no sign of Stephen Messner and Mosby guessed the Union colonel had, by that time, reached Underwood and relayed his story.

He glanced over his shoulder. Kidd Jackman had reached the open ground, was then swerving to give pursuit. He was still unaware of the calvary's presence. Mosby grinned again. It would be a tight squeeze, their being caught in the middle, but it would solve all their immediate problems.

The Messner party would end up safe. Jackman and his men would either be dead or prisoners; and he, with Rutledge and Frost, would be free to complete the mission. That is—if they managed to pull off the trick.

"Bluebellies!" Ben Frost yelled as they swept around a stand of wild berry bushes and came into the open.

"Right flank!" Mosby sang out and cut back toward the mountain.

He threw a glance toward the Yankee cavalry. The abrupt appearance of the three Rangers had taken them unawares. Evidently they had expected Mosby and his men to be riding hard in an opposite direction, not come charging straight for them. Messner, Mosby saw, was beside the Yankee captain, was at that moment in a voluble discussion.

Mosby watched Tom Underwood raise himself in his stirrups. The early morning light gleamed dully on his drawn saber. He raised it, began to wave it over his head. The line of blue horsemen surged into a fast gallop. Mosby looked for the outlaws. They were approaching at a dead run. Jackman and Underwood both were yet oblivious of the other's presence.

"That grove ahead!" Mosby shouted to his men. "Meet there!"

Frost and Rutledge waved their acknowledgment. They were enjoying the moments, conscious now what their major had in mind. Underwood and Jackman, if they continued, were following a collision course that would bring them together at the termination of a long thicket.

Three riders appeared suddenly on the far side of the field. Alarm rose within John Mosby. He had not anticipated Jackman's splitting his force, sending a part to circle wide and come in from the west. He calculated the position in which it put him and his Rangers. Where they had clear, open ground ahead that led to safety, there now was danger of being cut off. They could not veer right. That would throw them into the muzzles of Jackman's guns. And there was no turning back, not with Tom Underwood and a dozen cavalrymen rushing in for the kill.

The three renegades opened up with their pistols. The range was too far and the bullets fell harmlessly to the intervening ground. But they would soon be close enough to present a grave danger. Mosby swung his eyes to Jackman, then to Underwood. Another hundred yards and they would meet. He came to a decision. He drew one of his revolvers, twisted about to face Frost and Rutledge.

"Only chance we've got is to ride through them," he said. "Let's go!"

He began to fire at the oncoming trio. Immediately Frost and Rutledge started to shoot. For a dozen yards the opposing groups thundered toward each other, firing as rapidly as they could press the triggers of their weapons. One of the outlaws sagged forward on his saddle. He clung desperately to his horse's neck for a few jolting steps, then fell heavily to the ground. Immediately his companions wheeled off. They slowed momentarily as though undecided what they should do. Then, side by side, they raced on to rejoin the remainder of the Jackman party, now almost to the end of the thicket.

"Keep going!" Mosby shouted to the Rangers.

They hurried on, pointing for the thick stand of trees along the foot of the mountain. A staccato burst of gunfire broke out behind them. Mosby glanced back. Tom Underwood and his men had connected with Jackman and the renegades. All was a confused milling of horses,

61

boiling dust, yelling men. Pistols were cracking and the brittle clang of sabers was loud on the morning air.

"It's Underwood's party now," Mosby said, as Rutledge and Frost moved up to side him.

They galloped on across the clearing, gained the trees at the base of the slope. Mosby slowed the pace. Their horses were sucking deep for wind after the fast, continuous sprint.

"One way to fight a war," Jess Rutledge said, smiling broadly as he looked back.

"Was a mighty cute trick, Major," Frost added, a note of admiration in his voice. "Couldn't have worked out better. Reckon we won't have no more trouble from either one of them. Ought to get to that bridge now without them botherin' us. Good thing, too; we're plenty late."

"About eighteen hours," Mosby said, soberly. "Only good thing about it is that we've probably put an end to Jackman and his gang."

"And got that Yankee cavalry out of our hair."

Mosby nodded and urged his horse to a slow trot. Off to their right movement along the edge of the trees brought all three of the Rangers to attention. *More of Jackman's renegades,* Mosby thought. But it was only Orville Cole and the Messner women. As they watched the three lifted their hands in a farewell.

"Glad those ladies came through this safe," Rutledge said, waving a reply.

"So am I," Ben Frost added. "The Major was right • about helpin' them, even if they are Yankees."

11

THEY RODE north, crossing scarred, untended fields that showed the ravages of war, skirting deserted farm houses, following along stone hedgerows and innumerable creeks that still flowed lustily from the spring rains. Near noon they reached the slightly higher grading upon which the twin steel tracks of the railroad had been laid.

"Be easy to follow them in, Major," Rutledge said when they halted. "Take us right to that bridge without any more wandering around."

"And straight into a Yankee patrol or two," Mosby said. "You can bet they're guarding it close all the way to Washington."

"Somebody comin' down there now," Ben Frost warned, squinting into the distance. "Looks like soldiers."

Mosby procured his telescope from the leather bags of his saddle. He studied the small, moving dots far down the valley. "Yankee infantry," he said, finally. "Heading this way. We'll drop back and keep in the brush."

They wheeled about, ducked below the rising and galloped across the soft, gently rolling land to the trees and thickets that covered the nearby slopes. Once there, Mosby saw it was possible to proceed unnoticed and still maintain visual contact with the rails.

"Keep a sharp watch for videttes," he said. "They'll be taking no chances on that bridge. Probably sentries posted all through the woods."

"Maybe we ought to spread out," Rutledge suggested. "Keep a better lookout that way."

"Good idea," Mosby agreed. "Only stay in sight. We don't want to get separated."

An hour later they topped a long, high running ridge and looked down upon a deep valley. Mogatawny Bridge lay on its far edge, nearly half way up the towering mountain whose name it bore. Now the real danger of running into Yankee pickets and patrols faced them. Mosby waved in Frost and Rutledge.

"Bridge is on the side of that mountain," he said,

pointing across the broad swale. "You can judge the location by following the railroad tracks to where they dip below that hogback you see straight ahead."

The Rangers studied the country for a full minute. Frost said, "Be no chance to cross the valley. It will be crawlin' with Yankees. We circle clear around, that it, Major?"

Mosby said, "Only way. Keep on this ridge but stay below the summit. If we follow it we should end up near the top of Mogatawny Mountain. From there we can look down upon the bridge."

"You ever been here before?" Rutledge asked, digging around in his saddlebags for some of the hard biscuits and dried meat they had brought along.

"Once, a couple of years ago. I'm remembering the country as we come to it. I do recall the way the bridge was placed—but of course, they could have changed it some."

They pushed on, excitement and tension growing within each man as they drew nearer to the object of their mission. Twice along the ridge they caught sight of videttes and were forced to retreat lower on the slope to avoid being seen. Once, when they crossed the cleared ground where the grading cut a path through the forest, they almost ran into a cavalry patrol of five men and a sergeant. But they managed to remain unseen behind a thick stand of hemlock and the soldiers moved on by.

They gained the top of the mountain and halted. While Mosby secured the horses in a well hidden place, Ben Frost and Rutledge made a quick scouting survey of the immediate area.

"Bluebellies lower down," Frost said when he returned. "Don't think there's any up here."

"Reckon they figure nobody's going to get by their outposts and reach the mountain," Rutledge said.

They crossed a shallow basin and topped out another ridge that traversed the slope a short distance below them. They were careful to keep well down, not wishing to become silhouetted against the skyline. The upper reaches of Mogatawny Mountain were thick with brush, rock and dwarf trees and they had no difficulty in making the descent to the lip of an encampment from which, Mosby believed, they could look down upon the trestle. Coming to that point, they dropped flat and worked their way to

64

the edge of the cliff. He had guessed right. Mogatawny Bridge, while a considerable distance away, was plainly visible.

There had been several changes, he saw. The bridge had been strengthened: new timbers were evident in its underpinning. Most apparent, however, were the additional steel tracks that lay at both ends of the structure. Spur lines now circled out and back at both approaches.

John Mosby studied that through his glass. He finally realized their purpose. The heavily loaded steam trains that were using the trestle were often too much for the wooden structure. Rather than completely rebuild the bridge to greater strength, the railroad would simply sidetrack half the cars onto the spur, draw or push the remainder across and then return for the others. In such a way the strain on the timbers was reduced by half.

"Plenty of soldiers down there," Rutledge commented. "Looks like a regular encampment."

"Probably is," Mosby replied. "This bridge is a mighty important link in the Union supply line to the south."

There were several huts and a dozen or more tents on the flat area just north of the bridge. Smoke trickled from one of the squat structures; the kitchen, most likely. A flag stirred fitfully from a mast made from a tall tree, stripped of its limbs. Guards patrolled both ends of the trestle, and, far beneath, in the bottom of the one hundred foot deep ravine, other soldiers marched to and fro.

"Goin' to be a tough chore gettin' in there," Ben Frost observed. "Pickets all over the place. Man couldn't in no way sneak in without bein' spotted."

The tall sergeant was right. The bridge itself, two hundred feet long at least, and made entirely of timbers arranged in a three tiered network of cross members and uprights, would burn readily and collapse quickly under several well placed charges of blasting powder; but there lay the problem—affixing the explosives properly. Even under the cover of darkness it was doubtful if the structure could be approached.

And an answer must be found soon. Thanks to Kidd Jackman, their margin of time had been lost; the twenty-four hours Mosby had estimated they had to work with, were almost gone. The train carrying Grant's supplies and ammunition could not be far distant. Two perhaps three hours at most were all they could rely on.

Mosby drew back from the edge of the cliff. He sat up, his bearded face pulled into a tight frown as he sought to come up with a feasible plan. He glanced at the slope behind him. Several charges of powder would start an avalanche pouring down the steep grade and onto the bridge. But the damage would be only minor—and of a temporary nature. The Yankees would clean it up quickly and no permanent harm would have been accomplished.

It was impossible to come up from the floor of the ravine. Not only were there guards maintaining a line that traced directly beneath the bridge supports but there were more blue uniformed men marching in an outer ring that created a double cordon through which no one could pass unseen.

"What about fire, Major?" Rutledge suggested. "Not much of a breeze but, with the gunpowder, we might get things going."

Mosby shook his head. "They'd check it before it reached the bridge. And we would be out our explosive— the one thing we've got to work with. It's going to be a one shot proposition."

"Too far to just light the bombs and throw them," Frost said. "You think there might be a chance of—"

"Major—look!" Jess Rutledge broke in.

Mosby crawled quickly to the edge of the cliff. A dozen or more riders were entering the bridge from its southern approach. They rode single file down the narrow pedestrain walkway that lay beside the steel rails.

"Underwood," Frost murmured. "And he's got them Yankees with him. There's Jackman and some of his bunch, too."

MOSBY PLACED his glass on the officer at the head of the party. It was Stephen Messner. The Yankee colonel rode stiffly erect, looked neither to right nor left. Several of the soldiers lounging about the camp snapped to startled attention at his appearance.

A burly sergeant-major emerged from one of the huts and hauled up rigidly before Messner. Underwood, back in the procession, moved up beside the senior officer and dismounted. He returned the non-com's salute and stood quietly by while Messner talked. It meant further complications, Mosby realized. The camp would be put on the alert and, likely, patrols would be sent into the hills to search for the three Rangers.

Mosby allowed his telescope to run over the remainder of the party. He located Orville Cole and the two women. Then he saw Kidd Jackman. The outlaw's hands were bound behind his back and a short length of rope, looped about his neck, was tied to the saddle. There were two of his men with him. Either Underwood had succeeded in practically wiping out the outlaw gang or some of them had managed to escape. There were several wounded cavalrymen and one empty saddle.

At the sergeant-major's command, five soldiers marched up smartly and took charge of the renegades. They led them off to one of the huts that stood a bit apart from the others. The guardhouse, apparently. Jackman and his men would not long remain there. Stephen Messner would hold a hasty court martial and their lives would be quickly over.

From off to the north the melancholy wail of a steam train drifted across the valley. Mosby stiffened, instantly trained his glass to that direction. There was no engine visible yet but it was approaching. He was acutely aware of that fact now and the pressure to act, to complete the task assigned him and his men began to crowd him relentlessly.

He brought his attention back to the Union camp. Soldiers were now trotting toward the makeshift stable. Others were moving out along the bridge and descending into the ravine. The order was out to strengthen the guard.

"Looks like they're expectin' us," Ben Frost said.

"Be patrols scouting through the hills and down in the valley pretty soon," Rutledge said. "Surprise them some to know we're laying up here watching them."

"That train didn't sound too far off," Frost said then, stating a thought all three men were considering. "We better be gettin' somethin' planned out."

"That danged Underwood. Wished he had taken the Messners to some other camp. Makes things twice as hard for us now."

"Reckon that was that Yankee colonel's doin's. He had a hunch we were headed for that bridge."

John Mosby was only half listening. He glanced toward the sky. The sun was still several hours from setting; there was no possibility of waiting until dark to act. The train would have arrived, crossed the bridge and continued on its way by that time.

More soldiers were emerging from the tents and huts. They moved back onto the nearby slope of the mountain, reappeared shortly dragging brush and logs. Mosby watched as they began to erect piles at each end of the trestle. They were taking precautions against darkness, he realized. Huge watch fires would be kept burning thoughout the night.

He glanced to the bottom of the ravine. Similar measures were under way there, too. He swore softly at his luck. If Messner and Underwood had not shown up to warn the camp, their situation might be more promising.

But—regardless of their problems—the bridge must be destroyed, and, with it, the train with its load of supplies.

Rutledge, in a doubtful tone, said, "Major, you think maybe we better move on up the valley a piece and do the job there?"

Again Mosby refused the easier course. Such would create only a temporary delay. "Has to be this bridge," he said. "Only way we can really hurt them bad. If we can wreck it and send that train to the bottom of the ravine, we've as good as won an important battle. If Grant doesn't get those supplies by tomorrow, he's in serious trouble."

"I'm agreein' with the Major," Frost said. "It's the bridge or nothin'."

"There goes the colonel," Rutledge said.

Mosby swung his attention to where an ambulance had drawn up in front of one of the huts. He watched Nell Messner and her mother climb into the vehicle. They were followed by the Colonel and then Lieutenant Cole. As the driver gathered his reins, a cavalry escort rode into position. Mosby saw Underwood and the sergeant-major make their salute as the ambulance rolled off, headed, no doubt, for Washington.

The patrols that had been ordered out were lining up for instructions. There were at least two dozen cavalrymen. They wheeled off in squads of six, struck for the slopes that bordered the encampment.

"Goin' to have company," Ben Frost said.

"We'd better move the horses," Mosby added. "If that patrol to the left keeps on coming, they'll ride straight into that clearing where we left our mounts."

"Could bring them down this side," Rutledge suggested. "Doubt if they'll think of looking here."

"Be a good idea."

The shrill whistle of the train once more split the afternoon's hush. Mosby trained his glass toward the distant end of the tracks. Smoke was boiling upward as the locomotive labored along the slight grade. He could make out the sooty, diamond shaped stack, the red and gold circular trim, the huge, square headlight that fronted the boiler.

Sweat began to gather on the Confederate leader's brow as tension and the urgency of the moments bore down more heavily upon him. The train was less than an hour away.

"Major," Ben Frost said quietly, "I got me an idea."

Mosby turned to the sergeant. "Speak up, Ben. We haven't much time left."

Frost said, "It's like this: we get down on a level with them tracks. I take them bombs Jess made and when the train gets on the bridge, I ride like hell to it and toss the bombs into one or two of the coaches. I figure that'll get the job done quick."

"What do you figure those guards will be doing all that time?" Mosby asked. "You'd never get close enough

69

to throw the bombs. They'd cut you down before you were half way across that open ground."

"Maybe. But if you and Jess covered me, started in shootin' at the closest ones—"

Mosby reached out, laid his hand on the Tennessee man's shoulder. "Forget it, Ben. This doesn't call for suicide. I appreciate what you've got in mind but I'll come up with something else."

"Don't have to be suicide," Frost protested. "I can pull it off, with you two helpin'. And we sure got to blow that bridge and stop that train. You already said how important it is."

"I'll figure out a way. We better get to those horses. If that patrol should run onto them we'd be in a bad way since we'd lose our explosive as well as our means for escape."

They moved back up the slope, doing it carefully and quietly since they could no longer see the camp or any of the patrols that had ridden forth. There was now a very real danger of running headlong into a party of cavalrymen at 'most any point.

They reached the horses without incident and with no undue loss of time. Mosby waited while the Rangers released the animals. Once they were safe, he could return to the problem of how they would destroy the bridge and the supply train. He thought of Ben Frost's suggestion. It had merit but there must be another way the attack could be effected without paying so great a price.

But if it came down to it and there was no other course open, then it would be utilized. There would be one change, however; it would be he who carried the bombs, not Ben Frost.

13

THEY LED the horses down the same indefinite trail they had earlier ridden to gain the top. It was better to stay out of the saddle. Such a position raised a man above the surrounding brush and made him visible for a great distance on all sides.

The train was drawing nearer. The hollow, clanking noises of the iron wheels against the rails, the chuffing of the engine, the chink of couplers and creaking and groaning of the wooden coaches, began to fill the valley. Time was running out—the opportunity to act would soon be lost. Mosby, slightly ahead of the others, came to a sudden halt. He raised his hand for silence as Rutledge and Frost eased up to his side.

"What is it, Major?"

"Something's wrong," he murmured. "too quiet."

They stood in rigid silence, sweating out the fleeting irreplaceable moments. They listened. Except for the approaching steam engine and its protesting string of coaches, the world was hushed. There were no clacking insects, no twittering birds; even the rustling of the breeze had ceased. It brought to John Mosby a remembrance of that morning at Gettysburg—of those death-still seconds during which the universe seemed in breathless suspension just before it was suddenly ripped apart in a thunderous spasm of gunfire.

And then he saw the answer. Five Yankee cavalrymen, riding abreast and at slow, careful pace, emerged from the brush only a short distance ahead. They were moving at right angles to the Rangers, coming from the direction of the bridge.

Rutledge whistled soundlessly. "If we'd been a minute earlier, we'd have walked right into them."

"Probably another patrol back of us," Mosby said. "Should be clear ahead, though."

They resumed the trail, walking with infinite care, picking a path for their horses that would afford a minimum of noise. The sounds of the train were louder now, indicating that it could not be far from the entrance to the trestle. Mosby raised his head cautiously, looked ahead. They were almost to the foot of the slope—and to the end of the rock and brush that afforded such excellent cover. He turned his glance in the direction of the cavalrymen. They were just dropping below a low rise a hundred yards or so to the right. At least they need not worry about them for the time being.

He continued on, bearing for the point, selected earlier while on the brow of the hill, that would put them nearest to the steel rails. When they arrived at that position he lifted his hand for a halt. Cautioning silence, he moved to the extreme outer fringe of the brush. From there he had a broad view of the valley. Frost and Rutledge, after securing the horses, crawled to his side.

Mogatawny Bridge was a short quarter mile to their left. Directly ahead, little more than fifty yards distant, were the railroad tracks, gleaming brightly in the late afternoon sunlight. There were no soldiers evident except at the ravine itself. Four guards patrolled the near approach. A like number watched over the opposite side. No men were on the bridge itself but a considerable number still worked about the huts and tents. Although he could not see the bottom of the ravine, Mosby knew there were quite a few soldiers on duty at that location.

"There she comes," Rutledge said, pointing toward the far end of the valley.

The locomotive drawing the cars puffed its way onto the flats where the encampment lay, chugged wearily toward the entrance to the trestle. Behind it trailed a lengthy string of cars at the end of which another engine, a pusher, labored to do its part.

"Heavy load," Rutledge commented. "Takes both those engines to keep it moving."

The train ground to a squealing stop when the lead locomotive reached the cluster of tents and huts. Three soldiers moved out to talk with the engineer and fireman who swung down from their posts.

"No soldiers on it, only supplies," Ben Frost said. "One thing in our favor. You want to go ahead with my plan, Major?"

Mosby shook his head. A hope was springing alive within him—a possibility that would afford them just the opportunity they needed. "Wait," he said. "They're pulling a big train. Let's see if they break it."

"Looks like they're gettin' ready to do somethin'," the sergeant said.

Two more of the train's crew appeared, joined the pair talking with the Yankee soldiers near the engine. The discussion continued for a long five minutes, then the group moved back along the line of cars until it had reached a mid-point.

"Sure what they're fixin' to do," Frost murmured. "What've you got in mind, Major?"

"Watch," Mosby replied. "Let's be certain of what they're going to do."

The two locomotive men had swung about, were walking slowly back to their posts. The soldiers were drifting off to the camp, apparently no longer interested in the proceedings. The engineer, with his fireman, climbed into the cab of the diamond stack. Two short whistle blasts echoed across the valley. Then, with a sudden hammer of steam, the engine started across the bridge towing an exact half the number of the heavily burdened coaches.

The crew member who had been standing at the point where the uncoupling was done, swung onto the last moving car. The other climbed aboard the lead coach of those that remained.

"Brakeman," Mosby said, thinking aloud. "Once they cross the bridge and pull the grade a ways, he'll set the wheels."

"Believe I know what you're thinking, Major," Jess Rutledge said, his voice quickening with eagerness and excitement. "You're figuring to do something when they halt this first half of the train on the slope and go back for the rest."

"Exactly."

They watched the string of cars roll sluggishly across the trestle, the engine chugging mightily from its efforts. Although the bridge itself was near level, a slight upgrade in the tracks began at the southern end where they lifted to meet the climb out of the valley.

The lone locomotive immediately found itself in difficulty when it reached the slope and started the ascent. Smoke billowed from its stack and its drivers worked frantically. For several moments it appeared the pusher engine would be forced to shunt its cars onto the siding and come to the rescue but eventually the steady application of power caught and the coaches began to climb the grade.

The engineer tooted his whistle briefly to announce his success, and hurried on. The brakeman appeared atop the last car, took up a position beside the wheel he would turn to lock the coach and hold it stationary once they stopped. If luck was with them, Mosby thought, it would be only on the one car he would take such precaution; he was hoping the crew would consider the locomotive's brakes, combined with those of the end car, sufficient to hold the string in place until the remainder of the train could be brought across the trestle.

"Sergeant," Mosby said, his plan for attack now clear in mind, "we need to draw the attention of those Yankees away from the train. Take one of the bombs and get over to the far side of the valley as fast as you can. Explode it. I don't care how you manage it—just so you make a big noise. Then get back here. We may need your gun to cover our escape.

"Jess, when that explosion goes off, you'll ride for the end coach, the one where the brakeman is. He may still be there or he may get down and head back across the bridge to help the rest of the crew. If he's in your way, you know what to do.

John Mosby's eyes were alight as he talked. These were the moments he loved, the times when danger and excitement raced hand and hand at his side. "I figure the explosion Ben is going to set off will create enough confusion to allow us to act," he hurried on. "But we will have to be fast. While you're down there tossing your bombs into every open car you can reach, I'll be inside the locomotive. I'll get it into reverse and open the throttle. The brakes on that one coach will never hold and we ought to have a smashup right about the middle of the bridge!"

Ben Frost was already moving to his horse. "Be a beauty of a wreck!" he exclaimed. "Only one thing could go wrong. Locked wheels on that coach could cause it to jump the track. Too bad you won't have time to release them."

"Can't have everything our way," Mosby said and

grinned. He watched the sergeant remove all the bombs from his saddlebags except one. "Get that set off soon as you can. We want to catch the rest of those coaches while they're on the bridge."

"Won't take me long," Frost said and swung onto his saddle. "We meet here, that it?"

"Right here," Mosby answered as the Tennessean rode off into the brush.

Rutledge had moved to his horse. "I'll get ready," he said, starting to unload the balance of the explosive. "Think I'll pack them together, make myself three or four big ones. Like for them to hear this clear back in Washington."

14

"OUR SIGNAL to move out," Mosby said, his attention on the engineer and fireman who were then dropping to the ground from the cab of the locomotive, "will be the explosion that Ben sets off. We'll have a few seconds while everyone looks in that direction."

"We go it on foot or ride?"

"Be better to leave the horses here. Smaller targets that way. Tie them good. Don't want the bombs to scare them and cause them to run away. There goes that brakeman. Things are working for us, Jess."

"Leaves nobody aboard the train," Rutledge said with satisfaction, watching the three members of the crew stroll lazily toward the bridge. "Ought to be easy, Major."

"You ready?"

"Almost. Got to be sure these babies go off like I plan. You figure the end car is the best bet?"

"Yes. It will be the one that smashes into the other coaches on the bridge. I'm hoping one of them is loaded with gunpowder."

Rutledge, finished, got to his feet. He slung the saddlebags containing the explosives over his shoulder, felt in a pocket for matches. Satisfied everything was in order, he said, "Got them all in these bags. I can use them as one bomb or two or three, whichever seems the best when I get in close."

"Can you gauge the length of fuse so the explosion won't happen until the coach is on the bridge? That's where we want it to happen."

"Easy," Rutledge said. "But I need to wait until you get the cars rolling. Have to judge their speed before I cut the length."

"Engine will be at full throttle. Locked brakes on that end car will slow it down some but the grade is fairly steep and that will help us. They'll be moving at a good clip."

"I'll have time to judge," Rutledge said. "Won't take but a couple of seconds—and I want to be sure."

"They're bringing up the rest of the train," Mosby said, peering through the brush at the bridge. "Hope Ben hasn't run into trouble. Time is growing short."

"Ought to be reaching the other side of the valley right about now. Expect we'll be hearing the blast any second."

Mosby drew his pistols, examined both critically. With the engine crew away from their posts and now standing with the brakeman at the end of the trestle, there was little likelihood he would need his weapons. At least, not at the start. When they swung back for their horses, however, it could be a different story. The explosion would summon soldiers, on foot and in the saddle, from miles around. They could look for trouble then. He looked worriedly toward the opposite side of the valley. What had happened to Frost? What was holding him up? The blast was overdue.

Across the bridge, the pusher locomotive had its string of coaches rolling. In another half minute the first of them would be entering the framework of the trestle and starting the slow trip across its two hundred foot span.

He checked their position, mentally went over their plan to be certain there were no unconsidered possibilities. From where he and Rutledge waited, it was a good fifty yards to the tracks and the waiting coaches. The engine, for which he would race, was farther up the rails, possibly seventy or seventy-five more yards. The end box car into which Jess Rutledge would hurl the explosives was about an equal distance in the opposite direction.

"We break out of here, go straight across the clearing to the cars," Mosby said. "Sooner we get alongside them, the better. Not so apt to be seen. Then we split. You head for that coach and I'll get inside the locomotive."

Rutledge said, "Right, Major. Hope that door to the coach isn't locked. Be fine if I can get my bombs inside."

Mosby shook his head. "Probably is. Looks like an open window or a ventilator there at one end."

"Hard to reach," Rutledge said thoughtfully, "and I'd hate to throw and miss. But it won't be any problem. If

77

I can't yank the door open, I'll just drape the bags over the rods underneath. She'll blow—"

The valley suddenly rocked with a thunderous explosion. Across the way a portion of the hillside lifted into the air in a swirling cloud of dust and debris. Mosby flung a glance at the Union encampment. Soldiers had sprung into life, were now running toward the sound.

"Let's go!" he hissed to Rutledge, and leaped from the shelter of the brush into the open.

Shoulder to shoulder they sprinted across the cleared ground. They gained the shadow of the waiting cars. Down near the bridge voices were shouting questions. In the camp a bugle was blaring an urgent call.

"Good luck!" Rutledge yelled and swung off to the left.

Mosby made his reply and raced for the panting locomotive. Back, somewhere on the side of the mountain he could hear running horses. One of the patrols coming in to investigate. He wasted no time endeavoring to locate them. If they represented danger, it would simply have to come. At the moment his mind was concentrated solely upon the job at hand—upon getting into the engine's cab, releasing the brakes and starting the simmering machine down grade toward the bridge.

He could take nothing else into consideration now but his own chore; he must rely entirely upon Rutledge to do his part with the explosives, on Ben Frost to rush back across the valley and give them what protection he could with his gun. But there were no doubts in his mind; both were picked men, capable of doing all expected of them—more if need be.

The engine was before him. He grasped the iron hand railings, hoisted himself into the cab. The controls were familiar to him, just as they were to any member of the 43rd Battalion. On several occasions they had been called on to capture or destroy Union railroad equipment. He lost no time getting the engine into reverse motion.

A yell lifted from somewhere near the bridge. The train crew, he guessed, but there was no way of knowing if they had seen him or Rutledge. He allowed the engine a few moments to pick up momentum. The string of cars moved reluctantly, caused by the locked brakes of the end coach.

Gunshots rang out. They sounded hollow through the chugging and hissing of the straining engine. He heard a sharp spang as metal struck metal. A bullet had glanced against the boiler, ricochetted off into space. Mosby waited no longer. The moving train had been noticed. He opened the throttle. The drivers churned frantically, caught. The locomotive began to pick up speed. Mosby stepped to the side of the cab, leaped. He went to his knees at the impact, caught himself, plunged on for the spur of brush and rock where the horses waited.

From the tail of his eye he caught sight of Jess Rutledge, also legging it across the open ground in long, bounding strides. Beyond the Ranger, the train moved down grade with ever increasing momentum, the locked wheels of the end car screeching and smoking as they dragged against the rails.

Men were shouting. Gunshots erupted across the valley, somewhere near the point where Ben Frost had set off the decoy explosion. Mosby felt a surge of fear for the tall sergeant. Had he, somehow, gotten himself trapped? He gained the cover, wheeled to look back. Rutledge was no more than a dozen steps behind him. Mosby smiled grimly, pointed toward the bridge.

"They're trying to get the other cars out of the way!"

The frantic chuffing of the pusher engine laboring to reverse the forward motion of the string and draw them back off the trestle was barely audible above the racket of the runaway locomotive now rushing down the slope.

"They'll never make it!" Rutledge shouted, hurrying to the horses. Even as he spoke Mosby saw the figures of the engine's crew leap from the cab and go racing for shelter.

"Cavalry!"

Rutledge's cry brought the Confederate leader about swiftly. A half a dozen men were coming down the slope at reckless speed.

"Come on, Major!" Rutledge yelled. "Let's get out of here!"

Mosby vaulted to the saddle. "Cut staight across," he called to Rutledge. "Be too slow through the brush and rocks—and too dangerous for the horses. And we've got to let Frost see us. You hear those gunshots over there? He could be in trouble."

79

"Some of that shooting was him. The train crew headed for the engine when they saw it moving. Reckon they figured to stop it. Ben changed their minds for them."

They bolted from the brush in which they had been hiding, started across the open ground. Instantly gunshots broke out on the slope behind them but the bullets fell short.

The earth suddenly heaved. A tremendous sound filled the air, seemed to shake the very mountains. Mosby, riding slightly back of Rutledge, felt himself pushed sideways as though a mighty blast of wind had swept across the valley.

"There she goes!" Rutledge yelled triumphantly.

15

IT WAS an awsome sight. Black smoke, laced with blood red flames, soared toward the heavens. Bits of bridge timber, steam cars, crates, boxes and unidentifiable objects hurtled into space like shooting stars. Explosions began to shock the valley as ammunition in the coaches was caught up in a chain reaction of sound. A monstrous crackling and grinding filled the air, suddenly stifling and almost unbearably hot.

A whole freight car thrust itself upwards into the clouds of boiling smoke and flame. It burst outward with a roar, sides, ends, top and bottom flying into separate directions. A vivid shower of fire arched into the sky, looking much like an Independence Day rocket seen bursting over the county fair grounds. The flames seemed to remain suspended overhead for a brief time and then plunged downward into the ravine. Another deafening train of explosions errupted and then, abruptly, the entire valley was aglow as the trestle caught and began to burn fiercely.

Somewhere near the swirling mass of flames men were shouting, the sound of their voices sporadic in the cracking and popping of ammunition going off. A hissing arose from the doomed locomotive lying in the bottom of the gorge and the bugle at the camp still cried into the confusion.

"Everything's on fire!" Rutledge shouted.

Mosby turned his glance to the clearing beyond the inferno in the ravine. It was barely discernible through the smoke and fire. Several of the tents had been struck by the flaming torches hurled through the air. All were now lustily burning pyramids.

The hard pound of running horses brought John Mosby around quickly. Another squad of cavalry! They, too, had come off the mountain, apparently having been somewhere on its opposite slope when the explosions began.

"Run for it!" Mosby shouted. "Keep low—and head for the trees across the way."

81

Rutledge spurred his horse into a dead run. Mosby followed. He had drawn his pistol, was half turned on his saddle and ready to open up if the Yankees drew too close.

"There they are!"

The shout, only a few paces to his right, caught the Ranger's attention. A tall, blue uniformed Yankee infantryman stood at the edge of the brush. He had his musket up, was leveling it. Behind him other blue figures were materializing.

Mosby fired quickly. The soldier took a faltering step backwards, fell. Other Yankees ran into the open near him. Shots rang out in hasty succession. The whine of bullets was a clear, angry sound.

"Keep going!" Mosby yelled at Rutledge. He snapped a second and then a third shot at the infantrymen, some of whom had dropped to one knee for better aim. He saw another go down. The man beside him wheeled suddenly, plunged back into the safety of the brush. Mosby looked for Rutledge. The Ranger, bent low over the saddle, was racing for the shelter of the trees still some distance away.

What had happened to Ben Frost?

Mosby searched anxiously for the sergeant. He should have put in an appearance before that moment. A growing dread arose within the Confederate leader. Since the first inception of the Rangers, in early 1863, John Mosby had, himself, carefully chosen all men to serve under his command. As a result each was personally known to him and was as close, almost, as a brother. The loss of one was a heavy blow and cause for deep sorrow. Now, if Ben Frost were dead or captured—

"Major! More cavalry!"

At Rutledge's warning cry, Mosby whirled to the left. A half a dozen riders, attracted by the foot soldiers' gunfire and shouting, were rushing in, giving chase.

A fresh yell went up from the infantrymen when they saw the mounted men. Mosby crouched lower over the bay, pressed the striving horse for more speed. He began to shorten the gap between Rutledge and himself.

"Another bunch of cavalry!"

It was the Ranger's voice again. To their right now a new squad of blue coated horsemen were bearing down fast. It was Tom Underwood this time. Mosby quickly recognized the big redhead, leading his men at a hard run on a course designed to prevent the two Rangers from reaching the trees.

"Bear left!" Mosby yelled.

Rutledge immediately swerved off. Mosby swung with him. Gradually they widened the distance between themselves and the Yankee captain. But in so doing, the cavalry behind them gained perceptibly. Gunshots again rang out across the afternoon, and once more the vicious whine of bullets filled the Confederates' ears.

The roaring of the flames that engulfed the bridge and filled the ravine was a gigantic sound, not unlike the terrible winds that sometimes swept in from the sea. The air had grown increasingly hotter and sudden bursts of explosions still told of ammunition, touched by hungry flames, being set off.

A single horseman broke suddenly from the trees directly ahead. Relief flooded through Mosby. It was Ben Frost! The sergeant squared himself on his saddle. Ignoring Underwood, still a considerable distance away, he took careful aim at the lead cavalryman on Mosby's heels, and fired. The soldier buckled forward. His horse swerved off, slowed to a trot and came to a stop. The Tennessean's revolver barked again. Another Yankee clawed at his shoulder, dropped from the charging line. Mosby and Rutledge, not slackening their headlong pace, began to add their fire to that of Frost.

On ahead Mosby saw the railroad track grading. Beyond it, no more than a dozen yards, lay the edge of the slope with its densely growing trees and thick tangle of brush—the promise of safety and escape. Crossing the grade would be dangerous. For a few moments, while the horses scrambled for the top, they would be almost stationary—and perfect targets.

"Watch yourself!" Mosby yelled to Rutledge.

They reached the rising, built up a good six feet at that point as a precautionary measure against the spring floods that annually swept the valley. The horses dug in, fought to make the climb. Behind them the cavalrymen, quick to recognize the advantage thrust upon them, laid down a flurry of shots. Underwood, too, seeing the delay Mosby and Rutledge could not avoid, yelled to his men for greater speed.

Mosby gained the top of the grade. The bay was blowing hard. Rutledge was only a step away. Ahead he saw Ben Frost. The sergeant was half standing in his stirrups, coolly firing at the oncoming Yankees.

For a moment Mosby and Rutledge were silhouetted atop the rise. It seemed to the Confederate leader that they were caught there, suspended by some mysterious and powerful force in the hope that Yankee bullets might cut them down. A new burst of shooting lifted. Underwood was now close enough to open up. Mosby felt a ball pluck at his sleeve, another caromed off his saddle with a shrill, whistling sound.

He heard Jess Rutledge curse, saw him reel slightly on the saddle. And then they were going down the opposite side of the grade. When they gained level ground, he looked closely at the Ranger. In the last flurry of gunshots Jess had not been so fortunate. A red stain was forming on his broad back, just below the right shoulder. He was having difficulty staying on his horse.

"Hang on," Mosby cried, surging in close. "We're almost there."

Rutledge turned his head, grinned. "I'll make it!"

Frost galloped toward them. "This way," he yelled and spun about.

Mosby maneuvered Rutledge into a position ahead of him. They raced in behind the sergeant, now plunging into the shelter of the brush and rock.

"Trail goes up and over the top," Frost called back without slowing.

Bullets still sang angrily about them, clipped sharply through the leaves of the trees, screamed off rocks. Neither the cavalry that had been at their heels nor Underwood's patrol had reached the grading yet. That would delay them for several seconds, and would give Mosby and the two Rangers ample time to get well within the trees and thickets.

Rutledge suddenly wilted. He bent forward in his saddle, clawed at his horse's mane to stay aboard. The trail was steep and he was immediately in serious difficulty.

"Sergeant!" Mosby shouted, and drummed on the bay's

flanks until he was abreast the stricken man. "Give me a hand here."

Frost dropped back instantly. Together they steadied Rutledge. The Ranger was limp, seemingly without strength. The entire back of his coarse shirt was soaked with blood.

The hammering of hoofs at the foot of the slope meant that the Yankee cavalry had crossed the grading, was now rushing for the narrow trail. Mosby halted, faced Ben Frost.

"Keep on moving," he said. "I'll make a stand here and hold them long as I can."

16

BEN FROST's features gathered into a protest. Mosby cut away, rode off down the trail a dozen paces. When he glanced toward the two Rangers, they had not moved.

"Get going, Sergeant!" he ordered, and placed his back to them once again.

A flash of blue at the foot of the slope caught his attention. He fired quickly, hoping to bring the oncoming soldiers to a halt before they gained a foothold on the path. He saw the Yankee jerk aside and drop behind a rock. Whether it was hit or just a near miss, Mosby had no way of knowing. But the movements at the bottom of the trail ceased.

"Sergeant Walker!"

It was Tom Underwood's voice, urgent and authoritative.

"Here—sir!" the reply came.

"Take some men, move up the side of this mountain. Block the trail from above."

"Yes, sir!"

Mosby sent two more bullets toward the foot of the trail, paused then to reload. When both pistols were again ready, he began to drop back, retreating slowly up the path. It would not do to allow any of the Yankees to circle about, place themselves between him and the crest of the slope. They would have him neatly boxed. But he knew he could not pull entirely back yet, for the moment such a movement on his part became apparent to the Yankees, they would come storming in pursuit. Even now they had dismounted and could possibly be working their way to him. But he must hold as long as possible. Frost had to be given sufficient time to move Rutledge to the top, and safety.

A loud clattering, the sound of loose gravel sliding, the crackling of brush followed by a man's fervent cursing, positioned Walker and his men for Mosby. They were finding the climb up the mountainside, where there was no trail, a hard go. They were still below him, he saw.

He flung a glance up the slope. Rutledge and ·Frost were gone from sight, cut off from view by the thick brush. The Ranger chieftain snapped another bullet toward the foot of the trail, once again fell into a slow, careful retreat. He halted after a short distance. He was high enough now to look down into the valley and see the bridge, or the ravine where it had stretched its span. The area was still wrapped in billows of smoke and flames continued to leap upward from the floor of the gorge. There was nothing visible of the trestle. Even the approaches were gone, devoured by the fire that consumed the aged timbers like seasoned kindling wood.

The flames in the camp had been extinguished. Most of the tents and huts had burned to smouldering heaps and a dozen or so soldiers and civilians were gathered about the pusher locomotive. By quick action someone had managed to uncouple the engine before it had been pulled down into the raging inferno in the ravine.

It was strange. There was no shooting on the part of Underwood's men. Nor from the rest of the cavalrymen who had joined in the chase. The fact disturbed John Mosby, sent a vague warning through him. He withdrew farther up the slope, pondering the possible meaning. Was Underwood's entire force endeavoring to circle around and cut him off? Or were they all lying back, awaiting the moment when Walker could gain a position of advantage?

It came suddenly to Mosby that some sort of ruse was being perpetrated; Underwood's shouted command, loud enough to be heard across the mountain. Walker's reply, the noisy commotion to prove the sergeant-major and his squad of men were under way. It had all been for his benefit. The Yankee captain wanted him to believe in Walker's attempt, hoped he would confine his attention to that section of the slope. And since no attempt was being made to rush the trail itself, there could be only one answer; Underwood and a number of his men were moving in on the left, the opposite flank, hopeful of catching him unawares.

Mosby reacted fast. He swung about, moved hurriedly up the path after Rutledge and Frost. Within twenty-five yards he caught sight of the pair. Frost was on foot leading both horses. He had secured Rutledge to the saddle in some manner to prevent his toppling to the ground.

The trail had turned steep and the horses were having a bad time of it with their footing. Heedless, Mosby urged the bay on. He was thinking little of his own personal danger in those moments. He knew only that he must get the wounded Rutledge and Ben Frost to the top and start them down the opposite slope before Underwood and his men could effect an interception.

Frost heard the clattering of the bay. He glanced back, waved but did not halt. Rutledge appeared to be totally unconscious. He needed immediate attention, Mosby realized, otherwise he soon would bleed to death. And tending the wound would require many precious minutes. He drew the heaving bay to a stop, turned his attention down the trail. No soldiers were to be seen but he could not be certain they were not nearby. The path they had ascended twisted and turned sharply innumerable times as it cut its way through the rocks and dense brush.

He moved off to the left as far as the trail would permit, listening hard, probing the undergrowth for a flash of blue that would betray the presence of a Yankee soldier. He could neither hear nor see anything. He transferred his attention to the opposite side. There were only the dull, gray rocks, the silent twisted trees that fought one another for a glimpse of the sun, the matted tangle of vines and other growth. If the soldiers were advancing they were doing an unusual job of keeping quiet.

There were no more sounds coming from the area where Walker, with several men, supposedly was making the climb. He was more convinced now than ever that such a move had been faked action, that Walker had never intended to make the try. He turned about then, resumed the trail.

At that instant he did hear sound. It was a faint, distant rattling of rock. It seemed some distance away, much too far for any of Underwood's party. Of course, it could be more soldiers coming up from the camp to join in the hunt. He should expect that. The Yankees, infuriated by the loss and destruction of the train and bridge, would leave nothing undone to capture the men responsible for the disaster.

Mosby retreated steadily, his eyes sweeping back and forth across the cluttered slope below, ears straining for the least sound that would reveal the position of a blue clad enemy. Frost and Rutledge were again gone from view, the trail having made another right angle turn. But now and then the sounds of their slow progress reached him—a dislodged stone, the swooshing of a branch, the crack of a dead limb . . .

They should be near the summit. It seemed they had been on the side of the mountain for hours rather than a few short minutes. He could see the hard, slate colored rim of the palisades that stretched out on either side. A thought came to him; unless the trail they followed led to a pass through the towering cliffs, he and the two Rangers would shortly find themselves, literally, with their backs to a wall.

Mosby heard the enemy to his left at that point. It was the sharp click of metal, as though a musket barrel had been accidently swung against a stone. He checked both his pistols, again made certain they were fully loaded. He glanced up the path. Frost and Rutledge were out of sight, possibly on the summit. He could see a patch of blue through the lacework of tree leaves.

Soldiers suddenly burst into the open. They faced him from three sides. They were not shooting but bore down upon him with drawn sabers, or muskets upraised as clubs. He spun about, fired point blank at the man clawing for the bay's bridle. The Yankee went over backwards into the rocks.

"Get him! Get him!"

It was not Tom Underwood's voice. The order came from the burly sergeant-major who came plunging from the brush waving a pistol over his head. He would be Walker.

"Drag him off'n that horse!" he yelled. "Captain wants that Reb alive for hangin'!"

Mosby fired rapidly, keeping the soldiers back as he retreated steadily up the trail. The ambush had sprung from both sides of the path, and from below. It would appear none of the Yankees had yet been able to get in behind to cut him off from Rutledge and Frost. He took care that none would succeed now.

Walker crowded to the fore of his men, shouting curses as they fell back in the face of the Ranger's deadly shooting. He bowled one man aside, lunged for Mosby's wrist. The Confederate threw himself to one side to keep from being dragged off the saddle. With his free hand he brought his pistol down hard on the Yankee sergeant's skull. Walker groaned, released his hold. He went to his knees. The bay's churning hind legs caught him, knocked him sprawling into the brush.

Gunshots rang out from behind Mosby. He looked around quickly, fearful that some of the soldiers had managed to surround him. It was Ben Frost. The big sergeant was coming down the trail on foot, his pistol snapping wickedly. In his belt he carried a second weapon. Jess Rutledge's, Mosby guessed.

The Yankees recoiled at the new and sudden burst of shots. Mosby saw one drop to his knee, take aim at Frost's advancing figure. Mosby fired quickly. The Yankee cavalryman half raised, then pitched forward.

"Come on, Major!" Frost shouted, starting to retreat. "Top's only a few yards along. Good place there to hold them off."

Mosby turned. His guns were almost empty and there was no time to reload. He fought the frightened bay into motion, got him headed up the path after Frost, who was covering his movements with cool, appallingly accurate shooting.

Sergeant-major Walker was again yelling at his men. He had not been seriously injured, only stunned. He was trying to rally his disorganized patrols, keep them pressing the two Confederates as they fell back.

"Forget what I told you! Shoot—stop them any way you can! Don't let them get away!"

A twist in the trail cut off Mosby's view of the soldiers. He looked ahead. The way led to a narrow gash in the face of the cliff. Ben Frost had known of the opening, and, as he had said, it would be an ideal place at which to make a stand.

He spurred forward, caught up with the Tennessean. "What about Jess?"

Frost pointed to the cleft in the rock face. "Through there, Major. Got him restin'. He's in a bad way."

Mosby nodded. "We'll do what we can, then you're to light out for Dumfries with him. I'll stay here."

17

THE TWO men hurried to where the suffering Jess Rutledge lay. He was off his horse and sprawled full length on the hard ground. Mosby swung down and knelt beside him.

"Have you up and going in a few minutes, Ranger," he said. Then to Frost, he added, "Keep a watch on that trail, sergeant."

Rutledge roused. He twisted painfully about, grinned at his commanding officer. "I'll be all right, Major. Just help me back onto my horse. We got to be getting out of here."

"Not for a bit," Mosby replied. He rose, stepped quickly to the bay. From the saddlebags he procured several strips of cotton cloth that had been ripped into bandage widths. There was also a bottle of antiseptic given him by one of the surgeons. There were times when he and members of the Rangers were beyond contact with the main Confederate forces for days, even weeks, and medical attention was therefore not always available to them. He had found it prudent to carry a small store of simple necessities for use in just such emergencies as this.

He returned to Rutledge. Taking his knife, he slit the blood soaked shirt from collar to tail. The wound, he saw, was not too serious. It had bled copiously but fortunately, no bones or vital organs appeared to have been damaged by the musket ball which had passed entirely through. To that degree Jess Rutledge had been lucky.

"You'll be all right," Mosby said. "You've lost a lot of blood but I can stop that."

He set to work cleansing the wound. When that was done he applied a pressure bandage, using a liberal amount of the antiseptic in the process. It was necessary to raise Rutledge to a sitting position but the Ranger bore the pain without complaint.

Finished, Mosby got to his feet. He replaced the remainder of the bandages and antiseptic in his saddlebags and then moved to where Ben Frost maintained his vigil. The sergeant had chosen a point behind a large rock which afforded him an excellent view of the trail.

"Any signs of Yankees?"

Frost shook his head. "Nothin', but they're down there, and close. Thought I heard some movin' about a minute ago but I ain't certain. Major, you mean what you said about stayin' here?"

"I did. We'll get Jess onto his horse. He needs a surgeon soon as possible. About all I could do for him was stop the bleeding and that may not hold for long."

Frost rubbed his chin thoughtfully. "Be better for me to stay behind, Major—"

Mosby said, "No, I'm the honey that draws the flies. It's me Underwood wants. Even if I fail to hold them and they break through, I doubt if they will follow you and Rutledge."

"But, couldn't the three of us—"

Mosby did not permit the Tennessee man to finish. "We've got to get Jess to a doctor. And just as important, we've got to let General Lee know about the bridge and that Grant's supply train has gone up in smoke. He can then better figure how to proceed. It will be up to you, Ben, to see that he gets that word, as well as seeing to it that Jess gets help.

"Ride straight to Dumfries. Lee's courier will be checking with Carstairs. If he's not there, leave Jess and ride on and find the General yourself. I don't know where he will be. Somewhere between the Wilderness and Richmond."

"But, Major, be a dang sight more sensible—"

"Sergeant Frost!" Mosby cut in, his voice sharp edged. "I'm giving you an order. I expect to have it carried out to the exact letter."

Frost snapped to attention. "Yes, sir," he said and saluted.

"Good. Now, help me drag that old stump there into the trail. We'll block that opening between the rocks. It won't hold back men on foot, or horses either, for that matter, but they won't find it so easy to rush me."

They walked to where the stump lay rotting in the

sun. Together they managed to tumble it into the narrow pass.

"Now, let's get Jess on his horse," Mosby said, wheeling about. "I've got a feeling Underwood's going to try something mighty soon."

They hurried to where Rutledge lay. He seemed better. Color was returning to his face and he protested considerably when he learned of Mosby's order.

"No time to explain it now," the Confederate chief said, helping Frost lift the wounded man to his saddle. "Ben will give you the details later. We're going to tie you to your horse, Jess. Can't have you falling off."

Rutledge nodded his understanding. He swore softly at the ill luck that had overtaken him and now prevented him from taking part in the critical situation. Mosby patted his arm.

"Don't fret about it. You'll live to fight the Yankees another day. Anyway, you've done your share. The General will hear how those bombs of yours wiped out not only that bridge but the whole train as well."

"Thanks, Major," Rutledge murmured. "But I reckon it was only a piece of the plan—one third of it and no more. There was the getting in and the getting out. And I keep thinking—"

"Never mind the thinking. All you need do now is reach Dumfries and get that wound looked after. Then get on home and do that work you were talking about. I'll send for you when there's another chore to be done. You ready to move out, Sergeant?"

"Ready," Frost replied and swung onto his horse.

A sudden burst of gunshots down the mountain slope brought them all around. Mosby frowned, walked hurriedly to the opening in the cliff where he and Frost had thrown up the stump barrier. The sergeant dropped from his saddle and followed.

"Who would that be, Major?" Frost wondered. "Who'd them Yankees be shootin' at 'way over there?"

Mosby stared thoughtfully toward the valley. "Don't think we'd have any patrols in that area. The General brought in everybody when he decided to make a fight of it in the Wilderness."

"Reckon a couple of our boys just happened along, maybe lost, and are tryin' to reach our lines?"

"Possible," Mosby agreed. "Little far north but there could be a reason."

Again the rattle of gunshots broke across the late afternoon hush. The firing came from their right and a considerable distance lower. It was much farther away than it had seemed at first.

"Whoever it is," Mosby said, "makes a bit of luck for us. Maybe they will keep Underwood busy long enough for us all to get out of here."

Frost grinned, relieved. "Now, I'm hearin' you good, Major! Let's go!"

They wheeled, trotted to where their horses waited beside that of Jess Rutledge. Frost vaulted onto the saddle, spun about to herd the wounded Ranger's mount onto the trail that descended the slope and led to escape.

"The major's comin' with us, Jess," he said. "Them Yankees has found somebody else to shoot at."

The sharp crack of a musket punctuated the sergeant's words. Mosby, in the act of swinging onto the bay, sprang back. He heard a second report, this time the drone of the bullet. Without hesitation he leaped to one side, drew his pistol. On the run he snapped a shot at the barricade behind which a blur of blue had moved.

"Get out of here!" he shouted at Frost and slapped the sergeant's horse smartly on the flank.

The animal bolted forward, startling Rutledge's gray and sending him plunging down the narrow pathway. Again Mosby did not pause. He gained a clump of bushes, dived headlong into their thickness as the rifle barked again. He had not scored with his shot, he realized, or else there were a number of soldiers beyond the stump. He heard the musket ball thump into a tree, saw it send up a small explosion of dust and splinters.

He continued to move, not daring to remain motionless. He must reach a point where he could use his own weapons, prevent Underwood's men from climbing over the barricade and swarming in upon him—and giving chase to Rutledge and Frost.

His hope had been that the two Rangers could get started down the mountain unseen, thus precluding the possibilities of pursuit. But now that had all changed; their departure had been noticed.

There was a good chance that no effort to overtake

them would be made, that the Yankees would concentrate on him, as he had pointed out to Frost. At that moment it had been little more than a method for silencing the sergeant's protests, but now he found himself believing there might be more truth in it than he expected.

He reached the end of the brush, found himself against a solid wall of granite that lifted upwards for twenty or thirty feet. He could go no farther that way. He raised his head, peered toward the barricade. He could not see it from where he crouched. He was too far to the side.

But neither could the Yankees see him, he realized. Immediately he broke from the thicket, raced across the open ground and hauled up behind a bulge of loose rock and scraggly weeds. He looked again toward the break in the bridge. It was visible from his new position. He nodded in satisfaction. Let Underwood and his soldiers come. He could handle them, unless, he thought grimly, they all decided to come at one time.

18

OFF, DEEP in the valley, in the vicinity of the devastated bridge, John Mosby could hear men shouting. Their voices sounded hollow, oddly remote and detached. A gigantic smoke pall hung in the sky over the basin, so low the flickering flames mirrored against bellying clouds and turned them dull orange and yellow.

The mission had been successfully accomplished, he thought, as he watched the darkness slowly gather over the land. Even if he failed to live through it, and the odds now against that were great, he had been a factor in striking a tremendous blow for the Confederacy. The end result of it could be as beneficial as the winning of a decisive battle, and Lee's hopes to withstand the stolid Grant's relentless offensives should be materially improved.

If death were ahead it had never occurred to him that it would come in this manner—standing lonely sentinel at a mountain pass. He had always assumed that, when his luck ran out, it would happen one day in battle, or possibly while he was on a scouting expedition and was taken unawares by the Yankees.

Still—what difference how a man died so long as his life ended while he fought for the things he loved and believed in? What matter whether death claimed him as he charged across an open field in the face of enemy bullets, or while he slipped, silent as a summer shadow, through a Union encampment? All added up to the same total— and served an identical purpose; for the South, for the Confederacy. And a man should expect to die one day, he supposed, when he went to war.

There were few things in his life he regretted but he was sorry there had been no opportunity to visit his wife and children before this hour presented itself. It had been months since he had last seen them. Things would be greening up around Hathaway House. The warm, spring rains and the sun would have brought the trees into bud and leaf, the flowers would again be vividly spangling the gardens. Birds, despite the propinquity of war, would be singing in the boxwoods and hemlocks and other trees. And through it all the children would be laughing and playing, unaffected by the swirling tragedy that had caught up their elders.

For what had gone before in his brief thirty years of life, he was not sorry. Were the same problems and questions placed before him again, his answers woud be the same. Time had been good to him. He was thankful for the years with his wife and children, for the friends he had made, and if he never came down from the mountain top, he had those things to keep with him in memory when he fell.

He smiled, grimly, recalling the words of Jess Rutledge, or maybe it had been Sergeant Frost. They had been spoken when they were heading out on the mission to destroy the bridge and supply train; the desolation and death of the Wilderness was behind and they were moving into the quiet, seemingly untouched hills; *from hell to hallelujah,* the Ranger had said. There had been more truth in the utterance than any of them had supposed.

He wished, too, that he might have seen and talked with Jeb Stuart once more before it was all over. Always close friends, their parting at Lee's command post had been abrupt. Matters were so urgent there had been no time for the usual hour or two of conversation and exchange of thoughts and ideas.

Stuart would display a terrible anger when he heard of his friend's death. His red beard would bristle, his pale, blue eyes would snap and harden, and he would swear a mighty oath against the whole Yankee army for what they had done. But it would be only a show to mask the grief that enveloped him. To the world Jeb Stuart exhibited the steel-hard facade of a fearless, reckless soldier; to those who knew him well, as did John Mosby, that cold, almost brutal visage was sham: within him flowed the tenderness of a woman. The loss of any friend within his vast circle of acquaintances was always a personal diminishment.

Of late Stuart had changed. He appeared more thoughtful, often was moody and non-committal. There had been no alteration in the strong bond that existed between the two Confederate leaders but Mosby had been disturbed at times, had wondered if the cavalry officer were ill or unduly worried. Asked about it, Stuart had shrugged his thick shoulders and smiled.

"Forget it, John," he had said. "Reckon I've been doing too much thinking. You know how a man gets a hunch—a feeling of sorts. Well, one has been plaguing me. Could be I'm getting old."

John Mosby recalled his answer: "Who isn't? This war is making old men of all of us."

It was a strange turn of events, he thought, as he crouched there behind his shelter on the mountain top. Jeb Stuart had had the premonition he was about to die. It was the other way around.

He drew to sudden alert at a sound on the trail beyond the barricade. He strained to see through the hazy darkness. There was no movement around the stump; at least, he could detect none. Yet the noise had been unmistakable. It could have been a man's boot scuffing against the ground, a musket stock carelessly dragged across a rock.

The failing light had brought disadvantage to his position. He now needed to be in a more direct line with the cleft in the rocks if he were to see clearly any activity that took place around it. Now shadows were a hindrance.

Keeping close to the earth, he moved away from the mound of stones. A dozen paces distant in the small clearing, a fallen tree offered a hiding place. It was partially burned, attesting to the fact that once it had stood tall on the crown of the hill but had become victim to one of the wild storms that struck periodically. If he could gain the shelter of the log, he would command an excellent view of the barricade.

He gained the cover of the tree without incident. He had half expected a musket or a pistol shot, when he had bolted across the open. There had been nothing—only the night's silence filled with the expected drone of insects and rustle of small birds or animals in the dry brush.

How far would Rutledge and Ben Frost have gotten by this time? It was hard to estimate. They had been gone a good half hour but he was not familiar with the trail that descended the mountain's west side and had no way of knowing if their pace would be slow and cautious, or a good speed. He could only hope that all had gone well for them. Just how long he could hold out against a concerted attack by Underwood and his men, once they decided to make their move, was a matter of speculation. At least until his two pistols were empty.

He squatted on his heels, laid his twin weapons before him and tried to make himself comfortable. He stared at the pale skeleton of the stump, wondered if the Yankees beyond it were having their thoughts about what awaited them behind the barricade. The bullet he had fired earlier had discouraged any rash decision to climb over, at least for the time. But what were they waiting for?

Again he thought of the gunshots he had heard far down the slope and once more wondered who the Yankees could have been firing at. That it was someone of the Confederacy seemed unlikely. But if not, who? He listened into the night, strained to keep his mind concentrated on the root-snarled barrier, and on the trail back of it. Why didn't Underwood make his move? Mosby stirred impatiently. His nerves were beginning to wear thin. *Why didn't the Yankees attack?*

They certainly were there, hiding in the brush, watching his every move. There should be quite a number of them; Tom Underwood and at least eighteen or twenty men. The odds were all with the redheaded captain. Why was he delaying?

Earlier, Mosby had assumed the Yankees were awaiting sundown, when the men could move about more freely and perhaps scramble over the barricade with less chance of being seen. Now it was full dark, with only the starshine to outline them. And it would seem that Underwood would be anxious to break through and go in pursuit of Frost and Rutledge. Unless, as Mosby had reasoned before, the Yankee officer considered them of no importance.

The definite, hard clink of metal against stone brought John Mosby around. The sound had not come from beyond the barricade but from the west slope trail down which the two Rangers had disappeared. Mosby snatched up his revolvers, prepared to face the enemy from that unexpected quarter. A flood of dismay rushed through him. Underwood had somehow scaled the palisades with his men; he had circled, closed in from the rear. Likely he had heard Frost and Rutledge descending and had intercepted and captured them.

A riderless horse walked into the clearing. Mosby

stared. It was the one Ben Frost had been riding. He watched as the animal walked up to his own mount and halted. It looked around, as if assuring itself it had reached a correct destination, and then began to graze on the scanty grass that sprouted between the rocks.

What had happened? There had been no shooting on that side of the mountain. But, of course, Underwood's men, in force, could have taken the two Rangers by surprise and, in the ensuing struggle, the sergeant's horse could have broken away and trotted back up the trail.

Or there could have been an accident.

Mosby cast another close look at the barricade. He could see no signs of anyone. Keeping low, he crawled the length of the log. When he reached that point, he again checked the stump. Satisfied that his chances were good, he rose and ran across the open ground to where Frost's horse stood.

He caught the animal's bridle and made a careful examination of the saddle. There was no blood or other evidence of a fight. Something else must have happened, something that had no connection with Underwood and his soldiers. The thought that Frost, and even the wounded Jess Rutledge, might have been captured without a struggle was difficult to accept. Rangers were not that easily overcome. No, it was for some different cause that the horse had returned to the clearing. Frost had dismounted; perhaps Rutledge had needed aid. The horse had then become frightened and bolted.

A flare of light back at the barricade brought John Mosby up sharply. A yell broke through the night.

"There they are—by them rocks!"

Underwood and his men at last! The attack was on. They had tossed a bundle of flaming faggots over the tree stump as a means for lighting up the clearing.

Mosby jerked on the leather harness in his hand. He wheeled the horse about, headed him down the trail. He gave a shout, slapped the animal hard on the rump, sent him pounding off into the darkness. Likely Frost and Rutledge would be riding double. They would need the black.

"There they go!" Sergeant-major Walker's hoarse voice boomed. "Down the trail!"

Instantly half a dozen guns cracked. Bullets whipped

100

by Mosby. He paid them scant attention, swung instead onto the saddle of the bay. There would be no chance to stand firm in the clearing now. They had caught him in the open, away from any protective shelter. And he could not follow Ben Frost's horse; to do so would be to lead the Yankees to the escaping Rangers.

He spun the bay, raced across the clearing, to stop in shadow at its far side. The shooting ceased. The fire, flaring so brightly at the start, had abruptly died. But there would be more. A desperate thought moved into the Confederate's mind. He had one chance—one hope; surprise. Do something the Yankees would not expect.

He studied the stark, gnarled shape of the stump for several moments. It was not high. A simple jump for any horse. The problem would be the fire. Would the bay be able to clear it and the barricade both? Would he balk in the face of flames or would he take it all in stride?

He reached down, patted the horse's trembling neck. It might help if he took a strip of the bandage, and blindfolded the animal. But there was no time for that and there was no guarantee that it would work. There were horses that refused to move a step when their eyes were covered. The bay could be one of those.

Mosby took a deep breath. He checked both pistols, cocked them. He could hear the soldiers talking beyond the barrier. They were preparing a second bundle of faggots. That would be the time to act—the moment they tossed the torch over the stump and the glare of the flames was still in their eyes.

He saw the sudden rise of light. The bundle arched up and over. A shout broke through the night. Mosby leaned forward on the bay, spoke softly to the quivering animal. He drove his heels sharply inward. The horse sprang forward, fled across the open ground toward the stump.

Blue shadows began to clamber over the misshapen barricade. Mosby fired at them, instantly cleared the way. He hammered at the bay's ribs, urged him on. They drew near the stump. The pile of fiercely blazing faggots lay directly in his path. Beyond the flames Mosby could see several startled faces.

"Up, boy!" he cried to the bay and leaned into the jump

just as he had done a hundred times and more before in the quiet years when there was no war, no enemy.

The horse left the ground in a long, graceful arc. Like a soaring, winged Pegasus he cleared the fire, floated over the stump. And then John Mosby knew his luck had run out.

The gallant little bay was not going to make it.

MOSBY HAD a fleeting glimpse of shadowy figures, of pale, upturned faces. A burst of yells and curses broke out. In that fraction of the confused night, the bay seemed to halt momentarily in mid-air, remain suspended. He felt himself leave the saddle, hurtle downward. The hind legs of the horse had struck against an upthrusting root of the stump.

Mosby hit the ground on hands and knees. Momentum propelled him forward into a clump of thorny bush. He recoiled involuntarily, threw himself to one side. A pistol exploded close by, so near the crash of it almost deafened him. He rolled away, legs and arms driving madly as he sought to gain cover. He bounded to his feet as the pistol crashed again. He heard the bullet smash into a tree only an arm's length away. Behind him he could hear the wild thrashing of the bay, creating havoc among the soldiers who had been clustered at the base of the stump.

He plunged off into the tangle of brush. Darkness instantly cut off any view from the clearing but the noise of his flight was giving him away. Another shot ripped through the night. The ball passed only inches above his head. He dodged to his right, ran hard, ran blind. He knew he could prevent their seeing him but there was no way to avoid the racket his frantic passage was setting up.

"This way!" Walker's strident voice shouted. "You men —follow me!"

Mosby veered to his left, changing course. He could hear the soldiers now in pursuit, crashing, stumbling, swearing as they ran heedlessly. He was moving parallel across the slope of the mountain and the footing was dangerous. Loose rock, brush, exposed roots were a constant threat. He was continually off balance, struggling to stay upright and to keep running.

The Yankees were not slowing the chase. He altered direction again, this time heading straight down the steep grade, taking it in long, reckless strides.

"You see him, Sarge?" a voice called from off to the right.

Mosby endeavored to slow his downhill plunge. It was impossible. Speed and momentum combined to keep his legs churning. He strained his eyes ahead, sought to locate something by which he could halt his wild flight. Soon he would become over-balanced and a bad, possibly fatal, fall would be inevitable. A thick stand of low bushes loomed below. He made no attempt to avoid it, instead, permitted his hurtling body to rush full tilt into its depths. He tripped, went sprawling. The branches clawed at his skin but the cushioning effect saved him from any serious injury.

"There he is—down below us!" Walker sang out instantly. "Everybody stand quiet and listen. I heard him movin'."

"You all had better watch," another voice spoke up. "That's Mosby we're foolin' with. He'd as soon stick a knife in you as take a breath."

The dry rattle of displaced gravel and the snap of brush had ceased. Mosby, gasping deep for wind, lay quietly in the brush. A long minute dragged by.

"I don't hear nothin', Sarge. You reckon he could've reached the bottom?"

"Ain't had time. Anyway we'd still be hearin' him, was he movin'."

"Maybe. But they say them Rangers can get about quieter'n a mouse on a bale of cotton—"

"What about them other two, Sarge? Hadn't some of us better go back and get after them before they get too far?"

Walker's hoarse voice said, "Don't worry none about that. The captain sent some cavalry around the mountain to look after them. What we got to do is find the one on this side. He's the one the captain wants most."

"How we goin' to do that? So damn dark a man can't see his hand on his nose."

John Mosby listened and waited for the non-com to reply. He was a scant fifty yards below the Yankees and he could hear them plainly. As soon as Walker announced his plan for the search he would know what he must do.

He considered moving on while the soldiers prepared to act but quickly discarded the thought. In the darkness he could easily make a mis-step and tip off his position. It would be better to wait until they once again were searching. The noise of their own movements would cover his.

"Plunkett, stay up there by that old stump. Don't figure he'll try to escape that way but we ain't takin' no chances. Captain's goin' to raise holy hell as it is. You better build up that fire so's you can see good. And do somethin' about that horse. No use lettin' him suffer."

"All right, Sergeant," the soldier called Plunkett replied.

The fall had evidently injured the bay badly. It had probably broken both hind legs. Mosby felt a pang of sorrow for the little horse. He had done his job well, had come through at the critical moment. It also brought to John Mosby's mind an awareness of a new problem; he would have to find a new mount—assuming he managed to escape the Yankees and get off the mountain.

"Rest of you men string out. Keep about fifteen, twenty feet apart. We're startin' down slope. That Reb's hidin' somewhere in the brush and we'll flush him out like a bobwhite. Count off soon's you're in position. Lively now! Captain's due back here and I'm sure goin' to hate tellin' him we let that sucker slip through our fingers."

Mosby listened to the scuffling and rattling as the soldiers began to shape up a line. They would come down the slope in a broad sweep. Just how far the line would extend he had no way of knowing. That depended upon the number of men Walker had at his disposal. Mosby considered his situation. He had two choices. He could fade on down the slope ahead of the Yankees, keeping as quiet as possible, and follow a slanting course that, if he were lucky, would eventually take him beyond the end of the line.

Or he could lie quietly in the brush, gamble on the soldiers by-passing him in the darkness. The odds against the success of the second plan were high, he realized. He could be lucky and find himself in the middle distance between two of the soldiers; but it could easily be the other way around. He could end up directly in a Yankee's path. He would then have to show himself and make a run for it. And he would have small chance there. Sergeant-major Walker didn't sound like a man who was going to bungle his opportunities a second time.

A gunshot flatted across the night. It had come from the clearing. Plunkett ending the life of the bay. Up the slope above him Mosby heard the count-off begin; *one* . . . *two . . . three . . . four . . .* And finally, *eleven.* He had thought there would be more. But then he remembered that Walker had said something about Underwood sending some men to circle the mountain.

"All right!" the sergeant-major's voice echoed across the slope. "For—aard! Keep the man alongside you in sight. Keep your eyes peeled. We got to ketch that Reb."

Mosby heard the Yankees begin the descent. At the first rattle of loose rock he moved out of the bushes in which he had lain. The moon was out now and growing stronger but in the depths of the forest, its light failed to be of any appreciable help and he was compelled to proceed slowly and with extreme care.

He slanted down the slope, angled to the right. This route would take him in the general direction of the devastated bridge and, unquestionably, into territory where he could expect more soldiers to be in evidence. But, because of that very possibility, he felt his opportunities for finding a horse would be increased. To have gone the opposite way would have been much safer but his chances for escape to the Confederate lines would be proportionately smaller.

He wondered about Ben Frost and the wounded Rutledge. The Yankee sergeant-major, Walker, had said men were dispatched to capture them. He wondered now if the two Rangers had sucessfully eluded them or were they now prisoners, waiting to be hanged? He was positive now that the returning of Frost's horse had no bearing on the situation. The incident, whatever it might be, had occurred long before Underwood's cavalrymen would have had sufficient time to sweep around the mountain.

But the thought that the pair might be captives of the Yankees set off a steady train of worry within him. Captured, their fate was a foregone conclusion. Moreover, Mosby was depending on Frost to get through and carry the word to General Lee that Grant's supplies had been cut off. Now there was a good chance the Tennessee sergeant would fail. This made it imperative that Mosby escape and report to the Confederate Commander-in-Chief.

"Sarge! Down below—to the right!"

Mosby froze in the deep shadows through which he was making cautious passage. The warning shout of the men moving down the slope came to an abrupt halt.

"What was it? You see him?"

"Don't know. Was sure somethin'. Saw it dodgin' across a little clearin'."

"All right. Get down there and take a look. You men next to Billy, go with him. Rest of you hold your positions," Walker added, raising his voice so all might hear. "Now, you volunteers watch sharp! He's liable to come bustin' out there hell bent for 'lection!"

Mosby crouched in the blackness, endeavored to locate the three men who would be pushing forward to investigate. He wasn't sure if the Yankee called Billy had actually seen him or had caught a glimpse of something else. Regardless, he must be ready to act. Scarcely breathing, he rode out the tense moments.

Off to one side a twangy voice said, "Where was it at, Billy?"

"That there patch of bushes right in front of you. That's where he'd be, was it him."

"You ain't sure it was him?"

"Ain't sure of nothin'. I'm sayin' I saw somethin' move, quick like, in the moonlight."

"Well, come on over here with me. I ain't stickin' my nose in there by myself!"

Billy had not seen him. Mosby breathed deeper. The soldiers were heading for a thick stand of brush fifty feet or so on ahead. Either it had been the Yankee's imagination working overtime, or it had been someone else. He recalled the shooting that had taken place earlier in the evening. There could be some connection.

A route for escape suddenly appeared to the Ranger chief. Billy, and the men who had flanked him in the line, had pulled forward. Thus a broad gap now presented itself to the Confederate. He had only to head back up the slope, working toward his left, and, when he drew somewhere near a point abreast the remainder of the Yankees, settle down out of sight. Once Billy announced that it had been a mistake on his part, the sergeant would order the line to move on. Billy and the pair with him would not double back; they would simply wait until the others caught up.

It was absurdly easy. Mosby, moving like a wisp of smoke, turned back up the mountainside. On hands and knees he made his way through the dark shadows, carefully testing every hand place, every foothold before he trusted his weight to it.

"What about it, Billy?" Walker yelled. The non-com was so near that he startled Mosby.

"Ain't nobody down here, Sarge. Reckon I didn't see nothin'."

"Could have been a bird," someone else suggested. "One flying across open ground like that would have looked like a man running."

"Well, it wasn't our Reb," Walker said, "so let's be movin' on. Billy, you and them other boys wait right where you are. Don't want you gettin' out ahead of us. Everybody watch sharp. We're close to the bottom. We ought to be drivin' him out into the open purty soon."

Mosby, lying prone and still as death beneath a thickly leafed berry bush, heard the soldiers push on. He waited until they had picked up the trio who had advanced, and were continuing down the hillside. When there was no further danger of their either hearing or seeing him, he rose and struck out for the summit.

There would be only one guard at the barricade. Obtaining a horse and getting by him should be simple.

THE MOON lit up the area fronting the barrier with a strong, silver glow. Plunkett, the man detailed to stand guard, had built a fire and it, too, spread a bright fan of light across the rocks and over the brush.

John Mosby crawled silently to the edge of the clearing. Plunkett, at that moment, was crouched beside the luckless bay horse and was methodically ransacking the saddlebags. He was finding nothing of great value; a small amount of dried food, the telescope, medical supplies and a handful of spare ammunition.

The Ranger lay quietly in the thick brush for several minutes, listening and watching. He was certain there were no more Yankees in the immediate vicinity, but he could take nothing for granted. He studied the shadows beyond the flare of light, searching for horses. He located them a dozen yards down the trail. Would there be a man posted with them? It was customary but he doubted that the burly Walker would have taken such a precaution in this instance; he was too intent upon catching the Confederates who had destroyed the bridge and the railroad. He was employing every available man on the slope in the hunt with the exception, of course, of Plunkett.

Mosby reached into his boot, drew his knife. He must act swiftly and with certainty. A gunshot on the part of the Yankee would bring the others charging back up the slope instantly. He looked more closely at Plunkett, still digging hopefully through the saddlebags. The Yankee would not be easy to handle. He was a big man and would outweigh Mosby's slender one hundred and twenty-five pounds by half again.

Somewhere down near the foot of the mountain a shout lifted. Someone in the line had seen, or thought he had seen, motion. Another false alarm. That would work in John Mosby's favor. It would keep Walker and his men busy longer.

But the sergeant-major could not be expected to remain below indefinitely. When he and his men reached the flats and found no victim scuttling out before them, what would their next move be? Would Walker elect to continue along the edge of the mountain, or would he double back and return to the clearing? And what of Tom Underwood and his patrol? Where were they? Mosby felt a stream of dissatisfaction build and start to run through him. None of this was to his liking. He had faced similar odds before but always he had been aware of attending conditions. Here, conversely, he knew nothing definite.

But he could delay no longer. That much was evident. He must act to get Plunkett out of the way, sprint down the trail to where the Union cavalry horses waited. Then mounted on one, he would leap the barricade and start down the west trail for Dumfries. He would have to chance running into Underwood and his men. It was a calculated risk but he had no choice except to take it.

He drew himself to a crouch. Silently he glided from the brush, closed in on Plunkett. At that precise moment the Yankee soldier finished with his purloining of the saddlebags. He rose to his feet, half turned. He had a glimpse of Mosby rushing in upon him.

The man's eyes spread wide with surprise. A startled oath escaped his flaring lips. He tried to bring up his musket. Mosby struck him, knocked the weapon clattering to the ground. Breath exploded from Plunkett's lungs as Mosby drove his knotted fist into the man's belly and then they went over in a flailing tangle of arms and legs.

It took only seconds for Plunkett to recover from the initial surprise and shock. He wrestled about until he was flat on his back, began to fight. He caught Mosby's wrist in his powerful fingers and the Confederate leader became immediately conscious of the man's massive strength. The Ranger felt his arm being thrust up and back. But if Plunkett had the advantage of size, Mosby, skilled in the art of close, desperate in-fighting, was the better man in that.

He threw himself backwards, off the soldier. The sudden and unexpected move caught Plunkett unaware. He lost his grip on the Ranger's arm. He reached out, sought to seize Mosby again but the Confederate had rolled clear. He bounded lightly to his feet, stepped to one side. As Plunkett hastened to rise, Mosby caught the big soldier with a hard blow to the ear.

Plunkett howled and went over sideways. He scrambled to hands and knees, shaking his head savagely to clear away the gathering cobwebs. Mosby, like some swift bird of prey, surged in. Keeping beyond the soldier's reach, he smashed another crackling blow to Plunkett's face. The Yankee groaned, once more sought to shake off the clouds that were closing him in.

Mosby struck a third time, this from behind and with care. Adept, as were all men of the 43rd Battalion, in the ways and means for incapacitating an enemy quickly and silently, he brought the heel of his hand down sharply across Plunkett's neck. The Yankee dropped flat, a gusty burst of wind issuing from his lips.

Mosby wheeled to where the bay horse lay. He jerked open the saddlebags, reached inside for a strip of the cotton bandage. Crossing Plunkett's wrists behind his back, he bound them together securely. With a second length of the cloth he tied the soldier's ankles. A third went for a gag that would prevent his calling out once he regained consciousness.

That done, Mosby stepped back. Plunkett had not stirred. The Ranger chief stepped to the edge of the clearing, beyond the fan of light. He halted there, listening to the darkness. He could hear nothing, not even any sounds from the sergeant-major and his men somewhere down the mountainside. Apparently he and Plunkett were still alone.

He spun on his heel, trotted along the trail to where the horses were tethered. Exercising his usual caution, he approached them quietly, not absolutely certain there was no guard to be encountered. When he saw the animals were untended, he pulled free the halter rope of the nearest mount, a long legged sorrel, and swung onto the saddle.

He rode back up the narrow, twisting path to the clearing. Again using care, he halted in the shadows, first had his careful look about while he listened. Nothing had changed. Plunkett was still bound and gagged. He had regained consciousness and now was beginning to struggle against the strips of cloth that held him.

Mosby moved into the cleared area, dismounted, picked up his saddlebags, threw them across the sorrel. He leaned down to where Plunkett could see and hear him.

"You might as well be quiet, soldier. You won't get loose until someone comes along and cuts those strips."

Plunkett raged and swore unintelligible oaths beneath his gag. His eyes were hard and sparked with the anger that wracked him. Mosby grinned.

111

"When they let you free you can tell them John Mosby trussed you up. Tell them I'm not the cut-throat your sergeant-major claims I am. I could have killed you easily. I would do it now if I were the sort he and some of you think. But I'm not. I am a soldier doing my job and it doesn't call for cold-blooded murder. That's why you're alive and not lying there with your throat slit."

Plunkett struggled against his bonds. Beads of sweat stood out on his brow and the muscles in his neck corded into hard, round ropes. Despite his efforts, he made no headway against the tough strips of cloth. Finally he lay back in exhaustion, his powerful body trembling, barrel chest heaving.

Mosby nodded. "Take my advice, Plunkett: save your breath. Your friends will be along shortly and turn you loose. When they do, thank Sergeant-major Walker for the horse. Doubt if he's as good as my bay there, but he will have to do."

He stepped back, swung onto the saddle. Plunkett squirmed and threshed. Far down the mountainside Walker's hoarse shout sounded.

"Regroup! We've missed him somehow. The detail'll report at the clearin'. Hurry it up, now!"

Mosby looked down at Plunkett. He had wasted time but he had been unable to resist the opportunity to do what he could to dispell the prevalent story that he, as well as all Rangers, were bloodthirsty outlaws. He touched the brim of his plumed hat with two fingers.

"Good by, Yankee. Could be we'll meet again."

He trotted the sorrel down the trail for a short distance, seeking sufficient running room for him to clear the barricade. He paused there briefly, then, kicking the big red horse in the flanks, he sent him forward at a fast run. The sorrel soared over the stump effortlessly, came down on the opposite side—and shied violently to the left. The unexpected movement almost unseated Mosby.

Alarm burst through the Confederate like a fiery rocket. His hand streaked for the pistol on his hip. A horseman waited in the clearing; a tall man, stiffly erect with the moonlight shining brightly on his red hair. The metal of the revolver, held ready, glinted coldly.

Yankee Captain Tom Underwood.

112

21

"Don't reach for that weapon," Underwood said in a dead, level voice. "I will kill you instantly. Just raise your hands."

Mosby complied slowly. He let his eyes sweep the surrounding brush. Underwood apparently was alone.

"You wondering about the rest of my company?" the Yankee officer asked, reading Mosby's thoughts. "They're still below. Looking for those two men you sent on ahead."

Relief swept Mosby. Frost and Rutledge had escaped. Once they were off the mountain Underwood's men would never catch them. And evidently that had happened.

"Climb down," the officer said. "Stand where I can watch you. I don't trust you, John, so we'll wait right here until Sergeant Walker and his men get back."

Mosby's lips parted in a faint grin. Keeping his hands where Underwood could see them, he dismounted, took up a position beside the sorrel.

"Expect it would be best if you clasp your hands and put them behind your neck."

Again John Mosby smiled. Underwood, despite his outward calmness, was nervous. He was taking no chances. He did as his one time classmate directed.

"Been a long time, Tom," he drawled. "When we were back in the University I never thought one day we would face each other over a loaded pistol."

Underwood shrugged. "War has made a lot of difference—in many ways. Seems it's friend against friend, even brother against brother."

"Honest man fights for what he believes in," Mosby said.

"True," the Yankee captain agreed with a trace of bitterness in his tone, "but ordinarily in the usual fashion, not as a guerrilla skulking in the dark, thieving and murdering—"

Mosby's eyes flashed. "That what you think, Tom? You believe I could do that?"

"Of course. I've heard the reports and read a few dispatches. They're true, aren't they?"

"Matter of fact, they are not. I—the Rangers—have been blamed for a number of things we had nothing at all to do with. We've fought this war as Rangers, scouts, if you prefer, much the same as Francis Marion did in the Revolutionary War, and Robert Rogers in his time. I expect a lot of freebooters took advantage of the situation then just as they do now."

"Been several incidents I don't believe there was any doubt about," Underwood said, his voice stiff.

"Not that I personally was involved in. Oh, I don't say all my men are simon-pure. Things happen in the heat of battle—and war is a terrible thing no matter how you fight it. But it isn't all one-sided. There are a number of incidents perpetrated by Union Soldiers upon the South that I expect you would like to forget."

Underwood made no reply. Far down the slope where Walker and his men were making the climb, a whistle shrilled twice.

"They'll be here shortly," Underwood said then, his manner altering slightly. "Sorry I had to be the one who captured you, John. But it was bound to happen. If not me, it would be someone else—especially after what you did to the Mogatawny Bridge."

Mosby laughed. "That's one job you Yankees won't soon forget."

"And one that's costing you your life. You know my orders. They're the same that every other officer in the Federal army has received; we are to hang you and any of your men immediately upon capture. You knew General Grant had issued such an order?"

Mosby ignored the question. "I am entitled to the consideration accorded any prisoner of war."

Underwood shook his head. "You forfeited that right when you became a guerrilla. Grant would never have put out such an order if you hadn't hanged those cavalrymen of General Sheridan's."

"They received the same treatment he meted out to those men of mine he captured. I simply paid him back in kind."

Underwood was silent for a long minute. Mosby's thoughts settled and centered upon his predicament. His position was rapidly growing more critical and unless he could manage something before the sergeant-major and his men reached the clearing, the odds he would survive the dawn were near hopeless. He studied Tom Underwood closely, seeking an answer, a flaw or weakness that would lead to escape. Talk—keep talking. He might, in some way, throw the Yankee officer off guard. Three or four seconds—that's all he would need to duck back behind the sorrel, gain the brush.

"Saw you ride into camp with Colonel Messner and his party," he said. "Fact that I helped them escape from Kidd Jackman should prove something to you."

Underwood shifted his weight carefully on the saddle. "Could have been a matter of expediency. You were on your way to destroy the bridge and supply train. Maybe you didn't want to be bothered."

Mosby felt anger rise within him. He did not recall Underwood having been so unreasonable. In the University they had engaged in lengthy arguments and the big redhead had seemed a fair-minded man. But as Underwood himself had stated, the war wrought many changes: it seemed to have warped his process of thought considerably.

"A bit ridiculous, a statement like that," Mosby said. "We could have escaped from Jackman and left them behind. Instead, we endangered ourselves by taking them along. And if they had been in our way, and if we are as ruthless as you claim, wouldn't we have killed them somewhere in the hills?"

"You had reasons. The women, possibly. And couldn't my showing up with a patrol have prevented you from going ahead with a plan of some sort? My guess is that you simply hadn't had time to do away with them—"

John Mosby swore explosively. "Oh, Tom, for the love of heaven! You can't think that."

He took a half step forward, a calculated, testing movement. Underwood was instantly alert.

"Hold it!" he barked, and moved the pistol threateningly. "Don't try any of your fancy tricks on me, John! I'm onto you. I've heard stories how you always manage to squirm out of every bad situation you find yourself in—but it's different now. This time it won't work.

115

I warn you—I'll shoot if you make the slightest attempt to try something."

Mosby moved his shoulders indifferently. "Bullet would be better than a rope," he said, trying another tack.

Underwood studied him for a brief time. "I see. Well, if that's what you have in mind, trying to force me to shoot—forget it. I wouldn't kill you. I would only wound. General Grant wants you hanged as an example to the rest of your kind. I intend to follow orders."

The soldiers could be heard now on the slope. They were better than half way to the top, Mosby judged. In another five minutes they would reach the clearing. Tension began to build within the Confederate leader. It seemed he could almost feel the rough texture of the rope around his throat. He faced Underwood.

"You know your duty, Tom, and I can't blame you for wanting to carry it out to the exact letter. But in this you are wrong and I wish I could make you see it. I keep remembering that once we were friends—"

"Once," Underwood echoed. "You changed that when you chose to support a rebellion against our country. That ended it. And then to make it worse, you became a renegade. I could respect your beliefs if you were in the regular army fighting us like any other rebel. But as a guerrilla—"

"You walk both sides of the fence," Mosby broke in. "You ignore the fact that the Rangers are duly recognized by the Confederate government and President Davis as a branch of the army—the 43rd Battalion, Partisan Rangers. Lincoln and your Congress were notified of that."

Mosby paused. Beyond Tom Underwood his sharp eyes had caught vague motion in the shadows. Someone was there. His hopes soared. Was it Ben Frost? Had he returned to help?

"You say you respect Confederate soldiers in the ranks. Then why not show that same regard for Rangers? For my position as a Ranger officer? We fight the same as they do—and we're not murderers. There's a man named Plunkett on the other side of that stump who proves that."

The dark shape in back of the Yankee captain began to materialize. Mosby watched narrowly, careful not to warn Underwood in any way. He could not yet distinguish the person. A big man, tall, like Frost, but seemingly heavier, bulkier.

"I won't bite, John. I won't walk into one of your tricks. Nor will I argue the point of whether you are a legitimate army force or not. I simply follow my orders."

Horror suddenly gripped John Mosby. The dark figure moved into a shaft of moonlight—a huge, bearded man in a makeshift Confederate uniform. In his hand he held a pistol. It was pointed at Underwood's broad back. Kidd Jackman!

"Look out, Tom!" Mosby yelled.

The clearing rocked with the blast of the outlaw's weapon. Underwood pitched forward from the sledging impact of the bullet. Mosby dived for shelter in the brush as Jackman spun to face him. The pistol roared again.

Mosby struck flat on the ground, rolled quickly into the darker areas. He snatched his revolver from its holster, turned. Underwood was off his saddle, lay face down on the ground. Jackman had already swung onto the Yankee captain's horse, was wheeling about. Mosby brought up his weapon for a hasty shot but before he could press the trigger, the outlaw whirled away, plunged into the black void of the west slope trail.

Mosby leaped to his feet, ran into the clearing. The gunshots had aroused the men on the mountainside. He could hear them scrambling over the loose rock as they hurried to reach the summit. Dropping beside Underwood, he rolled the officer over. Underwood's eyes opened wearily. When he beheld Mosby, his features drew into a harsh sneer.

"In the back . . ." he muttered. "Should have expected it from guerrillas . ."

"Wasn't one of my Rangers, Tom," Mosby said firmly. "That was Kidd Jackman."

"Jackman?" Underwood repeated. He frowned. "Had just a quick look . . . Thought he was familiar . . . You're sure it was him?"

Mosby nodded. The soldiers were drawing closer. They could be no farther than the lip of the open ground beyond the barricade. "I'm sorry about this, Tom," he said. "And I'll even it up for you—for all of us. I promise that. I'll go after Jackman and I won't stop until he's

117

dead. I've taken enough blame for the things he's done."

Underwood forced a smile. "I'm—glad . . . glad it wasn't one of your men . . . Maybe I've been wrong. . . ."

The Yankee officer's voice trailed off into silence. His body went slack. John Mosby rose, moved swiftly to the sorrel horse. There was nothing anyone could do for Tom Underwood now—nothing except avenge his brutal murder. The Confederate vaulted to the saddle, wheeled toward the pathway down which the renegade had fled. Behind him a yell went up.

"There he goes! Get the horses!"

A SPATTER of gunshots erupted. Mosby, bent low over the sorrel's arched neck, heard the vicious moan of the balls as they passed overhead. He reached the first outcrop of brush, plunged into it.

"Here! Couple you men drag that damn tree stump out of the way!" It was Sergeant-major Walker. "And somebody take a look at the captain there, see if you can do somethin' for him."

They would find Tom Underwood dead, a bullet between his shoulders, Mosby thought. And he and the Rangers would get credit for the crime. He could thank Kidd Jackman for another cold-blooded murder that would be charged up to them. One small thing he could be grateful for: Tom Underwood had died knowing better, knowing that all the things he had assumed were true about his one time friend and the men who followed his lead, were not necessarily factual.

The sorrel headed down the trail at a reckless pace. Mosby drew him in, reluctant to take any greater chances than absolutely necessary. The west side pathway down the mountain, he noted, was much like that on the east. Narrow, confined, heavily overgrown along its edges. That was to his liking. Jackman would have to stay on it until the slope flattened out. This would give Mosby a better opportunity for overtaking him, or at least would narrow down the distance that had separated them before Jackman swung off and sought a place in which to hide.

The gunshots he had heard earlier that evening on the opposite slope made sense to Mosby now. Unquestionably it had been Jackman, escaped from the guardhouse at the encampment and endeavoring to get away. Soldiers had been in pursuit and had fired at him. Where were the men who had also been captured with him? Possibly dead in the escape break which probably had been effected during the fire.

He heard the sergeant-major and the soldiers at that moment. Just entering the trail, he judged. Soon they would come pouring down the slope after him. It would complicate matters a great deal. Mosby would have liked a free hand in hunting down Kidd Jackman. Having a dozen or more infuriated Yankee cavalrymen snapping at his heels, believing he had further added to his crimes by shooting their captain in the back, was going to make it a difficult task.

But he would find Kidd Jackman.

The outlaw had been allowed to live much too long. He must be brought to account with no further delay. There was no pressing need for Mosby to hurry on to Confederate headquarters and report to Lee. He was now certain in his mind that Ben Frost had been able to carry out that part of his mission.

That brought another realization to John Mosby as he raced on through the night. There were more of Tom Underwood's men on that side of the mountain. The captain had mentioned they were searching for Frost and Rutledge. A new worry lifted in the Ranger chief's mind. It would be fatal to blunder into their hands—and, if he calculated accurately, they were probably somewhere on the path ahead at that very moment, riding for the summit. The sounds of the gunshots would have attracted them.

He began to watch the shoulders of the trail more closely. In the darkness it was difficult to tell just what lay beyond the crowding wall of brush and rock that lined either side. He should get off the open trail though, and as soon as possible. The chances for running into an ambush were much too great.

A short distance later the trail began to widen. He was almost to the foot of the mountain. It should be possible to leave the path and move off to the brush shortly. The opportunity presented itself almost immediately. He swung the sorrel through a break, found himself in a badly overgrown but passable area where the horse could walk at a fair speed.

He was at a loss as to which direction he should take. Jackman could have followed a similar course, or taken an opposite one. In the darkness, and due to the roughness of the terrain, locating any hoof prints and pursuing them was out of the question, even if he waited until daylight. But it seemed logical to him that the outlaw would head southward. Jackman would point for a destination away from a section of the country where he knew a large number of Yankee soldiers were searching for him; thus he would not go left or continue straight on.

The hard pounding of running horses reached John Mosby at that moment. Sergeant-major Walker and his men were coming down fast. Mosby held the sorrel to a steady walk, pulling away from the trail at right angles. With any sort of luck at all, the Yankee cavalry, keeping to the path, would thunder on by.

He was a good two hundred yards off to the side when they drew abreast and swept on. Mosby, halted behind a low rise, could not see them but he heard all he needed to know. He breathed easier. There was no longer any reason to fear them.

He remained motionless, listened to the slowly diminishing hammer of the horses on the hard surface of the trail. When he could no longer hear them, he brought his thoughts back to the immediate problem—Jackman. He sought to put himself in the outlaw's position; where would he go if he were in the man's boots? To the west, north and east were the Yankee soldiers, all thirsting for his blood. Certainly not in any of those directions.

To the south were more soldiers, both Confederate and Yankee, but they were unaware of Jackman's most recent activities. To many he would be a stranger. Among them he would find some degree of safety and could travel, if he were careful, without too much difficulty. It sounded feasible—but travel to where?

The cave!

It came suddenly to John Mosby. Jackman undoubtedly would head straight for his hiding place in the low hills, the one where he and his outlaw followers had held the Messner party prisoner, where he had taken the Rangers. It was natural and logical. Jackman would feel he could best hide there and wait for those of his band who had also managed to escape.

The Confederate leader delayed no longer. He glanced skyward, squared directions in his mind and started off at once. The cave was a fair distance away but, by forced riding, he should reach it late that morning.

He misjudged by only an hour. It was high noon when he rode into the thicket below the ridge where, with

121

Ben Frost and Jess Rutledge, he had gone to investigate the screaming of a woman and found Nell Messner in the hands of Jackman's men. The same pair, dead, lay just as he had seen them last except they now had bloated and turned grotesque under the warm sun.

He tied the sorrel securely and began the short ascent to the summit of the ridge. He knew the approximate location of the cave this time and moved for it in a direct line rather than swinging wide, as before. When he came to the top, he dropped flat on his belly and crawled the remainder of the distance. He came to a stop no more than fifty yards from the outlaw's hideaway.

There was no one in sight. All appeared quiet and deserted. Mosby considered that for several minutes. He could have arrived before Jackman—or he could have figured wrong entirely. Jackman might have gone to some other place. But that did not seem reasonable. The normal thing for him to do would be to get under cover, wait for his men, and lie low until the search for him died off.

Mosby recalled then the corral where the outlaws kept their mounts while in camp. If Jackman were there, his horse would be in the enclosure at the other abandoned mine. He drew back into the brush, started to make his way to that point. A movement at the mouth of the cave brought him to a halt.

It was Jackman.

The bearded, barrel-bodied outlaw chief walked deliberately from the black depths of the mine shaft into the sunlight and stopped. He was picking his teeth, using the point of a knife that flashed in the sunlight as it was moved about. Evidently he had been having a noonday meal when Mosby first arrived. The Confederate watched the man stare off across the low hills and shallow valleys, shrug, and then turn back into the cave. It was apparent he expected someone. And it would seem he was entirely alone.

Mosby reversed himself. Moving swiftly and quietly, he skirted the open face of the rise upon which the mine shaft was located, came in toward it from its right hand side. Brush and rock extended almost to the opening at that point and it was simple to gain a position near its edge.

He considered the advisability of going in after the killer and discarded it. Jackman would have too great an advantage. Mosby would be silhouetted against the flare of light at the cave's mouth, offering a perfect target to the outlaw the instant he made his presence known.

He thought for a few moments, then, reaching down, he picked up a fist-sized rock. Holding it in his left hand, he drew his pistol with the right. When the gun was cocked and ready, he tossed the stone down the slope fronting the cave. It struck a dozen feet below, bounded about and set up a noisy clatter.

Kidd Jackman appeared instantly. He glanced warily about. Failing to see anyone, he walked into the open, huge head thrust forward on his shoulders, dark, evil eyes studying the bottom of the ravine for the cause of the racket.

Mosby stepped from the brush. "I'm behind you, Jackman," he said in a winter cold voice. "My gun's pointed at your spine. One move and I'll blow you in two."

The outlaw's ham like hands lifted slowly. He came around full circle, making no sudden motions. A frown knotted his forehead but there was no fear, only curiosity, in his granite-hard eyes.

"You, eh!" he said when his glance locked with that of Mosby. A half smile curved his thick lips. "Finally figured out who you was. You're Mosby, that Reb that's been givin' the Yankees so much hell. That you what blowed up that bridge?"

Mosby did not answer. He said, "Keep your hands up, Jackman. I'm going to tie you up and take you back to hang. It's what you have coming but don't think I won't use my revolver instead, if I have to."

Jackman's brutal features managed a look of surprise. "Now, what you want to hang me for? Ain't we fightin' for the same thing? Ain't we both agin the damn Yankees?"

"You fight anybody and everybody, including women and children," Mosby said. "Don't try to horse me, Jackman. I know all about you and your renegades. And I just had a first hand example of the way you do things."

"You mean that Yankee captain? Hell, man, I had to get me a horse. How else you figure I was goin' to do it, the place crawlin' with bluebellies way it was? Anyway,

123

you oughtn't to get riled up about that. He had a gun on you. I figure you're beholden to me for gettin' you off the hook. They'd have hung you sure if I hadn't come along. I know just how them Yankees feel about you."

"Thanks to you and few others of your stripe!" Mosby's bitter voice cut in. "But you're finished now. You won't be committing any more murders and passing off any more of your bloody raids as something the Rangers did."

"Well, maybe so," Jackman drawled, "but I don't figure it exactly that way. I learned that long as a man's drawin' breath he's livin'—and he's got some chance."

Mosby centered his attention on the outlaw's gross features. Jackman was as dangerous and as tricky as a swamp rattlesnake—doubly so in that he was cornered.

"Don't try anything, Jackman," he cautioned. "I warn you again."

Jackman shrugged his massive shoulders. "Now, I ask you, Mosby, what could I do with you standin' there pointin' that gun at my belly? What chance I got to do anything?"

In the next fraction of time he was jerking away, wheeling, amazingly fast for so large a man. His pistol leaped into his hand, came up in a metallic blur. Mosby fired twice, quickly. The outlaw's body jumped from the force of the bullets. Twin puffs of dust exploded from his shirt as the leaden slugs drove deep. Jackman's huge frame, responding to his tremendous strength, continued to move, to function. His arm came up. The weapon in his hand glinted in the sunlight.

Mosby fired a third shot. The outlaw's figure jolted visibly again. The arm that held the pistol seemed then to freeze, to become rigid. A great weakness overcame it and it began a slow descent. Jackman glared at Mosby through slitted, glittering eyes that were gradually starting to glaze. His stiff, spraddled legs suddenly were quivering. He took a short, backward step, another. Strength ran out of his huge body at that moment and he toppled over. He fell full length, his revolver clattering loudly against the rocks as he slid down the steep slope.

Mosby, knowing it to be unnecessary, but being the thorough man he was, descended the ravine. He knelt beside the outlaw, examined him briefly. Kidd Jackman was dead. The first bullet had been enough but it had taken three to drive the will for life from his powerful body.

He turned away, started back up the incline. Jackman and his army of renegades would haunt the hills and valleys no more. And Tom Underwood—and countless other persons—had been avenged. He hoped that somehow the Yankee captain was aware of that fact, and that it had been brought about by a Confederate Ranger.

23

JOHN MOSBY rode into the Carstairs' place at Dumfries from the river side. It was safer to approach the house from that direction and care was always prudent. With the tide of war surging back and forth a man could never know exactly in advance which force controlled any given area. He had seen no evidence of either Confederate or Union soldiers in the vicinity and that could be considered a doubtful sign.

He left the sorrel in the brush and started toward the low-roofed structure on foot. Carstairs was a Southern sympathizer and permitted the use of his premises not only as a central exchange point for dispatches but also for meetings and as a sanctuary for wounded men as well. Mosby intended to pause only long enough to get the news and inquire about Jess Rutledge. Then he planned to hurry on and rejoin Stuart and Lee, wherever they might be.

It had been a fruitful five days for the Rangers. They had succeeded not only in destroying the bridge and cutting off Grant's main supply line, as Lee had hoped they might do, but also they had removed that persistent and festering thorn that plagued army and civilians alike, Kidd Jackman, from the country. He was anxious to add that fact to the report he knew Ben Frost had already made.

He reached the side entrance, well hidden by huge lilac bushes, and rapped the customary signal on the thick door. It opened immediately and Henry Carstairs greeted him with a broad smile.

"Major! Glad to see you! Your men said I could expect you."

"They still here?" Mosby asked, entering the room.

"No. The sergeant went on shortly after they arrived. Rutledge pulled out early this morning, too. Was intending to go home for a spell. Until his wound healed, he said."

It had all worked out as he had hoped: Ben Frost had hurried on to Lee with the report. Jess Rutledge's injury had been cared for and he was by that time with his family.

"Got a dispatch for you, Major," Carstairs said, wheeling about. He was a small, quick man with snow white hair and brows that remained startlingly black. "Came a couple hours ago."

Mosby accepted the sealed packet from him. "What's the news? How has the war been going?"

"Don't know much, only what that courier said. Seems there's been quite a skirmish down Spottsylvania way. General Lee turned Grant back. The Yankees never got to Richmond. . . ."

John Mosby was only half hearing. His eyes were on the creased paper held in his hands. A terrible dread was moving through him as the words, penned by the precise hand of Robert E. Lee, sprang forth to strike his consciousness.

Friend Mosby:

It is my sad duty to inform you of the death of our esteemed and mutual comrade, General J. E. B. Stuart. In the sharp fighting at Yellow Tavern, where he successfully led the attack that drove off the enemy and prevented their entering Richmond, he was mortally wounded.

It is a grievous loss not only to us personally but to our noble cause as well. I fear we shall look long before we find a man so dear to our hearts and so dedicated to his beliefs.

I have taken the liberty of personally advising you of this tragedy by this means because I believe General Stuart would wish you to hear it from me rather than in the usual manner.

At your earliest convenience kindly report to me at headquarters.

Respectfully,
R. E. Lee

Jeb Stuart dead!

It was impossible—inconceivable. Jeb Stuart who had ridden into a hundred blazing skirmishes, who had led his men to victory time after time: he of the charmed life, the invincible warrior—dead? Big, laughing, red-bearded, reckless, generous Jeb Stuart—dead?

"What's wrong, Major? You look like you've seen a ghost!"

Mosby became aware of Carstairs' anxious voice. He

folded the dispatch from Lee, handed it to the man. He walked slowly to one of the windows in the east wall of the house, drew aside the curtain. In the far distance beyond the fields he could see the Potomac, a broad, silver sheet in the sunlight.

All the proud personal accomplishments of those past five days suddenly were ashes on his lips. Their meaning had dissipated, was lost: they now appeared only facets of the war, separate incidents that would aid in the eventual, overall victory.

With Jeb Stuart gone, the dash and excitement, the heady thrill of facing danger, had somehow vanished like sand castles on the shoreline left to the mercy of the waves. The bold, brave cavalier of the Confederacy had taken something with him in death. Henceforth to John Mosby, the war would be a matter of grim duty, one of dogged resistance, methodic attack. His thin lips twisted bitterly. Jeb's premonition had been accurate after all, for Jeb was dead and he still lived.

"I'm sorry, Major," Carstairs murmured haltingly. "I recollect how close you and the General were. Terrible thing when a man like him passes on. A mighty terrible thing."

John Mosby turned slowly about. His bearded face was set, his pale eyes suspiciously bright. "He had a feeling it was coming. I expect it happened the way he wanted it to—while he was riding at the head of his cavalry."

"Big loss to General Lee," Carstairs said. "I imagine he will be looking to you to take his place."

Mosby walked toward the door. He hesitated there, hand on the latch. He looked back, shook his head. "No man can take Jeb Stuart's place," he said and moved on into the yard where the sorrel waited.

RIDE TO THE GUN

Chapter 1

ONLY AT CERTAIN TIMES did his war wounds bother him. Usually it was just before a summer rain or during the rugged, penetrating cold of the winter months. Oddly enough, it was the healed over, commonplace injuries that distressed him most; the serious one, the deeply imbedded bullet doctors had said one day would kill him, troubled him little.

It was the hate, the ever bubbling bitterness that would not let him rest. He rose with it each morning, carried it about like a dark, malevolent shroud, through the waking hours; bedded down with it at night when the chore of living and working another day on the ranch was done. It was as much a part of him as his lean face, his cold, gray eyes. And it made of him a grim, silent recluse whose only contacts were those caused by necessity.

And why not?

A man had a right to feel as he did. There were good and ample reasons for it. Hadn't he given better than two years of his life for the cause of the Union, only to have circumstance rip from him and trample underfoot all the things every man holds dear and sacred? He had been innocent of wrong but they had accused him, turned from him and finally condemned him. They stripped him of honor, of rank—almost of sanity. If ever a man had cause to hate and be bitter, he guessed he, Dave Stanbuck, Sergeant, once of the fighting 20th Illinois Sharpshooters, had that right.

Perhaps. But it was wrong to take his spiteful moods out on the men who worked for him, as he had done that morning. He realized that as he entered his house, closed the door against the hot, noonday sunlight and paused there in the comparative, inner coolness, his shoulders pressed flat against the warped panel. After a moment he shrugged, as though weary of all thoughts, all things, and crossed the small room, the kitchen, to the cast-iron cook stove. Fitting the lifter to the forward lid, he set it aside. Using the short length of curved iron as a poker, he prodded the near-dead embers in the firebox. Reaching down, he picked a handful of wood chips from their box and dropped them onto the faltering coals.

They say a man cannot live with hate and bitterness, that in the end they will consume him. Of that he was fully aware. But it did not matter. Someday, when least expected, he would die anyway. Someday that slug in his body would complete its ultimate purpose and it would all be over and done with. Until that time, however, he would go on living and remembering and hating the man who had brought it all to pass; a man he did not know, had never seen clearly, but whose voice still echoed in his ears.

He would continue to run his small ranch in remote Mangus Valley, beat out an existence with the help of a handful of men who worked for him; who knew nothing of the past or of his background. They were conscious only that he could work harder and longer than any of them, that he was a strict taskmaster who expected full measure from them but who never failed to do his own, equal share.

In little more than a year's time he had built the ranch from the small, deserted, rag-tag spread it was when he took possession, to a going concern. He had accomplished it by sheer labor and determination. But mostly it had been the sheer labor. A man can keep memories in the background of his mind by burying himself in work.

He tried not to think of the war, of the times when he had devoted himself unstintingly to its prosecution, but there were moments when thoughts came unbidden. An infrequent passerby in Mangus Valley would pause, drop a few words of news. Or one of the riders, returning from Eldenburg, would have something to say about it. Never to him directly, however, but to one of the other men. They had long since learned he had no interest in the struggle, now in its last, frightful throes.

8

He did not resent Pierce or Wheelock, or either of the other two men who worked for him, when they left him out of such conversation. There was no feeling for the army left within him, no sympathy for the Union and its hopes. Once it had been all-important to him, but they had turned their backs to him, had cast him out as unfaithful, unwanted; he cared little how they fared now.

The day Charlie Pierce, as near to a foreman as Stanbuck had on the ranch, returned from the Fort and said, "Reckon old Lee and his Johnny Rebs are about on their last legs; they say Sherman's givin' them an awful beatin'," he had merely overheard. No question as to what actually had occurred, what forces were involved; what it meant, one way or the other, to Lee or Grant.

Grant. General of the Armies, Ulysses S. Grant. That was how it had begun. Grant, the finest, most able soldier he had ever known. He had respected him as a man, admired him as an officer. And when it was all over, he had been thrown out of the army because of Grant. It was an ironic twist. The soldier he had honored most became the emblem of his failure and disgrace.

The flames within the stove came to life finally. He added another handful of dry fuel, slid the round, iron lid back into the opening. Tipping back the top of the coffee pot, he glanced inside. There was water enough—he wanted only one cup of coffee. He centered the granite container on the slowly heating surface of the stove and turned away, his soul dark with its great loneliness. He should add more water to the pot, call in Pierce and Fred Wheelock—both were out in the yard somewhere—and ask them to drink and eat a bite of noonday lunch with him. But something inside him ruled against it; a powerful compulsion that held him apart, kept him aloof.

At such times he found it difficult to understand himself. He had always liked people, enjoyed friends. But after his experience with Grant and the subsequent hearings that evolved, he changed. The bitterness had set in and he became wary of others, mistrusted them and their intentions. It was a strange sort of fear. As a child, once burned, is forever after cautious of fire, he was chary of human association.

He sat down in the deep chair Charlie Pierce had made for him of cowhide and scrap lumber. He drew the makings from his shirt pocket and rolled himself a slim cigarette.

Lighting it, he glanced about the small, ill-equipped kitchen. Not much to show for twenty-five years of life. A weather-beaten, old house of discomfort, hot in the summer, cold in the winter. A few out-buildings in no better condition. Five hundred and sixty head of cattle and a ranch, for which the best that could be said was that grass and water were ample. But that was the hand that had been dealt him and Dave Stanbuck was man enough to play it out.

He guessed he shouldn't blame the army too much. He was a good enough soldier to realize the army goes by the book, mostly, and where Grant was concerned there was no deviation, not the slightest. But they could have given him a little time to try and clear himself, it would seem. He might have been able to prove he was telling the truth at the hearings, had he been allowed the opportunity. He had to admit his story was pretty thin, even a bit far-fetched. But it was true and they could have considered his past record and based some of their thoughts and decisions on that. They had not. And too, one word from Grant would have made a great difference, but it had not been forthcoming. The General had maintained a strict silence, left it completely up to those who conducted the investigation.

He would never forget the look on Grant's face that wet November morning when it happened. Nor his own feelings as he sighted down the barrel of his musket and centered it on the man he intended to kill. It was raining, a slow, monotonous, thoroughly soaking Mississippi drizzle. Dawn had not yet come and there was little reason to believe it would do much to alleviate the gloom when it did.

Stanbuck, with his platoon of Illinois Sharpshooters, had drawn up beneath a stand of trees and was awaiting the general order to move out, expected at daylight. Grant and some of his aides were rumored to be in the area; but it was rumor, no more than that. Yet it could be. Grant was that sort of officer, not afraid to get into the thick of things. Stanbuck hoped it was true and that he would again get the chance to meet and speak with the great General.

In the semi-darkness an officer suddenly presented himself to Stanbuck. He wore the dark blue, high-collared coat, flowing cape and lighter colored, yellow-piped trousers of the cavalry. The stripes on his sleeves proclaimed him to be a

10

field officer but the muffler about his neck and face hid the insignia of his actual rank.

"Sergeant," he had snapped in a peculiar, rasping voice, "get two men and follow me."

Stanbuck had turned without question. He ordered the ranking corporal to take over the squads and called out the names of two privates. They set off at once through the dripping brush, the officer in the lead.

They traveled a short quarter-mile, came to a halt in a low swale where rain water had collected in an ankle-deep pool. The officer, his hand raised for silence, spoke.

"Other side of that hill you'll see a dozen soldiers. They're Rebs. They were sent here to ambush General Grant who is expected along this way in the next hour or so. Our job is to clean them out before they can do any harm."

"Guerrillas," one of the privates had muttered and spat.

"Right. Guerrillas. When we reach the top of the hill, spread out. Go down on your belly."

"More men would be better," Stanbuck had pointed out. "Four of us against a dozen. Poor odds."

"Too risky to move up more," the officer countered. "Might draw attention. You won't have any trouble, Sergeant. There's three rifles and a pistol between us. And they won't be expecting an attack. That's what counts, Sergeant—surprise. The element of surprise."

"Yes, sir," Stanbuck had replied, bowing to superior rank and judgement.

They had waded across the pool, climbed the low hill and looked over its crest. There were less than a dozen men gathered below. Nine, perhaps ten. Although they were no more than fifty feet distant, they were indefinite shapes; only the yellow slickers they wore over their uniforms set them apart from the sopping, dark background that lay beyond them. They were crouched around a small fire which was having difficulty in burning. They were smoking, talking in low voices while a bottle of liquor was being passed between them.

"Pick your targets," the raspy-voiced officer ordered. "And don't miss."

"What about prisoners?" Stanbuck wondered. "Hadn't we better try to take them first, sir?"

"Not enough of us for that, Sergeant," the officer replied.

11

"Who takes guerrilla prisoners, anyway? Everybody set? On my command, stand and fire at will."

With the others, Dave Stanbuck readied himself. He did not like the situation much; it smacked too close of murder. But if Grant's life was at stake, he could understand why the officer was taking no chances.

"Now!"

He leaped to his feet, hearing the thunder of the private's muskets at one side, the sharper, more spiteful crack of the officer's pistol on the other. At the first blast the crouched guerrillas sprang to their feet—only they had not been guerrillas at all; they were Union officers. Stanbuck, his rifle, unaccountably, still unfired, stared in horror at the round whiskered face with the inevitable cigar protruding from the lips. Grant!

He wheeled, suddenly furious, realization coming to him in a wave of comprehension. The officer—he was the guerrilla! It was a plan to murder Grant and he had become a part of it! He had a glimpse of the man's shape as he ducked into the brush. Before he could fire there had been a tremendous crash of sound and the stunning impact of bullets plowing into his body as the survivors with Grant fought back.

He had awakened in an emergency aid station late that day. The two privates were dead. The fourth man? No one had seen him. Then had followed weeks in a base hospital while the army rocked with the story of the attempted assassination of Grant. He had recovered slowly. Two of the three bullets that had driven into him were removed and the wounds pronounced satisfactory. The third was a different story. It could not be taken out. As it was, he should really be dead from it. Likely he would be, in another month. Or it might take a year.

Then had come the hearings. Stanbuck had told his story but the two privates were dead and he had no one to verify his words. The platoon corporal and one or two soldiers remembered the incident of the officer coming for them, but only vaguely. The appearance and disappearance of strange officers among the troops was a common occurrence. But there had been an officer, the corporal was positive of that fact.

It probably was all that saved Dave Stanbuck from a firing squad. There was every indication he was involved in a plot to kill Grant, but no actual proof. He was then discharged, dishonorably. And four months from that cold, gray morning when he had sighted down a rifle barrel at a guerrilla who proved to be General U. S. Grant, commander of the United States forces, he was riding westward, seeking a new life, a place to hide, to lick his wounds—and forget.

But there was one thing he vowed never to erase from his mind; the recollection of the man who had deceived him that morning, the would-be officer whose face he had never seen but whose voice he would always remember. Somewhere, someday, sometime he would hear those harsh, grating tones again. And when he did he would have his moment of sweet revenge.

The lid on the coffee pot began to tremble. He got to his feet, moved to the stove, a faint limp evident in his step. He pushed the granite container to the side, away from the heated surface and reached for a tin cup that sat on the warming oven.

It was at that moment he heard the gunshot.

Chapter 2

IN THE HOT, midday hush the gunshot seemed abnormally loud. It set up a chain of echoes that knocked about the scattered buildings with restless insistence. Stanbuck remained where he stood, wondering as to its meaning.

"You there—inside the shack!" a voice rapped through the stillness. "Come outside! You don't we'll burn the place down around you!"

A sullen anger moved through Dave Stanbuck at the insolent command. He sought to place the voice. It was not familiar.

13

He had made few contacts with the three or four other ranchers in Mangus Valley but he did not believe it belonged to one of them.

"You comin' out? Last chance!"

Stanbuck dropped his hand to the gun at his hip, assured himself it was in place and ready. He stepped to the door. Fingers on the latch, he paused, having a second thought; better to use the side entrance. That way he could have his look into the yard first before showing himself.

He wheeled, crossed the kitchen, his mind still churning with questions and entered the small quarters where he slept. The adjoining room was used for storage purposes but it had a door that would let him into the open and bring him out behind the house. He turned the knob, stepped into the yard. There he halted abruptly. Three hard-faced riders awaited him. All were strangers. They had anticipated his move.

Anger rushed through him. "What the hell's this all about?"

"Just you drop that iron you're wearin', mister," one of the trio answered. "Then walk yourself around to the other side. Jaffick wants to see you."

Stanbuck's heavy brows came up. "Turley Jaffick?"

"The same. Now, get movin'."

Stanbuck dropped his pistol to the ground. He started along the path that led to the hard-packed yard on the opposite side of the ranchhouse. Turley Jaffick—the Butcher; one of the war's worst guerrillas. A ruthless killer who stopped at nothing. Daring and resourceful, he had professed sympathy for the Confederate cause, but later it was rumored he had switched his allegiance to the Union. Stanbuck had never come up against him, face-to-face, but the last he had heard, the man was carrying on his operations along the Tennessee border. What was he doing so far west?

He reached the corner of the sod and frame building, turned right and headed into the yard with the three toughs not far behind. Then he saw the limp, lifeless shape of Fred Wheelock sprawled in dusty disorder near the corral. That had been the shot he heard. His step slowed when he saw the young cowboy and the anger within him began to chill; then he continued on.

A dozen or more riders were in the yard. Two were a short distance out in front. Stanbuck recognized one as Jack Hazen, a gunman well known in the Territory; a sleek, dark, narrow-faced killer who wore two fancy guns and affected flashy clothing. At that moment he was sporting a bright-yellow shirt, heavy with Mexican embroidery, fawn-colored breeches with gold stripes down the seams of the legs and a white, wide-brimmed hat.

The other, he assumed, was Turley Jaffick. A big man, well over six feet in height with a good two hundred pounds of bone and muscle to go with it. He had red hair and a thick, full mustache. His eyes caught Stanbuck's attention instantly and held it. There was something vaguely familiar about the man; something in the flat emptiness of his stare.

"Just like you figured, Turl, he tried to cut and run out the back door," one of the outlaws standing at Stanbuck's elbow said.

Hazen, the outlaw, laughed. "Wonder he didn't tromp right over you, Jess, and get away. Would've been natural."

"Now, just a damn minute!" Jess exclaimed, and pushed forward.

"Shut up, both of you!" Jaffick's blunt command halted the outlaw, silenced the byplay. "He the only one in the house?"

Dave Stanbuck stiffened. His eyes drilled into Jaffick's face with a hard insistence, a steadily growing suspicion, while the short hairs along his neck began to lift.

"Only one," another voice confirmed.

There was motion off to Stanbuck's left, near the calf yard. He shifted his glance to that point. Charlie Pierce, his hawk face long and solemn, walked slowly toward him, arms uplifted. Back of him came two more of the Butcher's guerrillas.

They were looking at death. Dave Stanbuck realized that as he stood there in the center of the yard and viewed the savage, dour faces of the outlaws. These were the Butcher's trained killers; men who rode the land with their red-maned chieftain, robbing, burning and murdering. All but Hazen. He was a gunman of a different stripe but every bit as deadly and ruthless. But Stanbuck was not thinking of that in those tense moments; he was watching Jaffick, waiting for him to speak again.

But why had the Butcher come to Mangus Valley? There was little for a man such as Turley Jaffick to take. Only Tom Kinter had a ranch of any size and even he possessed little of the things Jaffick would be interested in. Kinter's wealth lay in cattle, in the good-sized herd he ran. Cattle! Could that be it? Was that the reason the Butcher had led his band of renegades into the Mangus country? Was he after the five- or six-thousand head of stock that could be rounded up from the ranches in the valley?

Jaffick pushed his battered campaign hat to the back of his head and rested his flat gaze on Stanbuck. "How many more cowboys you got around here, mister?"

It was the same voice! The identical raspy, harsh, sharp-edged tones he had heard that morning in the gloom of a Mississippi swamp. Jaffick and the unknown officer who had led the attempt on Grant's life were one and the same! He had found him!

Anger and hatred fused and burst within Dave Stanbuck in a sudden, violent explosion. "You!" he shouted, and lunged for the guerrilla.

He took three steps, long arms extended, fingers clawing for Jaffick. Something hard and solid crashed into the back of his head, drove him to his knees. He tried to rise. A second blow dropped him flat. He lay there, barely conscious, hearing the run of men's voices as if from a great distance.

Hazen wondered, "What's wrong with him, you reckon?"

And the hated voice of Jaffick replied: "Probably some jasper I come up against in the war. Could have something to do with a brother or maybe a sister or his wife. Don't remember him, though. Get him on his feet, Jess."

Dave felt hands at his shoulders, became aware that he was upright. He shook his head, cleared away the cobwebs. He focussed his eyes on Jaffick, hate and fury building inside him again as his mind stopped its spinning and returned to normal.

"What's eating you, friend?" Jaffick asked. "I know you from somewhere?"

"From a morning in Mississippi," Stanbuck answered in a voice that quivered with rage. "You ruined me, got two of my men killed. Grant—"

"Sure, I remember," Jaffick cut in. "You were part of that Illinois bunch. I slipped in during the night, made out like I was a cavalry major with a uniform I took off a dead man. Came within an ace of nailing old Grant's hide to the wall."

16

"Knew someday I'd find you," Stanbuck murmured in a low voice. "Killing you is going to be a sweet chore."

Jaffick shrugged his thick shoulders. "Well, I guess your looking is over with, sure enough, but you might find the killing a mite hard to come by. Sounds like I put you in a bit of trouble that morning."

"Enough—but not near as much as you've got!" Stanbuck yelled and tried to jerk free of the hands that grasped his arms. "I get a hold of you—"

"You won't," Jaffick replied coolly. "You'll never get the chance." The guerrilla leader swung his attention to Hazen. "How about it, Jack? Five men in this outfit? The soldier here, the old man, the pair we caught tending the cows and the dead one?"

"That's all," the gunman answered. "Never saw no more than that around here."

Jaffick nodded. "Guess that cleans up things at this place. Took less time than I allowed." He hesitated, threw an expressionless glance to someone beyond Stanbuck. "Earl, you ride over and see if the boys have that herd on the move yet."

One of the outlaws behind Stanbuck swung away, angling across the yard. At that moment Charlie Pierce, shoved hard by one of the outlaws, stumbled up to Stanbuck's side. The old man thrust his bristling countenance toward Jaffick.

"What you want around here, anyway?" he demanded. "Ain't no war in this country! Pickin's get so slim you had to move out?"

"They're a little slim back there, sure enough," Jaffick said, with a slow smile. "But this is a regular gold mine out here. With Fort Quinton ready to pay fifteen dollars a head for beef, I figure to do right well. With what I take out of this valley, old man, I'll have me a poke of seventy-five thousand good northern dollars. That'll set me and the boys up fine in Mexico."

Pierce choked on his words. "You mean you're cleanin' out this whole valley?"

"That's the idea," the guerrilla chief said.

It was not so difficult as it might sound. The Mangus country was an out of the way, seldom visited area. It was sixty miles to the nearest civilization, Fort Quinton to the east; better than a hundred and thirty-five miles to the nearest town, Eldenburg. And there probably were not twenty able

17

men in the entire valley. A cool and ruthless operator like Jaffick, with a gang such as he marshaled, could move in and have his way for weeks without the world beyond ever being the wiser.

"You won't get away with it!" Pierce declared, bobbing his head violently: "You can't do it!"

"Who you figure to stop me? Nobody ever comes this way. And when we leave there won't be anybody left to talk about it."

"Nobody left—" Pierce repeated. "You mean you plan on killin' everybody around? All them people?"

"All?" Jaffick echoed. "Not more than a dozen and a half in the whole country. Hell, old man, I've shot that many men personally in a skirmish."

"But that was warrin'! This here, it's just plain murder. Nothin' else!"

Jaffick shrugged. "What's the difference in being dead? Getting a bullet in your backyard is just the same as getting it in a war. Dead is dead, and it don't matter any to the man it happened to."

Dave Stanbuck heard the words through a hazy sort of vacuum. His mind was filled with one thing during those moments—the desire to get his hands on Turley Jaffick, to kill him, to avenge the long hours, the endless days of pain and mental torture he had undergone. But how? Faced with a dozen ready guns, he wouldn't stand a chance.

Jaffick had tired of bandying words with Pierce. He turned his attention back to his men. "Jess, you and Lee take this pair out behind the barn and get rid of them. Hide the bodies. Bury them. Drag that other one along, too. Don't figure anybody will be coming by here soon, but we won't take no chances on it."

Stanbuck felt fear rise within him; not for his own life but that he was to lose his chance for settling the score with Turley Jaffick. He threw himself forward, struggled to break free of the hands that held him. Someone clubbed him again, a hard blow to the side of the head. Stunned, he sagged back against the men behind him.

Two men on horses were suddenly before Pierce and himself. They drew their pistols, motioned for them to start towards the barn.

18

"Start walkin'," one of them ordered.

"And Jess," Turley Jaffick's discordant voice admonished, "be damn sure they're dead this time."

Chapter 3

JACK HAZEN LAUGHED, a hollow, mocking sound in the mid-day heat. He shifted on the saddle, resting his weight on one leg.

"Reckon you ought to hog-tie them first, Jess. Then hold the gun right against their heads. That way you're sure to do it right."

The outlaw called Jess, a short, heavy man with a long scar creasing the left side of his blotched face, halted abruptly. His eyes sparked hotly.

"Get off my back, Hazen! Had about all your mouth I aim to take!"

The gunman made no reply. He stared at Jess with an unblinking gaze, his lips set in a slight, down-curving smile. Although he had made no perceptible move, he was no longer the relaxed, indolent figure of moments past; now there was tenseness about him. He was coiled, ready to strike.

"Hold it!"

Turley Jaffick's sharp voice barked across the hush. "I'll have none of that! Leastwise, not until this job's done. Then if you two got something to settle, settle and be damned. Right now I've got other things for you to do. Understand?"

"All right, Turl," Jess said, his thick shoulders going down. "But I ain't takin' much more of this Fancy Dan's ridin'——"

"Maybe now's the time to do something about it," Hazen cut in softly. "Later might be a long time coming."

"Blast it all!" Jaffick roared, thoroughly aroused, "you both heard me! Cut out this bickering! Jess, get to doing what I told you. When that's finished, you and Lee join up and give us a hand with the herd."

Jaffick wheeled his horse hard about. He threw a cold glance at Hazen. "All right, Jack, let's go."

The gunman nodded slowly but did not move. He did not take his eyes off Jess, waiting until the outlaw and his partner, Lee, were directly before him. Only then did he straighten himself and settle in the saddle while some of the tense threat slipped from his hunched shoulders. He grinned at Jess, his thin lips pulling back over his teeth in a mirthless sort of grimace.

"See you later," he murmured to the scar-faced guerrilla.

Jess paused, ducked his head several times. "Any time you want, Fancy Dan. Any time you want."

Hazen, plainly not trusting the man at all, kept his glance on Jess as he pulled about and followed Jaffick and the others from the yard. Only when he was well away did he turn fully around.

"You got yourself a hat full of trouble there, Jess," the outlaw named Lee observed in a quiet voice.

"So I got trouble!" Jess shot back angrily. "You think I can't handle it? You think I'll back down before that prissy dude?"

"Never said that—"

"Everybody bowin' and scrapin' to that four-flusher! Runnin' around, kissin' his hind end. Well, not me, mister! And you got one thing wrong—it ain't me that's got trouble, it's him!"

"Sure, sure," Lee said, placatingly. "Come on, we better get on with this here chore. Turley comes back and finds these two jaspers still kickin', he'll raise holy hell. He'll be worse'n he was back there at that Rockin' S place, or whatever they called it."

Stanbuck's brain had once again cleared. His eyes followed Jaffick, now moving off into the distance with the rest of his crew. He thrust aside the glowing anger that racked him, cast about desperately for some means of escape, some way to get free of the two outlaws who held them, that he might over-take Jaffick and complete his avowed intention.

"All right," Jess muttered, his tone falling to a more agree-able tenor. "Let's get done with it."

Lee swiveled his attention to Stanbuck and Charlie Pierce. "Move out, you two. Head for that barn. And pick up your friend when you go by."

Stanbuck did not move. His brain worked fast now. He was thinking of the exchange between Hazen and the scar-faced outlaw, Jess, wondering if it might offer an opening. He glanced first at Lee, then to Jess. "Any chance of us talking this over?"

"Nope," Lee said, flatly. "Get movin'."

"Shooting us down in cold blood will get you hung," he continued. "Haven't got much money on the place, but it's yours if you want to take it and ride on out."

"How much money?" Jess asked, interested.

"Couple hundred dollars."

Lee snorted. "Couple hundred! Our cut from Turley will be ten times that much!"

"Still won't be enough to buy off the hangman," Stanbuck said, "once you're caught."

"Reckon they got a job of nabbin' us first," Jess said. "By the time they dig you and the rest up, we'll be so far down in Mexico they'd have to set up relay stations to reach us."

Stanbuck shook his head. "Like Charlie here said, you'll never get away with it. Somebody's bound to get through to the Fort and spread the word."

Lee grunted. He had a narrow, pinched face and his uncut hair lay upon his neck in a thick pad. "Ain't nobody leavin' this valley 'less Turley says so. Even if they was to try, they'd never get by the boys standin' sentry at the road to the east."

"Who's to try?" Jess demanded. "Never heard of no dead man yet ridin' a bronc!"

"That's for certain," Lee agreed.

"Well, come on, let's cut this yammerin'," Jess said then. "You was the one wantin' to hurry, now all you're doin' is standin' around gabbin' with these here cow nurses. You!" he said, pointing his gun at Stanbuck. "Start walkin' toward that barn."

Dave shrugged and turned about. There was no other choice but to obey—wait and watch. Charlie Pierce moved in beside

21

him. They started to walk slowly toward the structure. Stanbuck's brain was racing desperately against time. He and Pierce were doomed men, only moments from death unless he could come up with an idea of some sort.

"Grab hold of your friend there," Lee ordered as they came abreast of Fred Wheelock's lifeless body.

Stanbuck and the old foreman halted. They stooped, crouched beside the dead cowboy and lifted him between them. Regaining their balance, they continued on.

Jess said, "Mighty hot to be workin' out in the sun. Why don't we just put them inside the barn? Could pile a lot of hay and stuff on them. Hide them just as good."

"Sure," Lee agreed. "Then we could set fire to the place. Nobody'd ever find them then."

"That'd be a crazy fool stunt to pull!" Jess exploded. "Smoke would be seen ten miles off! Old Turley would peel our hides sure, was we to do somethin' like that."

"Reckon you're right," Lee mumbled. "Never thought about the smoke."

They reached the front of the barn. "Get inside," Jess ordered, again waving his weapon threateningly. "Little too hot, workin' outside."

Stanbuck and Pierce veered their steps toward the wide doorway, still bearing their burden between them. At the hitching rail their two horses, and that of the luckless Fred Wheelock, still waited. Had Jaffick and his guerrillas arrived ten minutes later, they would have found the ranch deserted. The three men had planned to ride out and help the other two punchers move the herd that afternoon. Stanbuck considered them closely. If only there was some way they could reach them, could get into the saddle before Jess and Lee could bring their guns into action.

The outlaws, still mounted, were just steps behind them. Each had his weapon out, ready. At the first move to break away, Stanbuck knew he and Pierce would feel a hail of bullets drive into their backs. No, there was no avenue of escape that way. Maybe some sort of opportunity would yet present itself once they were inside the barn. At least there would be a better possibility of it. The outlaws would be off their horses, on foot. That would equalize the odds some. They reached the door and entered the shadowy, cooler interior that smelled of hay and manure and dry, sun-baked timbers.

There was not much time left. Stanbuck lifted his eyes, glanced at Pierce. An idea had come to him, a wild, fantastic idea born of the last, final shreds of hope. The older man faced him across the body of Wheelock, still carried between them. His grizzled features were devoid of expression.

"Look alive," Stanbuck murmured.

The old foreman was instantly alert. He gave Stanbuck a tight, half-grin, signifying he was ready for any eventuality.

"Far enough!" Jess sang out from the doorway. He swung from his horse and waited while Lee followed suit. They left their mounts there, just outside the doorway, and came slowly and cautiously down the run.

"Over there—that back stall," Jess commanded, pointing with his pistol.

Stanbuck nodded. He turned to Pierce. "Let go, Charlie. I can handle old Fred." He took a better fuller grasp on Wheelock's body. Pierce immediately relinquished his hold.

"What you want to do with him?" Stanbuck asked, coming slowly around and facing the outlaws. The pair was standing shoulder to shoulder, little more than arm's length away.

"Throw him down here in that back stall, like I told you," Jess said, his face suddenly eager and shining with an oily brightness in the half-light. "Then you two set yourselves down right alongside him."

"Sure," Stanbuck said. He started to turn back, instead took a half-step to one side and whirled. With every ounce of strength he could muster, he threw the body of Fred Wheelock at the outlaws.

One of the guns exploded, the flash bright orange in the murky depths of the barn. Lee yelled and an oath ripped from Jess's lips as they both went down under the impact of the lifeless corpse.

Stanbuck, pushing Pierce ahead of him, lunged for the open doorway. There was no time to do anything else. "Their horses —take them!" he shouted.

Their own were waiting only yards away but they were tied to the rail. Getting to them, pulling free the reins would consume precious moments. They leaped to the saddles of the outlaws' horses, wheeled sharply away, driving hard for the corner of the barn. Behind them, Jess and Lee continued to shout their curses as they scrambled to gain the outside. The sudden smash of a gunshot shattered the day. Stanbuck heard the whine of a hastily fired bullet as it passed nearby.

Ten more feet to the corner of the building. Ten more feet and they would turn, would put the structure's bulk between themselves and the enraged outlaws. Only ten feet.

It seemed miles to Dave Stanbuck.

Chapter 4

BOTH OUTLAWS OPENED up in the next moment. The sounds of their crashing guns were a rapid staccato. From the tail of his eye Stanbuck saw Charlie Pierce jolt in the saddle and knew at once he had been shot. He started to yell but the old foreman steadied himself on his wild running horse, leaned forward and clung to the horn. They thundered on.

Suddenly they were at the corner of the barn, were curving around it in a close, tight arc. Stanbuck breathed easier. They were safe from the outlaws' bullets—at least for the length of time it would take Jess and Lee to mount up and give chase. With Pierce still hanging on, they continued, going the full length of the barn, breaking finally into the open field beyond.

Stanbuck glanced over his shoulder. No sign of the guerrillas yet. They had a good start on the pair—but a start for where? The valley was hemmed in by Turley Jaffick's men. The only route to safety, to the east and Fort Quinton was blocked. The town of Eldenburg, over a hundred miles south, could be reached only by first passing through that same gateway.

Mangus Valley was like a gigantic bowl with just one practical exit or entrance. Various trails did lead up and over the fringe of black, volcanic lava buttes, rising in frowning palisades on all sides, but they led to nowhere. To the west and north lay hundreds of unbroken miles before the first settlements were reached. To the south, forming the highest boundary of all, stood Mangus Mountain. It was a towering, cliff-racked formation rising to a narrow hogback generally referred to as the Ridge. One perilous trail ascended to that summit and a man, once on the Ridge, had no place else to go. That single, treacherous path was the solitary way both onto and off the mountain.

Stanbuck glanced at Pierce. The old puncher's face was strained, taut, reflecting his agony. His long, bony nose pointed straight ahead and the trailing ends of his straggling mustache lay back against his hollow cheeks. Back in the barn he had lost his hat and his snow-white hair shone silver in the driving sunlight. But he could not hold out for long. That was evident.

"Make it to the mountain?" Stanbuck shouted above the thudding of the horses' flying hoofs. "Looks like our best bet."

Pierce nodded his agreement. He began to veer his mount toward the huge pile of rock and brush, now five miles or so distant. Stanbuck again looked to their back trail. Jess and Lee were just rounding the barn, breaking into the field. Apparently they had taken time to reload their weapons. It had cost them several moments, affording Stanbuck and Pierce a greater lead.

But a bullet could quickly nullify that, Dave realized. One slug of viciously singing lead into a man's back or into the body of his horse could change the whole picture instantly. With a silent prayer on his lips Stanbuck crouched over his straining mount and drove on. All they needed was a bit of luck—good luck.

A short time later another hasty look told him they were holding their own in the desperate race. Their own horses would have been fresher than the sorrel and black that belonged to the outlaws, but they had not been given a choice. Still, their present mounts were showing no signs of weakening. They were strong animals, apparently accustomed to such emergencies.

No more shooting was taking place, indicating the outlaws knew they were well out of range and were wasting no ammunition from a position they knew was poor under the most favorable conditions. Stanbuck looked ahead. Mangus Mountain loomed nearer, its rugged slopes taking shape now as rocks and scrubby growth and long, steep canyons of trapped heat became visible.

Sweat glistened brightly on the neck of the black and occasionally a fine spray of foam dashed against Stanbuck's face. The horses were running fast and easy over the smooth roll of grassy plain. There were few rocks to endanger their flying hoofs, only the possibility of a gopher hole or a prairie dog's burrow. For those Dave Stanbuck maintained a sharp watch, carefully guiding the laboring black wide of any suspicious bulges in the earth's surface.

Gunshots suddenly began to crack hollowly behind them. There were no droning sounds and he knew the bullets were falling short. Again he looked beyond the black's pumping head, not having realized what the outlaws did; the mountain was directly before them. Another hundred yards and they would enter the first outcropping of glistening, black rock and sun-grayed brush.

He was thankful for that. The black, at last, was beginning to tire, to show signs of breaking under the hard, fast run. Pierce's sorrel, too, was nearly spent, running now with outthrust neck, head swung low. Neither animal could be expected to go much farther at such a pace. Nor could Charlie Pierce, Stanbuck saw. They gained the rocks, entered, and swung to their left on a faint path that led up to the trail.

Pierce swayed dangerously in the saddle. He clawed at the horn, letting the sorrel have his head and follow the trampled route on his own. Stanbuck threw a sharp glance at the man.

"Hang on, Charlie!" he yelled. "We've about made it!"

The path ended abruptly in a small clearing at the foot of the mountain. Both horses came to a sliding halt. Stanbuck immediately leaped from the saddle. He slapped the black on the rump and sent him trotting off to one side, his barrel-like body still heaving badly. Pierce struggled to dismount. He had difficulty getting one foot out of the stirrup. Stanbuck hurried to him and lifted him down. The sorrel followed the black and the two men started up the steep, brushy trail. Back at the outcropping there was a rushing thud of hoofs as the outlaws came in. It was that close.

"You bad hit?" Stanbuck asked, pushing the foreman on ahead of himself.

Pierce shook his head. "Don't rightly know. Bullet caught me in the side. Just sort of numb feelin' now."

Stanbuck, his broad hands securely hooked under the foreman's armpits, helped him as best he could. But the trail was steep, narrow and the footing uncertain, made so by loose gravel and shale.

"We get far enough up, we can stand them off," he said, the words loose and unjointed. He was running out of breath from the effort being expended.

"Go on—go on ahead," Pierce gasped. "I'll be all right. I'll hide out along here, somewheres."

"You keep moving!" Stanbuck snapped. "When you run out of steam, we'll stop and make a stand."

"Reckon—that won't—be long now!"

There was a clatter at the base of the trail. The outlaws had reached the clearing, were already starting to climb. The twisted, winding course of the path hid them from view but there was no doubt they were below, beginning to ascend. Stanbuck pulled back from Pierce, allowed him to struggle along on his own. He wheeled and picked up a boulder the size of a water bucket. He waited, the rock poised above his head, until he saw the first sign of the guerrillas, an extended hand reaching for a clump of brush. He hurled the stone with all his strength.

It struck just ahead of whichever outlaw had been in the lead. It smashed into a solid ledge of rock, shattering into a hundred sharp-edged bits of granite shrapnel. A man yelled in pain—Jess's voice, Stanbuck thought. It didn't matter to him which outlaw it was. He had stalled them, perhaps driven them back to the clearing for a time. Perhaps it would be long enough to allow Charlie Pierce and himself to reach the safety of the Ridge.

He turned to catch up with the old rider. He paused, his glance seized momentarily by the sight of a carriage and team below, just outside the clearing where the black and the sorrel now stood in head-lowered exhaustion. He studied the vehicle for some time, wondering who its owner might be—and why it was there.

A moment later he heard a groan and the sound of cascading

gravel on the trail above him. Pierce had fallen. He forgot the rig and hurried on, his breath quickly running out as he pushed himself to the limit up the punishing grade.

Pierce, sweat streaming off his blanched face, was on his feet by the time Stanbuck reached him. He was muttering curses, blaming his own awkwardness for the fall. Dave slid in beside him and again gave him his support.

"Just like a fresh-dropped calf," the foreman mumbled in disgust. "Can't keep my legs under me nohow!"

"Almost to the top," Stanbuck said, "Not much farther to go."

"I'll make it," Pierce said, grimly. "Don't go frettin' none over me."

"I'm not," Stanbuck replied and stopped short. Up the trail, ahead of them, he had heard something; a sound of some sort. He waited there on the tortuous trail, sweat pouring off his wind- and sun-darkened face, down his lean body, as he listened.

It came again. A muffled cough. The sound was plainly muted, as though an attempt had been made to smother it, hold it back. But, in the hot silence of the mountain, it had carried nevertheless. There was no doubt now. Someone was on the Ridge ahead of them.

Dave Stanbuck's mind raced on, probing the possibilities. Some of Turley Jaffick's men, placed on that strategic, high point as lookouts? Was that who it was? Or could it be others from the valley who had sought refuge on Mangus Mountain?

There was no turning back now, even if he thought it best. They could only go on. He motioned to Pierce to halt, to remain silent, indicating he was to wait and rest beside a huge, jutting boulder along the trail. He glanced back down the path. There were neither signs nor sounds that would lead him to believe Jess and Lee were making a second try. This immediately strengthened his suspicions that other outlaws were on the Ridge. Jess and Lee would abandon any thoughts of climbing the narrow trail if they knew other members of Jaffick's guerrilla band were above.

But he must know. He turned and started up the pathway, moving slowly and with extreme care. Charlie Pierce watched him pass with weary, pain-filled eyes, but he managed a tight grin.

28

Stanbuck nodded reassuringly at him, a confidence he did not completely feel. "Back in a minute," he said in a low whisper.

Chapter 5

THE TRAIL LEVELED off for a dozen feet or so, then again began to climb steadily. Dave Stanbuck, making his way slowly, placed each foot with utmost care as he sought to avoid displacing loose rock and setting up a clatter. He supported and pulled himself along by grasping the tough, spring brush that sprouted from the blistered slope, aiding himself by clinging to the burning surfaces of the huge rocks bordering the way. Forgotten momentarily was his need for vengeance upon Jaffick as he found himself lost in the furious turmoil of escape.

Sweat trickled freely from every pore in his body. He was thoroughly drenched. His feet and legs seemed to be on fire, and each time his bare skin came in contact with the rugged, heat-blasted boulders, he winced. But he choked back any sound. He sought to keep his breathing low, to stifle the rough rasping that his heaving lungs produced; if he were to have a cautious look at the Ridge, he must do it unseen. He halted, glancing upward. It could not be far to the top, not over a few feet, he thought.

He waited, allowed his pumping breast to quiet, permitted the crying muscles of his body to rest. He looked about, seeking some sort of weapon. There was nothing available, only rocks and small sticks, neither of any use to him unless he could come to grips at close quarters with whoever was on the Ridge.

Rested at last to some degree, he pushed on, moving even slower and with greater care. Light broke out ahead of him on the trail. He was almost to the top. He was seeing the sky beyond the summit. He halted again, listening. He heard voices. Several voices, all low and guarded and scarcely audible.

He crept upward another step. And another. Abruptly he was looking onto the narrow width and short length of the Ridge which ran an irregular, uneven course along the crown of Mangus Mountain. There was not just one man—there were three. And two elderly women and a girl. Stanbuck gave a sigh of relief. They were not of Jaffick's company of guerrillas, it was Tom Kinter, his wife, and a cowboy who worked for them, Ollie Dennis. The other people Stanbuck did not know.

He pulled himself up the final yard or two and walked into the open. His appearance caught them unawares, startled them. They fell back a step. Then Kinter recognized him.

"Stanbuck! Was that you on the trail?"

Dave nodded. "And I'm glad you're not who I expected to find up here, too. Figured it was some of Jaffick's bunch."

Kinter shook his head. "He hit your place, too, then."

Stanbuck nodded. He shifted his attention to Ollie Dennis, his glance sliding past the others. "Got a wounded man back down the trail. Obliged if you'd lend me a hand with him."

"Who is it?" the young cowboy asked.

"Charlie Pierce. Caught a bullet in the back."

Kinter said, "Help him, Ollie."

Stanbuck turned to the trail. Behind him he could hear the heavy-footed tread of the husky Dennis. He did not know the cowboy very well, having met him, as he had Tom Kinter, only two or three times in the years he had lived in Mangus Valley. Kinter used him more around the house and immediate yard than on the range, as a sort of handy man. Stanbuck became aware the puncher had stopped. He glanced back. Dennis had pulled a bottle from his pocket and was having a long swallow of whiskey. He met Dave's gaze, grinned and extended the bottle.

Stanbuck shook his head. "Not now. Little too warm for it."

He moved on, presently hearing Dennis fall in behind him again. They reached the point in the trail where Charlie

Pierce waited in silence. He was sitting on the rock, hunched slightly to one side. Stanbuck saw the deep, crusted stains on his shirt, well above his right hip. Pierce had bled considerably.

They got him to his feet and started up the difficult climb. The old foreman seemed to be in much greater pain now and they were forced to progress slowly. They came at last to the top and Stanbuck, moving ahead, lifted the old man bodily to the level of the Ridge. He nodded his thanks to Ollie Dennis and helped Pierce to a spot behind one of the larger boulders where shade was beginning to gather.

Immediately the two older women dropped to their knees beside him and began to attend his wound. Pierce groaned faintly. Tom Kinter's wife glanced to Stanbuck, her gray, thin features set in severe lines.

"There's not much we can do for him. We have no medicine, not even any water. We can bind it up to stop the bleeding, that's about all."

Over his shoulder Stanbuck said to Kinter, "Somebody keep a watch on that trail." Then he knelt beside his foreman. He looked closely at the wound. The bullet had struck above the hip. Luckily it had passed on through, missing bone and vital organs. He half-turned, facing Ollie Dennis.

"I'll have that drink you offered me."

Dennis stared at him blankly for a moment, but procured the bottle from inside his butternut shirt and handed it over, casting sideward looks at Kinter as he did.

Stanbuck pulled the cloth away from the bullet hole with his fingers. He spread the puckered, crusted wound a little and poured a small amount of the fiery liquor into the raw opening. Pierce groaned, writhed violently as the whiskey cauterized the torn flesh, but after a few moments he settled down and grinned weakly at Stanbuck.

"Reckon a little of that on the inside would do a mite of good, too."

Stanbuck held the bottle to the old foreman's lips and gave him a generous swig. Finished, he handed it back to Dennis with a laconic, "Obliged."

"If we just had some bandage," Kinter's wife said. "There's nothing we can use—"

The girl stepped up nearer. She was young, Dave saw, noting her for the first time, and very pretty with dark hair and deep, blue eyes. She was slender and well-shaped beneath an ankle-length, pink dress of some soft-looking material. Evidently she had begun the journey to Mangus Mountain in a hurry and had been denied the time to change to something more suitable than the low-necked party dress.

"Will my petticoat do?" she asked in a full, somewhat throaty voice.

"Be fine, Marissa," Mrs. Kinter replied, adding, "Don't know why I didn't think of that!"

The girl smiled, turned her back to the group. She busied herself for a minute, then stepped out of the snowy-white garment piled about her feet. She picked it up and brought it to the rancher's wife, her cheeks glowing faintly pink.

Mrs. Kinter at once ripped a wide length off the bottom of the petticoat and handed the rest back to Marissa. The girl folded the remnant into a triangular scarf, draping it over her head and bare shoulders.

Tom Kinter stepped up beside Stanbuck. "Reckon a few introductions are in order here, now that we've got your friend fixed best we can. You know my wife, Mattie. And Ollie Dennis, who works for us. Other lady there is my wife's sister, Mrs. McCarey. That's Corey McCarey, my brother-in-law, her husband."

Stanbuck shook the tall, broad-faced man's hand. He swung his eyes to the girl. Kinter, continuing his chore, said, "This is my niece, Marissa. She's the daughter of another brother-in-law, another McCarey. She lives with Corey and Esther. Her folks got killed accidentally at Sharpsburg. Cannonball overshot its target, hit their house—"

"Never mind, Tom," Mattie Kinter said quietly.

Stanbuck glanced at the girl. She was looking off into the valley, her face calm and withdrawn. He had not noted at first how thick and dark her brows actually were.

"Corey's home is in Boonesboro. In Maryland. It's not far from Sharpsburg," the old rancher continued. "Came out here to visit for a spell, just to sort of get away from the war—"

"And ran smack into something like this!" McCarey broke in angrily. "Just as well stayed home!"

Kinter shrugged. He removed his hat, exposing his graying hair to the streaming sunlight. "Trouble is everywhere nowdays, it seems, Corey. Man can't always sidestep it."

He brought his attention back to Dave. "They shoot up your place pretty bad?"

Stanbuck nodded. "Killed one of my riders. Not sure what happened to the other two. They got Charlie when we made a break. Guess it's the same story all through the valley."

"Bloodthirsty savages!" McCarey muttered in a low voice. "It's unbelievable in this day and age!"

Stanbuck was only half-listening. He was sorry for Kinter and his people but it was no worry of his. The one thing he must still do lay ahead of him; somehow get off the Ridge and catch up with Jaffick.

"Don't know about the Hamlins or the Rhodes but likely they got the same treatment as us. You know the bunch doing it?"

"I know the head man," Stanbuck said grimly. "Name of Jaffick. Ran into him a couple of years back. He led a guerrilla bunch along the border. Except this is pretty much the same gang he's got with him."

Tom Kinter had been studying the prone, quiet shape of Charlie Pierce. "Jaffick? That the one they call the Butcher?"

"The same."

Corey McCarey said, "A guerrilla fighter—like Quantrill?"

"The same, only worse."

"I believe that," Kinter said then. "They were strangers to me, except for Jack Hazen. Remember seeing him off and on around Eldenburg and in the valley. Wonder how he got lined up with Jaffick and his crowd?"

Stanbuck voiced a thought that had struck him earlier. "He could have been the one who brought Jaffick and his bunch here. Saw it would be a cinch to take over the valley, with everybody thinking about the war and only a small company of soldiers at Fort Quinton. Quick way to make a lot of money. Get in and get out fast."

"And it would all be charged up to the war, to guerrillas," Kinter added.

"About the way of it. But we've upset their plans a bit. Jaffick didn't figure to let anybody stay alive after he hit. And Hazen can't afford to let it happen either."

There was a long silence after that. McCarey broke it by saying, "You mean they'll come here now? They'll try to murder us so there will be no witnesses?"

Dave Stanbuck said, "The way I see it."

He glanced at the women, first to the two older ones still fussing about Charlie Pierce. And then to Marissa McCarey. She was a few steps farther along, her gaze now upon the shimmering surface of the desert lying to the west of the mountain. She was paying little attention to the conversation.

"Our chances are pretty good up here," he went on. "This ridge is like a fort. We can hold them off easy, since the only way up is by the trail."

"But this heat!" Corey McCarey protested, mopping at his flushed face. "And with no water or food! We can't stand it for long!"

"We'll have to try," Tom Kinter said. "Except they've got the entrance to the valley blocked. Not much hope of anybody riding by to give us some help."

"Maybe we can come up with an idea on how to get help," Stanbuck said. "Meantime, as I said, we can hold them off—"

"With what?" Ollie Dennis demanded suddenly. His face was a flaming red from the liquor and hot sun and his tongue was thick. "Unless you got a gun hid somewhere on you, there ain't one in the whole bunch of us!"

Stanbuck glanced quickly about. It was true. None of the three men wore pistols.

"Never carry one myself," Kinter said, almost apologetically. "And, of course, Corey doesn't. Reason Ollie doesn't have one is my fault, too. Never let him strap one on while he's working around the house. And Jaffick and his bunch caught us before we had a chance to do anything but run for it."

Stanbuck shrugged. "Well, can't be helped. Guess it doesn't matter too much anyway. Gun wouldn't be any big advantage up here. You can keep them off the trail with rocks."

"Unless they take a notion to rush us and come up shootin'," Dennis said. "We sure won't hold them back for long was they to do that."

Again Dave Stanbuck moved his shoulders, indicating it was no problem of his. He was going to find a way off the Ridge, somehow. Turley Jaffick was not getting away now, not after all this time. It was too bad about Tom Kinter and the others, but they would make out all right. They would have to. And Pierce would be all right too. As soon as he had squared things with Jaffick he would come back for him.

But they should be getting set. He would help that much; get a supply of rocks piled up at the head of the trail so they could be turned loose on anyone who attempted to ascend. Then he would start looking for a way off the Ridge.

"We'd a been safe up here if you hadn't come along!"

Ollie Dennis's remark came suddenly through the quiet. The liquor had aroused him and he spoke in a quick rush of words.

Stanbuck frowned. "How so?"

"How so?" the cowboy echoed. "That bunch didn't even know we was up here, that's how so! We got away from them before they ever saw us. Then we hid up here. But when you and Pierce, there, come a-chargin' across the flats, you led them straight to us. Now we're all in for it!"

Chapter 6

DEAD SILENCE FOLLOWED Ollie Dennis's words. In that hot, blistering interlude on the bald cap of Mangus Mountain, Dave Stanbuck's gaze moved slowly about, touching each of the persons there. Somewhere nearby, in the crevice of a heat-riven rock, an insect, encouraged by the breathless hush, began to buzz loudly. And in the heavens, far to the north, three vultures swung in low, graceful arcs as something in death caught their sharp attention.

It was the truth. Dave Stanbuck realized it in those moments. But how could he have known there were others on the

Ridge? Oddly enough, it was Marissa McCarey who came to his defense.

"You can't blame Dave—Mr. Stanbuck, for that," she said. "How was he to know we were already up here? And even if he had, there wasn't any other choice for him."

"Of course," Tom Kinter added. "Nobody owns this pile of rocks and anybody that wants to, can use it. We stood right here and saw what Stanbuck and his foreman were up against. Those outlaws were right on their tails and they had to come here. Wasn't no place else for them to go."

"Just the same," Dennis said, stubbornly, "he's sure fixed us good, comin' here. We'd a been all right, if he hadn't. By tomorrow that Jaffick and his bunch would a been gone and we could have rode back to the ranch. Now he'll camp right down there 'til he knows we're all dead!"

"That's enough, Ollie!" Kinter said, sharply, his face angry. "Forget it!"

"Forget it!" the cowboy repeated, his voice rising. "How can I forget it? In twenty-four hours I'll be dead most likely —and you tell me to forget it!"

"Ollie! You heard what I said!" Kinter snapped. "I'll have no more such talk."

Dennis relented, turning back to the trail. But he was far from forgetting their situation, as Kinter had ordered. Nor were the others, despite their pretense of viewing the matter as accidental and completely unavoidable. Stanbuck could read it in the tautness of their faces, in the bright worry that shone through their eyes. They had been safe; then he and Pierce had come, bringing the sure promise of death with them.

He wheeled about, slowly walked to the edge of the Ridge and looked down upon the flats. It was squarely up to him, he realized. He had got them into their trouble; he should get them out—at least, try. But that could mean missing Turley Jaffick. He might get away, get clear out of the country, lose himself again. Dave Stanbuck thought of all the hours he had spent hating the man, all the hell he had passed through because of him, and something inside rebelled at the idea of forsaking the pursuit of vengeance, even for a brief time.

But there were other things to consider. There were the people on the Ridge, Kinter and the rest, all trapped there with him. Their troubles and problems were their own; perhaps that was true. He had not asked others to assume his and there was no call for him to share theirs. Still, a man had an obligation to meet in such instances. He couldn't just turn his back and look the other way when help was needed. And maybe he was partly to blame for their being in the fix they were. Knowing something of Jaffick, he doubted that somewhat; the Butcher would never leave the valley without first being sure all the loose strings were tied, all the doors were closed. He came around and faced them, his mind made up; his accounting with Jaffick would have to wait.

He let his glance run over them, one by one. He said, "Sorry I caused this trouble. I'll do what I can to remedy it."

"We're all in this together," Tom Kinter spoke up at once. "Thing to do is get ready for them. You tell us what you want done and we'll start."

Stanbuck nodded to the rancher. He discovered he liked Kinter, wished now he had known him better. In the time he had lived in the valley he had kept pretty much to himself, confined his activities to the building up of his ranch—and to his own bitter thoughts. Now that he had found the man he sought and the prospect of cleansing his mind with revenge was at hand, things could change. He could live again, be a friend, a neighbor; start a new, whole life. It would be like being born again, a fresh beginning. He glanced at Marissa. He wondered if she would be staying on at the Kinter's for any length of time. If so he would—

He brought his thoughts back to the moment. Kinter and the others were waiting for him to speak up. He said, "Don't think that pair below will try anything until Jaffick and some of the others show up. One of them is hurt, how bad I don't know. I figure they'll sit tight down there until dark, anyway."

"You think Jaffick knows where we are—where his two men are, I mean?" Kinter asked.

Stanbuck said, "Certain of it. They weren't far away when Charlie and I made our break. He was sure to see Jess and Lee chase us toward the mountain. And when they don't show up like he told them to do, he'll come looking to see what went wrong. Those outlaws down there know that, too. They'll decide the best thing they can do is wait at the bottom of the trail, make sure we don't escape again."

"What happens when Jaffick gets here?" Corey McCarey, silent up to that time, asked.

"My guess is they'll try to rush us, send a half a dozen men up the trail at once, all shooting."

Kinter nodded his agreement. "Just about all he can do. You think we can stop them by rolling rocks down on them?"

"Nothing else we can do—and it ought to work. That trail is steep and plenty narrow with several sharp turns. There's one about twenty feet below the top. I think it's our best bet. It's a full, right-angle turn and the brush grows close on both sides, which will make it tough for a man to get out of the way of falling rocks.

"What we better do is gather plenty of ammunition in the way of rocks, pile them at the edge of the trail where they'll be handy. Ought to set up a watch, too. Don't want to get caught napping."

McCarey suddenly cracked the palms of his hands together. "It's unbelievable!" he exclaimed. "I just can't understand how a thing like this can happen! Why, this country isn't even civilized—all this killing and stealing! Where is your law?"

Dave Stanbuck said, "Man has to be pretty much his own law out here. He does what's right by himself and his neighbors, and when he comes up against a deal like this one, against Jaffick, I mean, he handles it the best way he can."

"But the law—don't you have a marshal or a sheriff or someone who represents the law?"

"Sure, we have a marshal but you can't wait on him. He has a good many thousand square miles of territory to look after and generally he's got his hands pretty full."

"But in Maryland—"

"You're a long ways from Maryland, Corey," Tom Kinter said gently. "Things are much different here. This is a new country and it will be a spell yet before your kind of law and civilization sets in."

McCarey wagged his head. "Well, I want no part of it. If we live through this terrible thing, I'm heading straight back to the place where a man can walk the streets in safety without fearing for his life or that of his womenfolk. I wouldn't live in a country like this!"

38

"You're wastin' your time, thinkin' you'll be goin' back to Maryland," Ollie Dennis said from his post at the top of the trail. "By this time tomorrow we'll all be bait for buzzards like them circlin' up there, thanks to Stanbuck and his friend."

Dave had a quick urge to cross over and smash his knotted fist into the cowboy's face and silence him. Not so much for his laying blame upon Pierce and himself—there was no denying he had spoken the truth in that—but for his continual harping on the inevitability of death for them all. It was doing no one any good, particularly the three women whose nerves must be near the breaking point, anyway. He glanced at Marissa, saw she was watching him in a grave, quiet way. He let his anger drain slowly off.

"Ollie, reckon you'll be gettin' there sooner'n the rest of us," Charlie Pierce said in a dry, tired voice. "If you don't quit nippin' at that firewater. Hot sun and that stuff sure won't mix."

"One way's as good as another to go," Dennis replied, and deliberately tipped the bottle to his lips to show his independence of mind.

After that, they set to work accumulating suitable rocks for the defense of the ridge, Stanbuck, Kinter and the Maryland man, McCarey, laboring side by side at the task. Ollie Dennis was kept at his guard post, watching the trail, although Stanbuck was certain no attempt would be made by the outlaws to mount it until the others arrived on the scene. It was a good place to keep Ollie, however. He would have been of little help. The combination of fiery liquor and sweltering heat would quickly prostrate him, had he undertaken any vigorous activity.

Within an hour they had a sizable pile of stones at the edge of the ridge overlooking the path, all large enough to do considerable damage but small enough to be easily handled. Stanbuck then descended the trail to the sharp turn he had mentioned earlier and had chosen as the point of no return for the outlaws; there he distributed a quantity of dry leaves, dead limbs, and loose shale and gravel over the uneven floor. Anyone moving across it could not fail to set up a racket easily heard by those on the rim above.

There was nothing left to do after that but settle down and wait. The afternoon wore on with no lessening of the brutal heat. With the sun's westward swing, shade began to develop on the near sides of the large rocks and this offered some relief. Stanbuck doubted if the women and McCarey could stand another day of the glaring sun. He decided that if they were still on the ridge and there was no rescue in sight by the following morning, he would suggest to Kinter that the petticoats of his wife and sister-in-law might be put to better use as canopies. They would provide some shelter from the sun. Marissa's thoughtfulness in offering her own under-garment as bandages gave him the idea.

He noted that Ollie Dennis had fallen asleep at his post. He was hunched against the pile of collected boulders, snor-ing lustily. Stanbuck removed him to the shade of a short ledge, dragging him the entire ten or twelve feet necessary without arousing the liquor besotted cowboy in the least. He did not trouble to station another guard at the head of the trail, still convinced no attempts would be made to storm the Ridge until later.

The need for water was beginning to tell on them all. It showed in the dryness of their lips and the gradually mount-ing, feverish glint in their eyes. He was not suffering too greatly himself, nor did Tom Kinter appear to be; but the women, the softly moaning Charlie Pierce, and Corey Mc-Carey were not so fortunate.

Watching them, Dave Stanbuck came to a conclusion. There could be no waiting around, no hoping to hold off. Help must be summoned, somehow. He had to figure a way off the Ridge, obtain a horse and bring aid. There were no other means open to him. He had thought of a signal fire, but discarded that suggestion when he decided it would be seen by no one but the outlaws. The only answer was to go for help—alone.

He arose, walked slowly along the Ridge, searching the down-flowing slope with his eyes for some break in its sur-face, some avenue of escape. With a rope there were one or two places where he might possibly descend—but there was no rope to be had and nothing with which to improvise one. There was no point in considering that method.

Near the end of the Ridge, he halted. Where the almost level top of the formation lifted abruptly to a rounded, smooth cone, a narrow channel cut by several hundred years of torrential rains sliced steeply downward. He studied it thoughtfully, a faint break of hope moving through him. A man might, with care, work himself down the groove in the cliff to the ledge below, a distance of fifty feet or so. From there it would be a gamble as to the possibility of descending to the next lower shelf of rock. The face of the cliff bulged outward, preventing him from seeing the exact formation at the next, succeeding level. But it might be worth a try.

He considered the best time to make an attempt. Late in the afternoon or early morning would be his choice. Night would be better, insofar as hiding his activities from the outlaws was concerned, but then his chance for success would be considerably lessened. In the darkness it would be easy to make a misstep, or misjudge a ledge or the location of a necessary pathway. And to do that meant death on the jagged rocks at the base of the mountain.

He did not think the outlaws, from their position at the bottom of the trail, could see him when he started to descend. A good two-hundred yards at ground level would separate him from where they waited and a large, rugged swell covered with rock and brush would lie between. He must be careful of noise, however; each step would have to be placed with extreme caution for sound carried extraordinarily well along the mountain. Rock and loose gravel, dislodged, would set up a noisy clatter that could easily be heard by the outlaws.

He came to a decision then; he would do it. He would leave soon, as soon as the sun dropped a little lower. He hoped Jaffick and the others would not put in their appearance for a while longer. Things would be much easier handled if he had only the two outlaws to contend with. With one of them injured, it should not be too difficult a job, even if he had no gun. He should be able to slip up on them, through the rocks and brush—

"Riders coming!" Tom Kinter sang out from the rim.

Chapter 7

THERE WERE TEN MEN in the bunch. Even from this distance, Dave Stanbuck recognized Hazen in the brilliantly colored shirt, and the guerrilla chief, Turley Jaffick, on his huge black-and-white horse. He watched them in silence for a time and then turned to the others.

"Stay back from the rim, out of sight. Could be they don't know you're up here. Maybe I can make a deal with Jaffick."

Tom Kinter threw him a keen glance. "You mean give yourself up? That it?"

Stanbuck said, "Just keep out of sight. Let me do the talking."

The old rancher shook his head vigorously. "You won't be making no such deal with Jaffick or anybody else. We're in this together, all of us, and we'll get out of it the same way. Anyway, Jaffick will know we're up here, too. They'll spot that rig of mine down there and add up two and two."

"How long had you been here when we arrived?" Stanbuck asked.

"Couple of hours. Maybe three."

"Figures out about right," Stanbuck murmured, more to himself than the others. "Likely you're right about the rig. Hazen would know who it belonged to and, since they didn't find you at your ranch, they'll guess you're up here on the mountain."

He paused, letting his gaze rest on the approaching outlaws. "Just the same, all of you stay down out of sight. We'll play it my way first."

"Maybe, if we just sit tight, this man Jaffick will take his crowd and ride on," Corey McCarey ventured. "Maybe he'll be satisfied to just keep us penned up here until he's finished with his business."

"Not Turley Jaffick," Stanbuck said. "He's got too much hanging over his head now to take any chances. One man left alive in this valley would talk. And that the Butcher can't afford to let happen."

The horsemen were almost to the mountain, just beyond the outcrop of scattered rock and brush. The first shadows of the westward-slipping sun were beginning to extend out from the base of the towering mass, but it would be hours yet before those on the ridge felt any surcease from the withering heat.

Stanbuck wished he had waited to scatter the leaves and loose gravel on the trail. It would be a good thing to know what Jaffick's plans were. He could slip down the path to within hearing distance and eavesdrop. But he would have to get beyond that turn without alarming the outlaws below.

He decided to risk it, anyway. He turned to the others, now waiting on the back side of the Ridge, heeding his warning.

"I'm going down the trail a piece," he said. "Want to get an idea of what Jaffick's got in mind, if I can. Keep back from the rim," he added, voicing his warning once more.

Kinter said, "We understand. Watch yourself, son."

Stanbuck grinned at the old rancher and made his way to the trail. Off to one side, Ollie Dennis slept noisily on, oblivious of the intense heat and the steadily closing danger they all faced. He heard a sound behind him and turned quickly, his nerves reacting sharply. It was Marissa McCarey.

She saw she had startled him and smiled faintly. "I'm sorry. Is there anything I can do to help?"

"No," he said, his tone unexpectedly harsh. "And be careful when you walk along that ridge. You could have been seen."

"I was careful," she replied, coolly.

Dave Stanbuck felt a light tinge of shame and embarrassment pass through him. He had not intended to be so curt.

But the pressures and tensions were beginning to bear down upon him, turn him edgy.

"Forget it," he murmured. "Guess I'm a bit jumpy."

"It's all right. Is there anything I can do?"

He studied her calm face for a moment, noting the intense blue of her eyes, the firm contours of her mouth. Her cheeks had taken on a higher scarlet from light sunburn and there were similar areas on her neck and shoulders, beneath the loose, improvised shawl.

He said, "I'm obliged for the offer but there's nothing." He paused. "Don't think I thanked you for the bandages they put on Charlie. Or for standing up for me back there."

She merely nodded. "Sometimes a woman can be of help," she stated, as though she believed there might be doubt in his mind on the matter. "I'll wait here at the top of the trail. If you need help call out. I'll hear."

He said, "Fine," and slipped off the ridge and started down the steep, trenchlike passageway. When he came to the turn with its trash and loose rock, he halted. From that point on he picked his way carefully, skirting the edges with deliberate caution. He discovered that by placing his foot solidly in the trail, after first burrowing his toes through the litter, and only then allowing his full weight to come down, he could proceed with surprising quiet and with no disturbance of the loose shale at all.

He descended to a point well beyond the halfway mark of the slope and there, hearing the voices of Jess and Lee plainly, stopped. It would be unwise to go any nearer. He reached his chosen station only moments before Jaffick and the others pulled up. The first words he heard, thin and pointed with sarcasm, were from Jack Hazen.

"Figured if there was any way a man could mess up a job, Turley, old Jess there would sure find it."

Jess said, "Aw, go to hell."

Jaffick asked, "What happened? Can't you two do anything right?" His voice was level, restrained, but there was an underlying thread of deadliness in it.

"They jumped us in the barn," Lee spoke up. "One of them was carryin' the dead man. Tossed him right at us. Got away before we could get back up. We winged one of them, howsomever. Saw him buck when the bullet hit him."

"What's wrong with your paw, Jess?" Hazen's lazy drawl came again. "You maybe bite yourself?"

A low curse rumbled from the outlaw's throat. Lee said, "We started up the trail after them but they rolled a bunch of rocks down on us. Jess got his hand mashed. Pretty bad, too, appears to me. And they ain't the only ones up there, either! There's somebody else."

"Who?" Jaffick's question was quick and urgent.

"Don't rightly know. We found a team and surrey over there. Horses got a sort of slanted S brand on them."

"Kinter, sure as the devil!" Hazen broke in. "That's why we never found them. They must have seen us coming and high-tailed it up here."

"Good, good," Jaffick said with satisfaction. "They had me bothered some. Now I know where they are—all cooped up nice. Makes it easy."

"Won't be easy, climbin' that there trail," Jess observed. "They can stand up there and keep the whole bunch of us off. All they need do is keep rollin' down rocks."

There was a silence after that. Then Jaffick said, "No other way to the top? This the only one?"

"Cliffs all the way, both sides. It's the trail or nothing," Hazen answered.

"No sense in anybody getting hurt like Jess did," Jaffick said. "Need all the men we got. We'll just wait here a spell while I mull this over a bit. Any water up there? A spring maybe?"

"Dry as a parson's prayer," Hazen said.

"If they didn't happen to carry along a canteenfull, they'll be getting in pretty bad shape about now."

"Maybe we could just stay here and let that sun take care of them," an unfamiliar voice suggested. "If that's that rancher up there, his womenfolk are along, too."

Jaffick said, "Can't spare the time, Keno. Already late getting that stock delivered. Jack, you know this country; got any ideas?"

"None, except to rush them," the gunman replied. "Send a half a dozen men up, shooting all the way."

"You be the first man," Jess said, pointedly. "About the fastest way I know to get your brains knocked out."

"Maybe," Hazen said. "And maybe not. Brains could keep

a man from getting his hand mashed up, was he to have some he could use."

Jess muttered something under his breath again, not audible to Stanbuck.

"One thing," Jaffick announced. "We keep them pinned down tight. Couple of you boys get out there on that slope with your rifles. You see anything on top move, blast it good. Nothing wears down a man's nerves like sniping. Meantime, I'll figure out something. We got to clean this up before we head for the Fort."

"Any of you got some grub in your saddlebags?" Lee asked in his plaintive voice. "Me and Jess is sure gettin' hungry. And we're about out of water. Like settin' at the gates of hell, out here all day."

"You and Jess ride on in and feed up," Jaffick said. "We sort of set up headquarters at Stanbuck's place. Plenty of grub there. Come on back when you get your bellies full."

Lee said, "Sure, Turley. Won't take long."

"Maybe find somethin' to fix up this here hand of mine," Jess muttered, hopefully. "Medicine or somethin'. Dang thing is givin' me fits!"

"Be better off if you'd find something you could use for a head," Hazen's sly voice remarked.

"By God!" Jess suddenly yelled, "I ain't—"

A blast of gunfire, two closely spaced shots, shattered the afternoon stillness. The reports set up a chain of echoes along the side of Mangus Mountain that rocked and bounced and rolled lazily off into infinity. The suddenness of it all startled Stanbuck. He crouched along the trail, wondering at its meaning.

"Damn it, Jack," Turley Jaffick's voice ripped through the stunned silence, outraged and harsh. "What did you want to do that for?"

"One-handed man's not much good to anybody," the gun-man drawled.

"You didn't have to do that. You know I'm short on men!"

"You saw him go for his iron."

"Sure, but you been prodding him to do it ever since you met. Now, don't you go picking any more fights, you hear? I'm still running this outfit."

"All a man needs to do to get along with me is keep his lip

46

buttoned," Hazen answered coolly. "Jess was one of them that couldn't understand that."

"Well, you lay off that rawhiding. I'm not furnishing notches for those fancy guns of yours. Next time you got to have trouble, come looking to me."

"Might be an idea," Hazen said softly.

"Remember it," Jaffick snapped. There was a long pause, then, "Couple of you boys drag Jess over there into the brush and cover him over. Use a lot of rocks. No use letting the buzzards and coyotes get to him."

It was clear what had happened, Hazen, spoiling for a fight with Jess had finally goaded the outlaw into it. And Jess had come out second best. The cold-blooded simplicity of it all chilled Dave Stanbuck. No stranger to death, the matter-of-fact, impersonal manner in which it was accomplished and then accepted by the others gave him a sickening feeling.

He heard Lee say, "Reckon I'll have to eat by myself now. So long. See you boys later."

Stanbuck turned and started up the trail. Little more was to be gained by listening to the outlaws who had fallen into a discussion of the day's events. He could get back to the Ridge, ease the worry he knew they would be undergoing after hearing the gunshots, and try to perfect some plan of defense and escape.

It was plain Turley Jaffick did not intend anyone should come off Mangus Mountain alive.

47

Chapter 8

MARISSA WAS WAITING when he reached the top of the trail. Her face was strained, her eyes filled with anxiety. Relief flowed instantly across her features when she saw him. She smiled.

"That shooting—I was afraid—"

Stanbuck, keeping low, crawled onto the ledge. "Private argument between a couple of Jaffick's men. One less to think about now."

She shuddered slightly. Beyond her Tom Kinter said, "Thought maybe they'd spotted you. Gave us a few bad moments."

Stanbuck told them what had happened in the clearing. When he finished, Corey McCarey stirred himself in agitated restlessness, slapping his hands together. "Hard to believe sane men would act like that! They're no more than beasts, quarreling and killing among themselves."

"Stay clear of the rim!" Stanbuck said quickly, afraid the greatly disturbed Maryland man would venture too close to the edge. "Jaffick's put two men on the slope below us, with rifles. He's hoping some of us will offer them a target."

"Unbelievable!" McCarey murmured. "Like living in the Stone Age again! Only one law—kill or be killed!"

Stanbuck moved to where Charlie Pierce lay. The old foreman slept, but it was not a comfortable sleep. He did not awaken Pierce but returned to where the others waited. He related then what he had heard below on the trail, finishing it by stating his own intention to try an escape as soon as the outlaws settled down.

Motion out on the flats caught their attention and Stanbuck paused, also letting his gaze follow the lone rider bearing northward. That would be Lee heading for his place, he knew. Jaffick, and most likely Hazen, would soon be taking a similar course. They would leave others to maintain a watch on the trail, preferring the comforts of Stanbuck's ranch to a night in the open. As soon as they had ridden out, the time to attempt an escape would be at hand.

He saw Pierce stir and turn toward him, favoring him with a glazed, wondering stare. Keeping well down, he moved to where the puncher lay. Pierce greeted him with a wary smile. His eyes were unnaturally bright. Fever was setting in, beginning to have its way with him. Charlie needed the care of a doctor, and soon.

"Hang on," Stanbuck said to him, laying his hand on the old man's shoulder. "I'm going for help."

Pierce nodded. "Reckon you can make it if anybody can."

"You know this country better than I do. There any way to reach Fort Quinton from here except by the east road through the saddle?"

Pierce shook his head. "Only way I know. Course, a man could ride north over the buttes and circle around wide after he's out of the mountains. Take about a week that way."

"No good," Stanbuck said. "Quickest and the shortest, that's the way I've got to go."

"East road, then. Your only bet."

That meant riding straight into Turley Jaffick's guards if he could successfully get by the men below, obtain a horse, and pass any other outlaws the guerrilla leader might have scattered about the valley. But there didn't appear to be any other answer. He would have to try—at least, try.

"Better you take the buckskin," Charlie Pierce said. "He's fast, mighty fast. And he's got good wind. I'll get him ready for you."

Startled momentarily, Stanbuck glanced sharply at the old foreman. In the next moment he understood. Pierce's mind was wandering; the fever was beginning to have its irrational way with him. He reached out and patted the man's bony arm.

"Never mind, I'll do it myself. You've had a hard day."

49

"Sure am obliged," Pierce muttered. "Reckon I am middlin' tired."

It was a little cooler, now the afternoon sun had begun to wane. It would be hours yet until dark, but by then Dave Stanbuck hoped to be down on the flats, streaking his way east for help. Jaffick might yet attempt to overpower them that day but he doubted it. Likely that following morning would be the deadline the outlaw chief would set.

He glanced at the people on the Ridge. Ollie Dennis was in his drunk slumber, the neck of the bottle clutched tight in his fingers. Kinter, McCarey and their wives sat in a small group on the far edge of the Ridge which overlooked the desert to the west. They were not talking, simply sitting in a circle, staring at the ground or off across the still gleaming wastes of mesa.

He saw Marissa then. She was a little apart from the others, as she generally was, sitting on a low rock at the foot of a short ledge. Her shoulders were pressed back against the rough wall. Her eyes still followed the departing Lee and, at that angle, the shadowing beneath them accentuated their size, made them appear larger, darker, and pointed up the perfection of her profile.

She was a strange girl, Dave Stanbuck thought, his gaze coming to full rest upon her. Touched by war's starkness, she had become withdrawn, aloof. She spoke little and when she did it was for a specific purpose and not just to idle time. She was withstanding the ordeal on the Ridge much better than her aunts or her uncle, Corey McCarey, he thought. She seemed more the child of Tom Kinter than of some other man.

She felt his glance upon her and faced him. She smiled and Stanbuck grinned. Then once again she looked away, her attention going to the faint dot that was a horseman disappearing into the north.

He should be getting ready to leave. Remembering the riflemen assigned to the slope by Jaffick, he stretched out full length and, on his belly, crawled to the edge of the Ridge. The sharpshooters would withdraw upon the coming of darkness but, since he planned to begin his descent before night settled in, he must necessarily know their exact positions. To blunder into or draw the attention of either would be fatal.

He spotted the first man immediately. He was sitting boldly in the open, perched on a huge slab of rock about one-third of the way up the mountain. He was just below the lower palisade of cliffs. At the moment he was gazing upward. Stanbuck could see the squarish shape of his brown face with its darker outline of uncut beard and hair. He was almost directly beneath.

He did not discover the second man until a sudden, bright glint of sunlight against metal snared his attention. The outlaw was farther along the mountain than he had expected him to be, although about the same distance below the Ridge. Stanbuck frowned at that discovery, searching along the rim for the crevice down which he hoped to make the descent. The sniper was almost on a line with it; only the natural, bulging contour of the slope itself hid the man from him. His presence could mean a serious problem.

At that moment two men, Jaffick and Hazen, came from the hidden area at the foot of the trail. They were walking, leading their horses. Evidently they were about to depart. They halted below the guard stationed on the rock, tied their mounts to a scrubby tree, and slowly climbed the distance to where the outlaw sat. They stopped there and began some sort of conversation with him. A short time later Jaffick's voice boomed through the quiet.

"You up there! You people on the Ridge!"

There was an immediate rustle and stir behind Dave Stanbuck. "Careful!" he warned hastily. "Stay back out of sight!"

"You hear me? I'm willing to let you come down! I'm ready to talk this over with you!"

"Answer him!" McCarey cried in an urgent, anxious voice. "He says he wants to talk—"

"A trick," Stanbuck said. "Nothing more. He'd like to talk us off of here. Save him a lot of time and trouble. But don't get any wrong ideas about what would happen once he did. Just keep remembering one thing—he can't afford to leave one person alive in this valley!"

"And knowing who this Jaffick really is," Tom Kinter added, "he sure won't."

"Can you be sure?" McCarey demanded in a lifting tone. "How do you know he would murder us? I just can't believe a man would kill in cold blood like that. Not people that can't hurt him, not women—"

"What about it? You want to hash this deal over? I'm giving

51

you a chance. You don't take it, I'll be back in the morning with a way to make you come down!"

"How do you know?" McCarey repeated his question. "Maybe he'll just hold us, keep us here until he's finished with what he's doing. Then we'll be free to go."

"You saw a little of the war," Stanbuck reminded him, quietly. "You think Quantrill operated that way?"

"But that was the way Quantrill fought—that was war—"

"So is this, far as Jaffick is concerned."

"Your last chance!" Jaffick's voice floated up to them hollowly. "Tomorrow will be too late!"

"I'm going to talk to him!" McCarey suddenly cried and lurched to his feet. "I think he wants to—"

"Stay down!" Stanbuck yelled in alarm and clawed at the tall man's legs.

McCarey took a long step forward. He faltered, his hands flew to his chest. Stanbuck heard then the delayed, flat crack of the rifle down the slope. A strange, wondering look crossed the Marylander's face. He staggered back a few, uncertain steps. Stanbuck's hands closed about his ankles. McCarey's wife screamed, a wild, shattering sound that rocked through the hush. She ran to his side, threw her arms about him as she sought to keep him from falling. She sagged against him, her head snapping back. Again Dave heard the dry, vicious snap of the gun below and knew the sniper had scored a second time.

"Keep down!" he shouted and began to work his way back towards the center of the Ridge.

Kinter and Marissa were on their knees, heeding his warning. The three of them grasped the McCareys, dragged them away from the edge to the safety of the opposite side.

Kinter hurriedly pulled aside McCarey's shirt front, glanced at the ugly wound almost in dead center of his breast. He laid his head over the man's heart, glanced at Stanbuck. He shook his head. McCarey still lived but it would not be for long. Nearby, Mattie Kinter worked over her sister.

"It's not bad," she said. "Bullet hit her in the shoulder. It's still there." She turned a questioning look at her husband. Kinter shook his head again. At once Marissa moved in beside McCarey, took his head in her lap and began to stroke his furrowed brow.

McCarey opened his eyes, stared at her, a look of wonder

still on his features. His eyes shifted to Kinter, then to Stanbuck.

"Can't believe it," he said, haltingly. "Just can't believe it! God in heaven—what a country!"

His body sagged, went slack. Marrissa stiffened for a brief moment and Stanbuck saw a sudden surge of tears glisten in her eyes. She bent swiftly and kissed the Marylander.

Mattie Kinter, now in command of the situation said, "Marissa, help me here."

Obediently the girl straightened up. She removed McCarey's head from her lap, placed it gently on the ground. Wordlessly, she turned and crawled on hands and knees to her aunt's side.

"We'll need more bandages," Mattie Kinter said. "And we'll have to take that bullet out. Get Mr. Kinter's pocket knife. And some matches."

"Yes, Aunt Mattie."

Ollie Dennis, awake now and weaving unsteadily on his feet, came in nearer. "What'd I say?" he demanded, triumphantly. "You wouldn't listen to me, but I told you! I said none of us would get off this old mountain alive! None of us! I told you!"

Dennis rattled on incoherently, addled by the heat, the whiskey, and now what appeared a verification of his own strong fears. Tom Kinter got to his feet, grasped the young cowboy by the arm and drew him back to the far side of the Ridge.

"Stay there," he commanded. "No time to listen to you squall!"

From his ledge Charlie Pierce suddenly yelled, "Watch that wall-eyed critter, Fred! Don't let him get behind you!"

The old foreman was far away, again herding stubborn cattle with his friend, Fred Wheelock. He was happily unaware of the actual moments, of the death that stalked the Ridge on Mangus Mountain and waited below for them all.

Bitter, angry, Stanbuck wheeled away, working across the flat surface of the Ridge to the rim again. Two riders were well out on the flats; Jaffick and Hazen, indefinite figures now in the failing light. He glanced below. He could scarcely see the two snipers, only darker blurs in the swiftly settling night. He glanced along the Ridge, along the shadow-struck cliff.

It was too late now to attempt a descent. Perhaps it would have failed anyway; the farthest rifleman had been too close, too near the crevice. And he had to be certain. He could not fail, if the others were to live.

He would start early in the morning, before the outlaws were up and had time to take their positions on the slope. It meant traveling in broad daylight, but he would have to chance it. Actually, the odds could be in his favor in that. He knew the country far better than the outlaws did and his chances for crossing it unseen would be good. When he reached the east rim of the valley, the only gateway to the outside, it would be a different matter. It would be difficult to slip by men stationed at the narrow mouth. He shook his head. He wouldn't worry about that now. He would meet that problem when he got to it.

He turned, crawled back to the center of the Ridge. Kinter had pulled McCarey off to one side and had covered him with branches and leaves, partly hiding him. Marissa and Mattie Kinter worked over Esther who sobbed in a low, choked way. And off to their left Ollie Dennis had started again on his bottle, his overbright eyes fixed upon Marissa's bowed shoulders.

Chapter 9

It was late, near midnight, Dave Stanbuck judged. Almost time to awaken Tom Kinter for his turn to stand the watch. The others on the Ridge had finally quieted down and dropped off to sleep; even the wounded Charlie Pierce and Esther McCarey. Dennis, drinking steadily again, was off somewhere in the dark, apparently wishing only to be left to enjoy his bottle. Unfortunate that Ollie had resorted to his whiskey;

they could use another man. As it was, Kinter and himself were forced to bear the entire load.

It had come to him as he sat there in the pale starlight, that it might be worthwhile to drop down the trail sometime during the night hours and see how well guarded it was. Knowing the reputation of Turley Jaffick, and what happened to his followers who failed in their responsibilities to him, he was fairly certain of what he would learn; there would be not the slightest possibility of escape. Still, it was worth the effort. To get off the mountain by that route, rather than attempt the dangerous descent of the cliffs, would save a vast amount of time. When Tom Kinter took over he would have his look below, he decided.

His glance swung then to Marissa McCarey. She was sitting near the fire and, at that moment, had leaned over to toss more fuel into the dying flames. Marissa had surprised him. She had taken all the terrible moments of the day, all the hardships, without a murmur of complaint or despair. As the hours had passed since he first met her, his opinion of her had risen, just as had his interest. Now he found himself looking at her with a great admiration.

A woman any man could be proud of; one he could make a good life with, raise sons and daughters that would be a credit to everyone. Life would be a wonderful, happy thing with someone like Marissa. Dave Stanbuck's thoughts came to a full halt. What was he thinking? What was wrong with him? No woman ever looked twice at him—and besides, there was no place for a woman in the harsh, grinding life he had chosen. Particularly a fine, eastern-bred girl such as Marissa McCarey. She was accustomed to the kinder, easier ways of civilization and the attentions of cultured, polite gentlemen. She would have no time for a man such as he.

He shrugged, seeking to throw aside the persistent thoughts that clung to his mind. Perhaps, if they got off the Ridge alive, Marissa would stay on with the Kinters for a spell. If Esther McCarey failed to survive her ordeal, she might even stay on for good. He doubted if she had any love now for the West, after experiencing what she had, but perhaps that would change. Given the chance, he could show her what the country was really like, that there was a beautiful and good side to it, also.

It was something to think about and he found himself

looking forward to better times, when they could be together and there was no threat poised above them. But first came the all-important matter of staying alive, of keeping Marissa and the others alive.

He settled back against the pile of stones and drew out his tobacco and papers. He spun up a cigarette, smoking it thoughtfully down to a stub. He tossed it to the ground, sat staring at the faint, red coal as it gradually died and became dark. He must get Marissa and the others off the Ridge, help them to safety, somehow. He had to beat Turley Jaffick at his own game. He paused suddenly as a realization struck him. Somewhere along the line, in the hot afternoon hours, or perhaps in the darkness of the night, some inner change had taken place. He was considering Turley Jaffick in relation to Marissa and Tom Kinter and the rest of those persons imprisoned on the Ridge to whom he represented a vital danger. His own personal, faithfully nurtured hatred had faded into the shadows, into the background. That was strange. How could anything so strong—

"Dave!"

The frantic summons from the night brought him to his feet in a single bound. He stood there, near the top of the trail, listening, seeking to locate the source of the cry. His eyes swept the Ridge but the rocks and brush were cloaked in shadows, were distorted and masked beyond definition. Only the small, circular area in the short fan of firelight was clear. Anxious, disturbed, he moved away from his post, drifted in nearer to the flickering flames. The others still slept—but one was missing. Marissa. He threw his glance along the Ridge again, frantically probing for anything that would indicate her presence. He strained his ears for sound.

"Dave!"

He located her by her desperate cry, saw the vague blur of her struggling shape off to the left a dozen yards or more. He rushed toward her in long strides. It was Ollie with whom she fought. The liquor had twisted his mind, set him off. He reached the swaying couple. With a broad sweep of his hand he slapped Dennis soundly across the face. The cowboy staggered back, releasing his grasp of the girl.

"Damn you—stay out of this!" he shouted.

Stanbuck grabbed the shirt front of the man and shook him

hard. "What's the matter with you? Haven't we got enough trouble without you pulling something like this?"

"My business," Ollie muttered and started a long, right handed swing.

Stanbuck blocked it with his left arm and came up fast with a knotted fist to the cowboy's belly. "Stay away from Marissa, you hear me? I find you've bothered her again when I get back, I'll kill you! Understand that?"

Dennis, doubled over, clutching at his stomach, mumbled incoherently. Tom Kinter and his wife, attracted by the noise, came up.

"What's the trouble here?" the rancher asked, looking closely at the cowboy.

Stanbuck shook his head. "Little too much whiskey in Ollie."

Kinter glanced at Marissa. "You all right?"

The girl nodded. She moved up beside Stanbuck. "Thank you, Dave," she murmured.

Mattie Kinter crossed to where she stood. She took the girl by the shoulders and turned her around gently. "Let's go back to the fire. You're cold."

They all walked out of the hollow, leaving Ollie Dennis still standing alone in the darkness. Marissa, Mattie Kinter's arm encircling her waist, found a place beside the flickering flames. Kinter threw more wood onto the fire.

Stanbuck, wondering then if the noise of the brief encounter had reached the outlaws below, continued on to the top of the trail. He listened for a time but, hearing no out-of-the ordinary sounds, assumed it had gone unnoticed. He leaned back against the mound of stones, drew his tobacco from a pocket and began to fashion himself a cigarette. Tom Kinter strolled up.

"Just talking with Marissa. Appreciate your stepping in."

Dave nodded. "Forget it. Too bad Ollie's in the shape he is. We could use him."

"Ollie's not too bright," Kinter said. "Reason I've always kept him close to the house. Sort of a handyman."

"He'll behave himself now. Don't think you need to worry any more about him."

"Was sort of hoping he'd straighten up enough to give you a hand. You still figure to try and climb down that cliff when it's light enough?"

Stanbuck took a deep drag of his cigarette. "Unless I can find some other way."

Kinter frowned. "Another way?"

"Thought I'd try getting by them on the trail."

The old rancher studied him for a moment. "Seems to me that would be a mite hard to do. You think there's much chance of doing it?"

Stanbuck said, frankly, "Doubt it, but I figure it's worth a look. Most likely Jaffick's got the bottom of the trail well guarded. He's army enough to see to that. But it's a thing I ought to check. If I could get by them, catch them asleep or careless for a couple of minutes, it would save a lot of time."

"Sure would," Kinter agreed. "How about me making the try? You look like you could use some rest."

Stanbuck grinned. "Obliged to you and I appreciate the offer, but I'd better do it myself. Main reason is that if the opportunity is there, I'll have to grab it right then. By the time you could get back up the trail and tell me, and I could get down there, the chance might be gone."

Kinter said, "True enough. Seems like this whole load is on you, however. Like to carry a little of it myself."

"Your time will come. If I manage to get by them, your job starts. Be up to you to hold them off until I get back with the soldiers."

"Shouldn't be too hard to do. Ought to be able to keep them from climbing that trail."

Stanbuck nodded. "But watch out for Jaffick. He's tricky. He may come up with a different idea."

"I'll remember that," Kinter said.

Stanbuck tossed aside his cigarette. He leaned forward and removed his boots. Kinter watched him pull the uppers beneath his belt and anchor them securely.

He said, "You saying good-bye to Marissa? She'll be expecting you to."

Stanbuck glanced at him. "Why?"

Kinter grinned. "If you're so all-fired blind you can't see how she feels about you, ever since she first laid eyes on you, then you better go ask."

Dave Stanbuck held silent for a long minute while his thoughts went back swiftly to a time earlier that night when the girl had occupied his mind. He shrugged. It had been foolish to think of Marissa, to have any such hopes. Even though she believed she cared, she could never be happy with his way of life. There was no point in considering it, in allowing it to progress further. Better it ended now than produce heart-break and unhappiness later.

"No use her wasting time thinking about me, Tom," he said. "I'm not the man for her." He turned to the trail. "I'll be back in a half an hour, if there's no chance to get through."

"I'll be waiting right here," the old rancher said. "Just in case you need me."

Dave let himself off the Ridge quietly, being careful not to dislodge gravel or rattle the dry, noisy brush. The descent of the trail was not difficult. He found he could travel silently without his boots, the only problem presenting itself being the sharp-edged stones and pointed sticks that gouged at his unprotected feet. It was not too bad, however.

As he had feared, Turley Jaffick covered the possibility of escape during the night with customary thoroughness. Before Stanbuck reached the last turn in the trail, he became aware of illuminating firelight which exposed the mouth of the trenchlike passage with bright clarity. He halted there, just beyond the fan of light, and surveyed the clearing ahead.

Two guards, rifles lying across their knees, faced the trail. Both men were far from sleep and they watched the opening in the rocks and brush with a steady intent. Each knew well the penalty for carelessness if he failed at his post.

Back and around them, in a half-circle, the rest of the party slept. Each would take his turn at guard duty, Dave surmised, and none would be required to remain overlong at his post, thus avoiding the danger of dulled senses and the possibility of unwilling drowsiness.

He looked down at the cartridge belt about his waist. There were a few brass shells in the loops. The old ruse of tossing several into the fire might create a moment of diversion and distraction. But not enough, he readily saw. He could not hope to get past the others before he would be cut down by a blast of gunfire.

He studied the sleeping men for another ten minutes and then gave it up. There was no avenue of escape possible at that point. He turned quietly and started up the trail. He made it without incident.

When he reached the top he found not only Kinter awaiting him but Marissa McCarey as well. She smiled when she saw him, the welcome in her manner unmistakable. He pulled himself onto the Ridge and began to draw on his boots.

"No chance, I take it," the rancher said.

Stanbuck shook his head as he stamped his feet into position within the boots. "None. Far as the trail is concerned, we're sealed in tight. Only way is down the cliff."

Marissa moved quickly to him. Still smiling, she said, "I'm glad. I was afraid you had gone. Now, I can go with you."

Chapter 10

DAVE STANBUCK STARED AT THE GIRL. He frowned. "Afraid not. It will be dangerous—and plenty rough going."

She said, "I know, but I want to go anyway, Dave."

"Not even sure I can get down that cliff," he persisted. "May be a way and I might wind up at a dead end. And there's no guarantee. I won't be spotted by the guerrillas when I'm somewhere on the slope. I'd be like a sitting duck on a pond."

Marissa shook her head. "Please, Dave."

He was equally stubborn. It would be difficult enough to get himself off Mangus Mountain unseen by the outlaws without the extra responsibility and burden of the girl's presence. Almost brusquely, he said, "Sorry. Best you forget it," and started toward the campfire.

A few steps along, Tom Kinter halted him with a hand on his arm. "Might be a smart idea to take her with you. If anything happened to you she could be of help."

Stanbuck had already realized that; but he had been thinking in terms of Ollie Dennis, not Marissa. He stared at Kinter. "You actually think that—that I should take her along on a deal as risky as this will be?"

Kinter nodded slowly. "Don't underestimate Marissa. She's

no ordinary woman. She'll be right in on the finish, every time. And I'll take it as a personal favor, Dave. I'd like to be sure one of my family gets off this Ridge alive."

"Not much guarantee I'll make it either," Dave said.

"I realize that, but I figure the odds are good."

Stanbuck considered for a moment. He thought he saw through the rancher's way of thinking; that the girl would be better off making a desperate break for freedom with him than in staying behind, relying on the possibly false security of the Ridge and ending up, perhaps, in the hands of Turley Jaffick and his crowd. He wondered if she knew the way her uncle felt.

"You been talking to Marissa about it?" he asked. "That the reason she wants to go?"

Kinter said, "Her reasons are her own. She doesn't know how I feel."

Dave Stanbuck had a swift surge of pride, of happiness at the thought that Marissa wanted to be with him, wanted to share his danger. And just as quickly he thrust it aside. He should not permit her to feel as she did. It was not good. There was no future for her in it—for either of them. But he could not deny her, just as he could not refuse Tom Kinter's request. Perhaps, during the hours that lay ahead he could make her understand.

He turned to her, glancing at her clothing, the gay, rose-pink party dress, her thin slippers. "You can't move around very well in that outfit," he said. "You need something else."

She flashed her smile at him. "Is that all that worries you? Let me have your knife."

Stanbuck produced one from his pocket and handed it to her. She opened the largest blade and, leaning over, slashed the hem of the garment front and back. She returned the blade to him and then ripped the dress to a point half way up her thighs. She took the separate halves of the desecrated garment and wrapped them about her legs, forming a sort of pantaloon. Tearing several narrow strips of cloth from the remainder of her petticoat, she secured the legs of her improvised breeches by tying encircling bands, one just above the ankle, another near the knee. Finished, she stepped back for his inspection. It was a practical, if startling, arrangement.

"Not a Fifth Avenue riding habit," she said. "But just as good."

Dave Stanbuck agreed. Marissa could now climb about the cliff, make her way through brush and rock or ride a horse with no hindrance from a full-flowing skirt.

He glanced down. "The slippers?"

She turned and went to where her aunt sat. She was back in a few moments wearing a pair of shoes of heavier construction. "I made a trade with Aunt Mattie," she said.

He grinned in spite of himself. "I guess you're ready, then. We'll have to leave in a few minutes. It soon will be light."

Marissa moved up close to him. "Thank you, Dave. I'm glad you understand. And if we don't make it, don't blame yourself. It's just that I want to be with you, no matter what happens."

"No," he said quickly, firmly. "It can't be that way, Marissa. You're going with me only because I think you will be safer. Your uncle thinks so, too. It has to be for that reason, and no other."

She regarded him soberly for a long minute. Then, "All right, Dave. That's the way it will be. As soon as I've told Aunt Mattie and Aunt Esther good-bye, I'll be ready to start." She did not wait for Stanbuck to make any reply. She moved forward, kissed Tom Kinter on the cheek and whirled to the older women. Dave and the rancher watched her cross over to the other side of the fire.

Kinter swung to the problem at hand. "Figuring you get through, how long will it take to get back with help?"

"Sixty miles to the Fort, sixty back," Stanbuck said. "With luck and fresh horses, we ought to make it by sundown."

Kinter's thin face looked old and worn in the pale light. The lines about his mouth were deep and, for the first time, there was a hopelessness in his manner. "A long time," he murmured.

"I'll make it fast as I can," Stanbuck promised. "Don't figure you'll have any trouble keeping them off the trail, however."

The rancher sighed. "Not the problem, as I see it. No water, that's where we're hurting. My wife's sister and your friend, Pierce, there, need it bad now. Come noon today, we'll all be in bad shape."

"Do what you can to stay out of the sun," Dave said. He remembered an earlier thought. "Might take your wife's petti-

62

coat and stretch it between the rocks, like a canopy. Be a little cooler under it."

"Good idea," Kinter said. He smiled. "Petticoats keep coming in handy up here. I live through this, I'm going to see that it's renamed Petticoat Ridge!"

Stanbuck grinned at the rancher's show of humor. "One thing that will help, once Marissa and I are on the way down, will be for you to roll a few rocks off into the trail, every now and then. Not many, but enough to attract the outlaw's attention and hold it. They'll be wondering what's going on and maybe the snipers won't get out on the slope so early."

Kinter indicated his understanding. "Won't know when you've reached bottom, but soon as I hear that bunch below stirring around I'll begin." He stopped and extended his hand. "I'll say my *adios* now, son. And good luck to you. Hope you make it—for all our sakes."

Stanbuck shook the rancher's hand gravely. "I'll do the best I can," he promised in a low voice.

Kinter said, "I know that and I figure you'll get through. After this is all over I'd like for us to get better acquainted. No sense in people living out here like we do, one man every thirty miles, and not getting to be friends. Fact is, I started to ride over to your place once or twice but, somehow, something always came up. You know how it is around a ranch. Always a chore to be looked after."

Kinter was just being polite, Stanbuck knew. It had been he, not the old rancher, who had kept to himself, maintaining a rigid seclusion. He regretted it now. It would have been nice to have known Kinter and his family better. But after his time in the war was done and he had ridden west in search of a new life, he wanted only one thing—to be left alone; to surround himself with hard, demanding work that would never allow him to pause and think. In such a scheme there had been no room for casual acquaintances.

"Right here and now," Tom Kinter went on, "I'm extending you an invitation to come to supper—the night after we get home from this fix. My wife will cook up the best fried chicken and milk gravy you ever sat down to!"

"I'm accepting that invitation right now, before you change your mind!" Dave said. He threw his glance to the eastern horizon. "Now, think I'll see if Charlie Pierce is awake."

He walked to where the old foreman lay and dropped to a

crouch beside him. He looked closely at his friend's wan face. If he slept he did not wish to awaken him. But Pierce opened his eyes immediately.

"Thought maybe you were having yourself a nap," Dave said.

Pierce grinned faintly. "Nope, just layin' here, thinkin' mostly."

"Feeling some better?"

"Some. Everything's kind of easy like inside me. Don't know if that's good or bad but it sure is comfortin'."

Stanbuck reached out, laid his hand on the man's forehead. "Fever's down. Looks like you're going to make it, sure enough."

"Could be so," Pierce answered. "Guess a man never knows for certain about a thing like this. I always figured when a man's time come, it come and nothin' he did was goin' to change things any."

"Maybe, but you'll be sleeping in a bed with a doctor looking after you, come this time tomorrow. You can plan on it."

Pierce's brow furrowed into a dark corrugation. "You goin' to try and slip by that bunch down trail?"

"Not the trail. Think I found a place where I can get off the cliff. At least, one where I can start. Can't see below the first ledge."

"Recollect your sayin' somethin' about it last night—or maybe 'twas yesterday. You figure it smart to take the little gal with you?"

Stanbuck looked at him, surprised. "How did you know that?"

"Hearin's still pretty sharp! Sure was some fancy pair of chaps she rigged up."

Stanbuck smiled. "Don't know how good an idea it is, but I couldn't talk her out of it."

Pierce studied Dave's face for a long time. Then, "Kind a nice, son, seein' you grin like that. One thing you ain't never done much of. Always figured there was somethin' chawin' at your innards but I didn't say nothin'. Reckoned you'd tell me about it if you wanted me to know. But then, you never was much for talkin'."

Stanbuck said, "Things will be different around the place, Charlie, once this is over."

"Good. No sense in a man eatin' his own insides out. Got somethin' to do with that feller Jaffick, ain't it?"

Stanbuck nodded. "Goes back to the war. I'll tell you about it someday—after I've squared up with him."

"Fine. When you figure to leave?"

"Right away. Been waiting for daylight."

"About time you was leavin' then. Before you go, sort of like to say I'm real obliged for the job you give me. Workin' for you has been plumb pleasurable."

"You're still working for me," Stanbuck said, finding his words stiff and hard to get out. "Soon as you're on your feet again, there's a lot of things around the ranch that we got to get done. I'll talk it over with you tomorrow when you're feeling better."

"Sure," Charlie Pierce said. "One thing I most forgot. There's a jag of stock, five maybe six head, up in that little canyon on the north corner of the range. You know the place. Old dead juniper tree standin' on a short hill—"

"I know the spot," Stanbuck said, gently.

"Good. Like I said, there's some stock there, along with an old blue. He's sort of set himself up a private little harem. Me and Fred was goin' to roust them out today but looks like we ain't goin' to get to it. Ought to be done, too. Saw some cat tracks up there once."

"I'll take care of it," Stanbuck said. He reached for the foreman's hand, shook it. "Time I was going, Charlie. See you later."

Pierce grinned. "So long, partner. Good luck to you and the lady."

Dave Stanbuck turned quickly away, his face set in stern, solemn lines, a thick lump blocking his throat. He looked up. Marissa was standing before him, waiting. She smiled.

"I'm ready, Dave."

Chapter 11

DAYLIGHT WAS NO MORE THAN A FAINT, gray line stretched along the eastern horizon when Marissa and Dave Stanbuck started up the Ridge. It would be well over a half an hour before any appreciable illumination struck the rugged, irregular terrain. Their passage was slow and difficult. Deep shadows smoothed the ground beneath them, hid the sharp, loose rocks and dead branches, masked the treacherous holes and low places which continually caused them to stumble and reel as though they were without sight.

Twice Marissa fell, going to her knees. She made no outcry nor voiced any complaint. Stanbuck was careful not to set too hard a pace for her; there was no great need to hurry. They had left the others early enough to allow ample time for reaching the crevice where he hoped to begin the descent.

With each step he became more aware of the fallacy of his plans, however, even granting that he and Marissa were able to escape the cliff and obtain horses upon which they could ride to Fort Quinton. Turley Jaffick would not permit another complete day to pass in a stalemate at Mangus Mountain. He would return that morning, just as he had promised, and he would bring with him some sort of plan, or means, to force Tom Kinter and those with him to yield.

Butcher Jaffick would waste no more time on two or three persons. He would close the matter, one way or another, and by the time Dave and Marissa could reach the fort and return with soldiers it would be all over and done with. It would be too late.

Of course, he could then demand the arrest of the guerrillas when they arrived at the fort with the stolen herd; he could accuse Jaffick and his men of ruthless murder and cattle rustling, and prove all of it. He would have the satisfaction of seeing Jaffick and Hazen and all the others pay for their crimes—but that would be of no help to Tom Kinter and the others.

They would be dead, and what vengeance Dave Stanbuck could exact by due process of law upon their killers would be little more than tasteless ashes in his mouth. He needed to come up with something else, a different plan; one that would enable him immediately to effect a rescue before Jaffick and his bloody-handed followers could strike at the Ridge.

They reached the end of the narrow, tablelike plateau along which they had traveled. Light was growing steadily stronger and Stanbuck was pleased he had figured the time element almost to the moment. In a very short time they would be able to start down. He glanced back along the Ridge—Petticoat Ridge now. A faint, orange glow marked the location of their camp. Marissa moved by him and stood for a time gazing upward at the towering butte which terminated the Ridge, then went on to higher, soaring peaks.

Stanbuck's gaze followed Marissa. Her face was uptilted to the fading starlight. It appeared soft and creamy, her eyes were deep and luminous. She was a beautiful woman and something within him stirred deeply. He remembered what Tom Kinter had said, of her own words and the way she had looked at him. And he recalled his own thoughts. He brought himself up short, mentally shook himself impatiently and with anger. Marissa McCarey was not for him, he again reminded himself. He must remember that—and somehow, he must make her understand it.

He became aware then that she was looking directly at him, her lips faintly parted, her eyes issuing their invitation. He did not move. She came closer, until she was before him.

"Dave—kiss me," she murmured.

For a moment there was indecision within him, but for only a moment. He looked away, off towards the east. "Time we started down," he said quietly.

A small sigh of hopelessness slipped from her and she turned away. He had an almost insurmountable urge to reach out, take her in his arms and crush her to him, but that, too, he thrust aside. He moved by her, led the way to where the crevice slashed its way into the mountain's body. He halted there.

"I'll go ahead and pick the way," he said in a low voice. "When I give the word, you follow. Quiet now, and careful. Can't afford to start a rockslide and draw the attention of Jaffick's men."

She only nodded, apparently mistrusting her voice.

He let himself down into the narrow gash, shallow here and barely wide enough to accommodate the breadth of his shoulders. Marissa followed immediately and they began to slowly work their way downward. It was surprisingly easy; the rough surface of the crevice allowed them to find footholes with no trouble and they descended the first thirty feet, to the end of the crevice, without incident.

There good fortune ended. Dave Stanbuck found himself poised fifteen feet above a narrow ledge of rock with no alternative but to drop or else climb back up into the slash. He studied the shelf below him. It appeared to be fairly smooth with no treacherous, loose shale on its surface. Moreover, it looked to him as if it sloped inwardly, toward the face of the cliff and not to the opposite and the precipitous drop which plunged off on that side.

He glanced to Marissa. She had halted directly over him, was watching him, waiting for him to decide their next move. She could not see the ledge below, nor the sheer cliff that lay beyond its edge.

"Got to drop to a shelf that's under us," he explained. "It's a pretty good jump, but not too bad. When I've done it, you wait until I call out, then, work your way down to where I am now."

"All right," she said, her voice faint. "Be careful, Dave."

He grinned and set himself for the drop. It would be simple enough; just let himself hang straight, then release all holds. The natural contour of the cliff itself would tend to throw him towards it. The great danger lay, not in projecting himself over the ledge into empty space beyond but in falling wrong; if he struck unevenly he could easily break a leg, or, at best, sprain an ankle.

It was growing lighter. The entire face of the cliff was now visible through a smoky sort of haze. Back toward the south end of Mangus Mountain he could hear an occasional

68

hollow thud and realized Tom Kinter was following out his instructions and was now rolling boulders down the trail to hold the outlaws' attention to that point.

He turned his glance to the east. Long shafts of purple and orange were fanning into the sky. Sunrise was not far off. He took a deep breath, relaxed his long body and let go. He plunged straight down. He remembered to keep his knees bent slightly and struck on the balls of his feet. His knees folded with the impact and he jacknifed to a squatting position. It was done. It had been easy.

He turned his eyes upward. Marissa was already in place, awaiting his instructions. She was wondering about him.

"Are you all right?"

"Fine," he answered. "You can make it easy. Just let yourself drop. Keep your knees bent a little. I'll be waiting to catch you. Ready?"

She said, "Ready."

"Let yourself drop."

He caught her as her feet met the rocky shelf. They both swayed back against the face of the cliff.

"That wasn't hard," she began and then noticed the sheer drop beyond the ledge. Her eyes flared, then shut tightly. Her fingers tightened involuntarily about his arms. "Oh—if I had known—"

"No point in thinking about it now," he said with a short laugh. "All over and done with no harm."

He turned, took a swift survey of their location. The ledge itself ran off in both directions, climbing gently toward the south, sliding off at a faint angle to the opposite, northern way.

"Couldn't be better," he murmured and with the girl close at his heels, started along the shelf's course at a fast walk.

It followed a slight decline, sometimes widening, other times slimming down to little more than a pathway but always gradually lowering toward the floor of the valley. After a time Stanbuck glanced over his shoulder. They had covered at least a quarter of a mile. He halted, not liking that. At such a slow rate of fall they would come out much too far along the mountain.

He studied the steep grade that fell off below the ledge. It was not sheer, as was the cliff above the rocky shelf, only steep. He doubted if a man could either climb or descend it,

69

however, without experiencing a considerable amount of trouble and many dangerous falls. Then he saw a wisp of smoke, snaking skyward from somewhere near the lower end of the mountain. That would be the outlaws' camp. They were preparing breakfast. He realized they were already much too far to the north.

"We've got to get off this ledge," he said. "We keep on as we are and we'll end up ten miles away. But I still don't think we could make it down that slope."

She said, "There was a place further back that might do. The rain must have washed down the side and cut a little valley out of the mountainside. If we could get down into it, I think we might reach the bottom."

"Sounds like what we need," he said. "Show me."

They retraced their steps a few hundred yards. There Marissa halted and pointed to the arroyo she had noted. Many wild rains had poured off the cliff, gouged into the slope with torrential, cascading force and carved a route downward to the valley floor below. It would be easy to descend the balance of the way by it, Stanbuck quickly saw—if they could get to it.

It was not less than forty feet below the ledge upon which they stood and Dave Stanbuck could not help but marvel as he visualized the waterfall the formation must present when the rains flooded down the mountain and poured over the rocky lip. Unlike the drop they had made above, they would strike upon a slanted surface, the very angle of which was certain to catapult them forward, off balance, into a rugged assemblage of jagged boulders and clawing brush on the far side.

Yet there could be a way. Stanbuck let his attention dwell upon the problem. By leaping outwards, as the surging water would do, he could project himself to a small, island-like knoll upon which a stunted juniper tree grew. If, at the moment his feet touched that solid ground, he could grasp one of the tree's outthrust branches and maintain that grasp, he could prevent himself from being hurled into the rocks.

It would take perfect timing and all the strength he had in his arms, he realized. But he could do it, he was certain; that Marissa could not, he was equally sure. Immediately he had the answer to that problem. He would block her with his own body, stay her forward momentum.

He said, "I'm going to jump to that tree. After I get set, you follow."

He did not go into details or possibilities. Better she did not know the depth of the danger, that if he failed to check himself with the juniper, he would end up in the rocks below, seriously injured if not dead.

He glanced over his shoulder. "Don't move until I give you the word," he said, and leaped.

He struck the hard surface of the small hill, almost forgetting this time to relax his knees. The impact jolted him solidly. He clawed at the juniper, felt a rough barked branch scrape skin from the palms of his hands as he was thrown forward. His fingers involuntarily released their grip, tightened again as he sought to check his fall—or die. A heavier, thicker limb of the tree came between his fingers. He seized it, this time ignoring the burn of the ragged-edged bark as it ripped through his clenched hand. He swung widely, like a gate, as by sheer strength alone he hung on. His half-bent body described a tight arc. He crashed into the main trunk of the stout, old tree.

He pulled himself about slowly, sucking for the breath that had been driven from his lungs by the solid collision with the juniper. His hands smarted from the bits of pointed wood that had been ground into his skin. He brushed his palms together briskly, easing the pain. He moved back to the opposite side of the tree and looked up at Marissa. She was watching for him, one hand held against her lips as if to stay her breath.

"All right," he called out as he came into view. "You're next."

A smile spread across her face when she saw he was unhurt and relief slackened her taut shape. "I thought for a moment—"

"Don't worry about that tree," he said, cutting through her words curtly. "Jump straight for me. I'll do the rest."

"I'm ready."

"Jump!"

He had anchored himself firmly, both feet braced solidly on the uneven ground. His right hand was locked securely about one of the juniper's tough limbs. When Marissa, light as she was, came up against him, he went down full length, carrying her with him. They skidded the distance of a buckboard, came to a jolting, dusty stop against a clump of mesquite. Stanbuck, on the bottom, took the brunt of the brutal fall.

For a minute they lay there in stunned silence. Then they sat up slowly and looked about. On, down the arroyo, no more than a hundred yards, they could see the beginning of the valley's level floor.

They were off the mountain.

Chapter 12

DAVE STANBUCK PULLED HIMSELF TO HIS FEET and helped Marissa to hers. She was still slightly dazed from the furious moments, but she smiled gamely at him, her eyes dark and deepest blue when her glance met his.

He said, "Looks like we've made it—at least, this far."

She turned, lifting her gaze to the Ridge where they so lately had been. It towered overhead. Sunlight, although not yet touching the lower reaches of the slopes, was now full upon the steep and rugged formation of the mountain, pointing up the stark bleakness of it. She shuddered.

"I never realized it was so high!"

His features were serious. "Sometimes it's better if a man doesn't know what's ahead of him. Leaves him no room to think about it."

"Perhaps," she murmured. "But where a woman is concerned, I doubt if it would make any difference. A woman would go with the man she loved no matter where it took her."

He made no answer. They turned and started down the

72

slope for the valley. It was a short, if uneven distance. It did not take them long to break out of the arroyo.

He halted there. Cover behind which they could move was scant, he noted. There was only the welter of rocks that had, in storm-ridden times past, rolled off the mountain and come to rest along its foot and the scrubby, thin growth that eventually had managed to sprout and maintain life on the barren ground in the heat-blasted summers and bitter cold winters. Stanbuck motioned to a large boulder a few steps to one side.

"Wait there," he said. "I'll have a look at what's ahead."

He moved off at a good trot, pressed by the urgency to act, to accomplish something for those trapped on the Ridge before it was too late. He kept low, skirting the confusion of rock and brush, heading for an outthrusting point which promised an unimpaired view of the farther contours of Mangus Mountain. He again saw the twirling column of smoke lifting from the outlaws' fire; it was much closer now. He reached the jutting of stones and worked his way to its edge. He had a fair, if somewhat distant, view of the outlaws' camp.

They were grouped around their fire. He could not determine exactly how many were present, eight or nine, including the two who sat a few feet apart, nearer to the mountain. They were the guards, keeping their close watch on the mouth of the trail. He looked for the horses. His hopes plunged. They were picketed not between the guerrillas and himself, as he had wished, but beyond, in a small, open clearing. This meant he and Marissa must somehow completely circle Jaffick's men to reach the animals.

It would be easy to get nearer the camp itself. He saw that at once. Enough rock and scrubby growth lay scattered along the base of the slope to provide a sufficient screen for masking their movements. He withdrew from the point and hurried back to Marissa, aware again that they must move quickly if they were to get anything done before Jaffick and the rest of his riders returned.

He told her briefly what he had learned. They started out at once. They walked fast, kept low and well within the protective cover. How to get help to Kinter and the others was the problem that plagued Stanbuck now. He had succeeded in getting off the mountain, but what could he do now? His original thought of obtaining horses and riding to the fort for help had lost its appeal to him; there simply was no time for such a lengthy ride.

But with no weapon he faced a seemingly impossible task. If he had a gun—just one gun. An idea suddenly flashed through his mind. A weapon was the answer, and he just might be able to get one! With it, he could move in behind the outlaws and disarm them. Once that was done and the Ridge was no longer sealed off, Kinter and the others would come down. Then all could escape before the Butcher and the others arrived. He halted briefly to allow Marissa to rest and he went quickly over the plan forming in his head.

When he had finished, she posed one question: "Where will you get the gun?"

"Bound to be a rifle left on one of the saddles. They'll be using their handguns. All we need do is get to the horses, find a rifle still in its scabbard, and we're in business."

But he should have a weapon of some sort in the meantime, in the event they blundered accidently into one of the outlaws. He reached down and picked up a stout length of wood, once a branch of a tree somewhere back up on the slope. It was fairly straight, the diameter of a hoe handle and the length of his arm. He took his knife, opened the largest blade and trimmed the limb to smoothness. With a strip of leather sliced from his belt, he secured the knife to the branch, improvising a crude but effective spear.

"Now we've got something, at least," he said.

They moved out for the camp immediately after that. Stanbuck, in the lead, again took care to keep from any possible view of the guerrillas. Marissa stayed close to his heels, obeying his every motion without question. They came at last to the edge of the camp and halted behind a large mound of rocks and low brush.

The outlaws were no more than fifty feet away. Eight men about the fire, taking turns at drinking coffee from a blackened pot which they passed back and forth. Two more were at the mouth of the trail where they maintained a steady, unswerving vigilance. Stanbuck could hear the sounds of their talking but the distance was too great, their voices too low, and he could not make out what was being said.

He turned his attention to the horses. They were in a small cluster somewhat back and a long fifty feet farther on. Stanbuck counted them absently. Thirteen. He had a moment's wonder at the extra animals and then recalled the outlaw Jess and that man's sudden death. His horse was the odd one, plus, of course, those of Charlie Pierce and himself.

He mentally traced a course to the animals, picking each step that would take them to where the horses waited. The scattering of brush and rock was such that they could make it easily except for the last dozen strides. There, they would be faced with open ground, devoid entirely of cover behind which they could hide. Their only hope in crossing unnoticed at that point lay in a continuation of the outlaws' attention being focused elsewhere; at that moment all ten men faced the mountain, their backs toward Marissa and Stanbuck.

He motioned to the girl for extreme caution and they glided silently forward, making their way to the last patch of sheltering brush. They halted. Ahead lay the open stretch; to their right were the outlaws, as yet unaware of their presence and still watching the entrance to the trail.

At the moment Tom Kinter, faithful to his assigned task, sent another boulder crashing down the steep and narrow pathway. It was what Stanbuck had hoped for, had counted on. He touched Marissa's wrist.

"Now. Fast and quiet."

They stepped into the open and raced across the barren ground. It required only seconds but to Dave it seemed much longer. They reached the thick screen of junipers and other growth on the far side behind which the horses stood. They halted, breathless from the hard run. They delayed there only moments. Time was precious. Turley Jaffick and his followers would not be long in coming.

Stanbuck moved silently through the brush, his long shape like a weaving shadow. Marissa was at his side. He swung a few yards wide of the picketed horses, approaching them from the front, fearing to startle them and set up a racket that would draw the guerrillas' attention.

He paused again and faced the girl. "Once I get my hands on a rifle, we'll move in on them. There's no time to spare. But it will have to be handled just so. There will be ten guns against our one."

"I can handle a rifle," Marissa said quickly. "Uncle Tom gave me lessons—"

"Better you leave that part to me. I'll make them stand up, with their hands over their heads. When I give the word, you move in, take their guns. Throw them back into the brush, out of reach. But be careful while you're doing it. They're all desperate men, killers. Don't get too close to any of them—and don't walk in front of me."

"I understand," she murmured.

He turned his attention to the horses. They had been secured to a rope picket line, stretched between two stout trees. He moved in among the animals, clucking softly as he went, keeping them quiet and at ease. He stepped quickly from one to another, examining their saddles briefly. He reached the last, wheeled slowly about and faced Marissa. He shook his head wearily.

"Not a rifle in the lot," he said in a voice heavy with disappointment and disgust.

Chapter 13

THIRTEEN HORSES, thirteen saddles, four of which had rifle scabbards slung at their skirts—but there were no guns in them. If there had been at the start, when the outlaws rode in, they had been withdrawn and the riders now had them in their hands at the camp. Dave Stanbuck stood in the steadily growing sunlight and considered his next move. Back on the side of the mountain another rock clattered down the steep pathway and thudded solidly against something immovable at the bottom. One of the guerrillas laughed, a harsh, grating sound that somehow rankled Stanbuck. He walked slowly to the girl.

She said nothing, asked no question, merely waited for him to decide what they should do next. That they must abandon the plan to overcome and disarm the outlaws and free those on Petticoat Ridge before Jaffick and his men came, was apparent. Without a gun it was impossible. But perhaps there still was a way to obtain one; Stanbuck, his solemn face suddenly alive, turned back to the horses.

He motioned to Marissa and together they went to where the line of animals waited. He untied the ends of the picket rope and, moving softly, led them farther away from the camp. When he was certain they could not possibly be heard, he stopped. He began to look over the animals.

He chose a mount for Marissa and one for himself. Both were long-legged bays that had a capacity for speed and endurance. That done, he released the remaining horses, all but one; he took up the reins to it, a stocky little buckskin, and returned him to where the outlaws' mounts had been tethered originally. There he anchored him securely to a tree.

He trotted back to the girl and helped her mount up, not taking time to shorten her stirrups but showing her, instead, how to tuck her feet inside the fold of the leather itself. He could feel her eyes upon him as he swung onto his own bay and thrust his spear into the empty rifle scabbard of the saddle. She was wondering about the buckskin.

They circled around the remaining horses and prodded them gently into forward motion, pointing them for the heart of the valley. They did it quietly, for he felt they were still too close to the camp to draw attention.

"That one horse—why are we leaving him?" Marissa asked, unable to suppress her curiosity longer.

"We'll stampede the rest. With just one left, only one man will be able to chase after them. I'll try to get my hands on him and take his gun."

They maintained a slow paced drive for another two hundred yards, then broke into the open. He glanced about and saw immediately there was no more cover to be hoped for. He pulled off his hat, slapped it loudly against the rump of the horse nearest him. The animal bolted forward, startling the others and suddenly they all were running hard for the open country.

"After them!" Stanbuck shouted. "Keep them going away. Can't let them cut back!"

Marissa nodded her understanding. Together they broke onto the level ground, riding close behind the fleeing horses.

77

Back toward the camp, yells broke out as they were seen. A moment later Stanbuck heard the flat, distant spat of a rifle. But they were well beyond range and they had nothing to fear from bullets.

He half-turned in the saddle, glancing toward the clearing. Two or three of the outlaws were running toward the lone horse that stood there. Stanbuck grinned. They were rising to the bait. He continued to watch. A short time later the little buckskin burst from the screen of brush and was in full pursuit, his rider bending low over the saddle.

"Here comes our pigeon!" he sang out to Marissa. "Bear to the left slightly—there's some choppy hills and arroyos in that direction."

The running horses tried again to curve in sharply and double back toward the mountain. Stanbuck and Marissa had to swing in and force them back. The buckskin came on fast but Stanbuck was keeping a sharp watch upon him. He did not want him too close, not until they reached the more broken area where it would be easier to ambush the man and drag him from his saddle.

The trap was working perfectly. The horses were staying ahead at just the right speed, were driving now for a series of small hills and swales. The rider on the buckskin was getting nearer, but just enough to keep him coming on. As soon as they topped out the first ridge, Dave would cut away, leaving Marissa to follow on after the horses while he doubled back and waited for the outlaw. It would be simple.

They mounted a long, gentle swell which rose to a low height and sloped off on its opposite side into a shallow bowl. The horses slackened their pace as they neared the crest—and quite suddenly threw back their heads and veered sharply.

Dave Stanbuck had a glimpse of half a dozen riders, perhaps more, directly ahead of them. They had met almost head on as they climbed the opposing side of the same hill. He saw the florid, startled face of Turley Jaffick with its bristling, red mustache; a wide splash of bright color that was the Mexican shirt Jack Hazen wore; and beyond them other outlaws, one of whom was carrying two small, black cans of blasting powder taken, undoubtedly, from Stanbuck's own storehouse.

Dave saw all this in one fleeting, panoramic glimpse. The terrible danger that faced Marissa and himself struck him in that same instant. He lunged forward in the saddle, lashed at the bay she rode with his broad-brimmed hat. The horse plunged off to the right, down the slope. Stanbuck was after her, flogging his own mount unmercifully, demanding every bit of speed the huge bay possessed.

"Ride for the rocks!"

He yelled his order to the girl as they thundered down the grade and leveled off on the straightaway that led to the brakes. Their horses were going at top pace, long legs reaching out beneath them, devouring the earth in tremendous gulps.

Behind, Stanbuck heard Turley Jaffick's wild howl of rage as he and his riders fought to bring their horses out of the confusion.

"Cut 'em down! Shoot, you blasted fools! Shoot! Shoot! Knock them out of their saddles!"

A spatter of gunfire rippled through the morning air. Stanbuck heard the angry buzz of bullets passing nearby. He risked a glance over his shoulder. Jaffick's party had recovered itself and was now coming down the hill in a wide fan as it gave pursuit.

He swung his attention toward the rough land toward which they were heading. It seemed no nearer despite the fact their horses were thundering for it at top speed. They were holding their own, and that was good; the lead they had garnered at the initial collision had been enough to allow the long-legged bays to get underway. They were within shooting range. That troubled Stanbuck most of all. The bays likely could hold their lead but they were making no progress in widening the gap that lay between.

Turley Jaffick's voice was shrill, cursing, threatening, commanding his men, now strung out behind in an irregular line. Jack Hazen was slightly ahead of the others, his yellow shirt a bright splash as he hunched over his mount's extended neck; his white hat sharp and definite against the darker background that was the rider behind him.

They topped out another rise and plunged down into a shallow basin. Jaffick's voice floated to them, beat into their ears as they surged over the far crest.

"Cut 'em down! Aim for the horses!"

Worry began to tear at Dave Stanbuck; worry not for himself and his own safety but for Marissa. The possibility of a bullet striking her or felling her mount was very real now. He sought to veer his horse to the left, to get the bay's huge bulk behind her as a shield. The bay flatly refused to accept such a maneuver. He clamped the bit in his iron jaws and rushed on, neck and neck with his counterpart.

Stanbuck gave it up and glanced ahead. They were not far now from the rocks and brush. There would be no guarantee of safety in the depths of the brakes, he knew, and they would have to slacken their headlong pace, travel more slowly and carefully. But at least there would be less danger from bullets. They could dodge in and out of cover, offer only fleeting, difficult targets and, with a bit of luck, eventually elude Jaffick and his bunch.

"Dave—to the left!" Marissa cried suddenly. "Soldiers!" Stanbuck's attention swiveled sharply to that point. His heart lifted and a wave of thankfulnesss swept through him. At least two squads of blue-uniformed men were bearing down upon them from the east. Cavalry from Fort Quinton, out on patrol! It was a break of good fortune he could not have dreamed possible.

"Head for them!" he shouted to the girl and together they swung their horses for the oncoming soldiers.

Stanbuck threw a glance over his shoulder. Jaffick and his men had ceased their shooting. They had settled back in their saddles and were coming on at a gallop. Butcher Jaffick was a cool one. Soldiers were not frightening him off, apparently.

The cavalry halted ahead on a small knoll and waited. With Marissa a length in front of him, Stanbuck rode up and stopped. The officer in charge was a major who wore the insignia of the Quartermaster Corps. That fact immediately struck Stanbuck as odd but he passed it by. Frontier duty sometimes altered the usual system. Further along he saw a red-faced, buck sergeant, sweating profusely on his McClellan and, back of him, a collection of privates and corporals.

Twelve men in all, counting the narrow-faced major. Not many but enough, if handled right, to effect the rescue of those waiting on Mangus Mountain and take Jaffick and his guerrilla bunch in tow. Stanbuck kneed his horse to where he could face the officer.

"Major—quick! These men chasing us are killers! There are more of them west of here, at Mangus Mountain. They've got several people trapped on it and they plan to kill them, too.

80

Throw a squad around this bunch and I'll lead you to the others. We move fast, maybe we can prevent any more bloodshed!"

Chapter 14

THE OFFICER LOOKED DAVE STANBUCK OVER COOLLY. "Who are you, mister?"

"Name is Stanbuck. Lady with me is Miss McCarey. We both live here in this valley. You're from Fort Quinton, I take it."

The officer nodded. "I'm Major Roebling."

The steady thud of Jaffick's horses grew louder as they rode in, suddenly ceasing when they halted. Roebling made no move, gave no signal to the soldiers beyond him.

"We need help," Stanbuck persisted. "This whole valley—"

"Mornin', Major." Jaffick's voice cut through Dave's words in a strong, confident flow. "Lucky you came along. These rustlers were about to give us the slip!"

Stanbuck, at first startled and then outraged by Jaffick's bald accusation, whirled in the saddle. The guerrilla chief and his men regarded him with sly, amused expressions. He turned back to Roebling. The officer's features had not altered from one of cool disinterest. Behind him, however, the cavalrymen now regarded Marissa, in her flamboyant costume, in a different light.

"Danged if rustlers ain't gettin' purtier all the time!"

"Wish't I had me some cows to get rustled," another voice added. "Be a real pleasure, catchin' rustlers like little pink britches there."

"Quiet there in the ranks!" the red-faced sergeant barked. "The major needs none of your lip, Patterson. Nor yours either, Higbee."

Roebling swung his agate eyes to Jaffick. "Am I to understand you are accusing these people of rustling?"

"Of trying to," Jaffick said, smoothly. "They've been nipping at our flanks for two days. So far it's got them nothing but a few bullets."

"He's a liar!" Stanbuck burst out. "He's nothing but a killer and a thief, himself! I can prove—"

"One reason why we're running late," Jaffick said. "They've slowed us up some."

Roebling nodded. "Wondered about that. Where's your herd now?"

Jaffick waved to a dust pall in the north. "There. My boys will push them hard tonight. Should reach the fort by midday tomorrow."

"Major—" Stanbuck said, striving to keep a tight rein on his anger. "You've got to listen to me! I—"

The officer waved him to silence. To Jaffick he said, "Good. I will expect delivery tomorrow then. How many head? The full five thousand?"

"May fall a bit shy of that."

"Shy? How many?"

"Probably a thousand."

"A thousand! Your agreement with me was to drive in five thousand, not four! If I had known—"

"Now, hold on!" Jaffick said. "Five thousand was the deal, sure enough. But not necessarily in one bunch. You'll get the rest. Even more if you find out you need them. Figured the smart thing to do was to deliver what I had on hand so's you could load them up and start shipping. Then I'll take my crew and roundup the strays and stragglers and finish up the order. This time of year, a man's herd is mighty well scattered!"

"Not a single head of that herd belongs to him!" Stanbuck shouted, forcing himself to be heard. "He's no rancher! He doesn't even belong in this country!"

Roebling swung his hard gaze around, settled it upon Stanbuck. "Who are you, mister?" he demanded, as if noticing Dave for the first time.

"I said before, name is Stanbuck. Own a ranch here in

this valley. The lady with me is Miss McCarey. She is the niece of another rancher, man named Kinter. Right at the present, Kinter and some others are hiding out on the top of a mountain, trying to keep from being—"

"You say Mr. Jaffick here has no ranch in this valley?"

"He doesn't own one square inch of this country! And every steer he's driving in to you has been stolen, either from my herd or some of the others around here."

Roebling shifted his gaze to Jaffick. "Well, Mr. Jaffick?"

The guerrilla leader shrugged in resignation. He smiled. "What did you expect him to say? Man knows he will be swinging from a tree limb, soon as I can find one big enough. Reckon he'd say anything to try and get out of that." He stopped, ducked his head at Hazen. "Jack, how long you lived around here?"

The gunman thought for a moment. "Better than five years now."

"You ever see this man or woman before?"

"Only since they rode in here with some others a week or so ago."

Jaffick turned a satisfied face to Roebling. "Hazen, here, is my foreman, Major. Expect he knows just about every man in these parts. How long you worked for me, Jack?"

Hazen shrugged. "From the day you started ranching, Mr. Jaffick," he said in a respectful tone.

"That's a lie!" Stanbuck said flatly, his voice trembling. "There's not a grain of truth in anything either one of them is saying. I can prove it—"

"I'm satisfied," Roebling said, ignoring Stanbuck. "Long as I get the beef I contracted for and there's a bill of sale to cover the transaction. The army requires nothing more."

Marissa, silent up to that moment, rode in nearer to the officer. "You must listen to us!" she said earnestly. "Dave is telling you the truth. We're not outlaws and my uncle and others are up on that mountain. And there have been others killed—murdered by these men . . ."

"Sure," Jaffick said smoothly, "and you're all pure and white and never did nothing like I've said. I suppose those horses you're riding came right out of your own corral. They don't belong to two of my men you probably shot down in cold blood."

Roebling's attention swiveled once again to Dave Stanbuck. "What about that? Is it true? Do those horses belong to Jaffick's men?"

Stanbuck, suddenly helpless in the face of the charge, said, "Yes, but we had to take them—"

The officer turned away, closed the subject from his mind. As far as he was concerned there was nothing more to be said on the matter.

"Look at me!" Dave shouted, still hoping to convince the man. "I'm not even armed! If I was all Jaffick says, you think I'd be going up against his crowd with no gun?"

"He had a gun," Jaffick explained with affected patience, "and we took it from him. We bottled up him and some more of his hardcases yesterday after they tried a raid on us. Somehow he managed to escape, along with his woman there. Naturally he would have no gun."

Roebling only shrugged. "I've neither the desire nor the time to become embroiled in such a matter. Settle it yourselves. I'm interested in seeing that the meat I've contracted for is delivered as agreed."

"And it sure will be, Major," Jaffick said quickly. "You can depend on it. Tomorrow we'll be at the fort and you can make your own tally when my boys show up with the herd. Soon as I know how many short of five thousand we are, I'll get busy and bring in the balance."

Roebling said, "Fair enough, Mr. Jaffick."

"Now," the outlaw leader continued, "about the payment. You got that set up like we agreed?"

Roebling said, "Just as you wanted. Cash."

"Good. Nothing wrong with government vouchers, you understand. Good as gold, far as I'm concerned. But out here they're a little hard to handle. And I likely will have to do a bit of buying to make up what I'm short in steers. Cash always talks loud when a man's doing business."

"You'll get it in cash," the officer said. "And at fifteen dollars a head, as stated."

Stanbuck squirmed in his saddle. He had gotten nowhere with Roebling. Everything he had said had been ignored or else deliberately explained in a light that favored Jaffick. It came to him then that there might be more to the situation than met the eye; that there could possibly be something between the officer and Jaffick.

Roebling was too willing to accept everything and anything the guerrilla told him while being patently unwilling to hear anything else. Dave cast about desperately for something that might force Roebling to listen, that would pin him down and in some way throw a shadow of doubt upon Turley Jaffick. In the presence of the waiting cavalrymen, the officer would hardly dare to ignore something clearly evident.

He glanced at the sergeant. The non-com was watching the proceedings with disinterest, as were the troopers beyond him. One soldier dozed in the gradually increasing heat of day, his head slumped forward, shoulders down. He could expect no aid from them, Dave knew. They were under Roebling's command and, while they might dislike the surly, hard-faced officer they, nevertheless, were soldiers enough to back him as their superior.

He swung his attention to Jaffick, probing his mind for a possible, overlooked fact that would help. The outlaw chief was talking with Roebling, having some discussion as to the handling of the herd when it arrived at the fort. His men would turn the stock over to the army, he said, and they would then leave immediately in order to get the second roundup underway. He, Jaffick, would remain at the fort long enough for the tally and to settle up and collect. That was to be expected. Jaffick would be certain to get his hands on the money as quickly as possible, just in case something went wrong later.

That was it!

A shaft of hope broke through Dave Stanbuck's thoughts. Perhaps, if Roebling knew with whom he dealt, a doubt might be cast that would cause him to listen, to consider the proof Stanbuck offered to produce.

"Major," he said in a voice designed to reach the furthermost cavalryman. "You ever hear of a guerrilla they called the Butcher?"

Chapter 15

MAJOR ROEBLING, in the act of saying something to the outlaw chief, paused. He came slowly around, his thin face twisted into a frown. Behind him the sergeant, as if light had suddenly burst across his consciousness, spoke up.

"The Butcher—sure! Knew I'd heard that name of Jaffick somewheres! I know him, Major!"

"Sergeant Bayes!" the officer snapped. "Keep it quiet back there!"

"Yes, sir," Bayes replied briskly, embarrassed by his momentary lapse.

Jaffick's smile was a hard-cornered, fixed expression on his florid countenance. He said nothing; only his pale eyes betrayed his pulsing anger at Stanbuck's continuing insistence.

"He tried to murder General Grant. I know now he's the man because I was there at the time. It cost me my place in the army. But that's something else. Main thing I'm telling you is that he's a guerrilla murderer. You ever hear of him?"

"Few have not," Roebling admitted.

But it was evident he was not too well acquainted with Jaffick and his bloody record. "You see any field duty, Major?"

Roebling shook his head. "No, I'm afraid I didn't."

That explained it. Behind the lines officers, being too engrossed in their desk operations and the huge mountains of red tape attendant to government functions, or else too involved in the complicated manipulations of power politics for their own advantage, seldom were aware of what the actual fighting man was up against or of what took place beyond their immediate circle.

"Ask your sergeant then. I think he knows him!"

"I do that, sir!" Bayes said at once, his voice quick and loaded with venom. "This Jaffick, or the Butcher as everybody called him—"

"That will do, Sergeant," Roebling checked the non-com's words. He glanced at Stanbuck. "It's your contention that Mr. Jaffick is the same man you knew as the Butcher. Is that it?"

"The same. I knew—"

Roebling cut him off again. "And if he is? What does his past history have to do with the United States army contracting with him to supply meat? We have to get supplies from any source possible. It's a matter of dealing with whomever we can, and at the best price obtainable."

Stanbuck stared at the officer. "That may be one way of looking at it, but a strange one! Point I make is why you will take his word over mine, knowing what kind of a man he is. I can prove everything I've said if you will give me the chance."

Turley Jaffick lifted his hands, then let them fall in a gesture of resignation. "Damn it all, Major! We have to go through this again? Sure I did army service once. I admit it. I even admit I served the Confederacy at first, until I realized they were wrong. That's when I lined up with the Union. As for fighting—I fought the way I knew best."

"You didn't fight," Stanbuck said in a metal-sharp tone. "Leastwise, not like a soldier. You put in your time raiding defenseless towns, robbing and burning and murdering helpless people who couldn't stand against you and your pack of killers."

"Matter of opinion," Jaffick countered.

"Matter of record! You never served either side in the war. You served yourself. You were doing it to fill your own pockets while you hid behind one flag or the other all the while. The very uniform you and your bunch wore came off the bodies of soldiers you murdered!"

Turley Jaffick's face was bleak. His eyes were empty, flat, and he looked at Dave Stanbuck in baleful silence.

"Everything I've said about this man is in the records," Stanbuck rushed on, "And now he's adding more to it. That herd he is selling you is not his, it never was. Not one steer in the whole four thousand! And to get them he has murdered a half-dozen people, maybe more. He's not finished yet. He will have to get rid of me and Miss McCarey here. And those people he's got trapped up on Mangus Mountain. You let him get away with this and you'll have the slaughter of a dozen or more men, women and children on your conscience!"

"Silence!" Roebling roared, suddenly aroused.

"You'll hear what I've got to say!" Stanbuck shouted. "I'm not in the army and I don't take orders from you or any other brass-button popinjay! I insist you follow me back across this valley and let me prove what I've told you. I'll show you the men killed by this guerrilla cutthroat. I'll take you to the ranches he's raided—"

Jaffick drew his pistol. He spurred his horse in behind Stanbuck and jammed the muzzle of his weapon into the rancher's spine. "I've had enough of these insults! I'll not sit by and be cut to ribbons by a stinking thief trying to save his own hide!"

Stanbuck knocked the weapon aside with a backwards jab of his arm. "What about it, Major? You willing to let me show you?"

Roebling shook his head. "What this man did in the past has nothing to do with the moment at hand. Perhaps he was a guerrilla fighter. I don't know and I don't care. We had such on our side. So did the Confederates. A lot of men did things during the war they aren't proud of, but that's no sign they can't change, can't become useful, decent citizens. You can't hold against a man something he did—"

"Hold against him!" Stanbuck echoed. "You take him with you, turn him in to army headquarters, either side, and I'll guarantee they will hang him within twenty-four hours! That's what they think of him, Major. Both sides, Union or Rebel."

"Neither here nor there," Roebling replied, unruffled. "I'm not concerned with what has happened, only with the present and the fact that this man can supply beef to the Quartermaster Corps."

"I think your interest in him is more than just as a supplier." Stanbuck said hotly, unable to contain himself longer. "I think the pair of you have a special deal of some sort cooked up. How much commission he giving you, Major? How much?"

"Sergeant Bayes!" Roebling shouted, his face going purple. "Put these people under arrest! Charge them with attempted cattle stealing. If that's not enough, I'll add interference with a government contractor in the performance of his agreement!"

Bayes kneed his horse up beside Stanbuck. He nodded to Marissa and then to the rancher.

"Over there," he said, his moon face blank and betraying none of his feelings. He pointed toward the waiting troopers. "Open up ranks."

Marissa and Dave Stanbuck walked their mounts into the small enclosure formed by the soldiers. Bayes shut them off effectively, pulling his own thick-bodied horse around until it closed the only exit from the formation.

Turley Jaffick sighed heavily. He replaced his pistol in its worn, well-oiled holster. "The way it always goes," he said. "Man makes a few mistakes and never lives them down. Even the ones he makes fighting for his country in the only way he knows how. All I've asked since I got out of the war was to be left alone, to do my cattle raising and live like any other man. But there's always some jasper, like this one here, popping up to remind me of the past and set things to simmering again."

Roebling did not answer. He still smarted under Stanbuck's accusation and, true or not, it was plain it galled him deeply. There was something to it, of that Dave was positive. Turley Jaffick was too sure of himself and Roebling too reluctant to delve further into the matter. He turned his attention to the soldier beside him.

"Who's commanding the Fort?"

The cavalryman looked at him for a moment. "Colonel Milroy."

"Joe Milroy?"

The private nodded. "Know him?"

"Once knew a Joe Milroy. Don't know if it's the same one."

"Well, you better hope this is the one. You're sure goin' to be needin' a friend."

"Quiet back there!" Bayes's voice shouted. "Be no talkin' to the prisoners!"

Stanbuck lapsed into silence. It would make no difference if it were the Milroy he knew. No officer would listen to him, once he learned Stanbuck's identity. Like the mark of Cain, he was branded with the stigma of murder—or attempted murder. He could expect no help from that point. It would come too late, anyway. Jaffick and his men would have long since ended things for Charlie Pierce and Kinter and all the others on Petticoat Ridge. He had to come up with some means for helping them now—before Jaffick and his crew could return and complete their plans.

A curious thought occurred to Dave Stanbuck at that moment. A transformation had taken place within him he had not thought possible. He no longer viewed Jaffick as the object of a personal feud; he had become, instead, the symbol of a threat to certain innocent people—friends, actually. Friends. He found the word strange, almost unfamiliar, but it stirred him in a way he had not felt in many months.

He glanced at Marissa. Her face was stiff, showing the strains of the hours. Her eyes were heavy and mirrored the weariness that dragged at her slim body. He reached out, laid his hand upon hers.

"Don't worry, we'll come through this yet."

She looked at him and smiled. "I'm all right."

He grinned, his own words mocking him. *Come through it how?* With a dozen armed cavalrymen escorting them back to Fort Quinton, how could he do anything? If he tried to bolt, he wouldn't make fifty yards before they cut him down. And even if he were fortunate enough to escape their bullets, what could he accomplish? He would be no better off. He glanced at Sergeant Bayes, assessing the possibilities that might lie there. Instinctively, he felt the non-com sympathized with him, perhaps even believed all he had said. But Bayes was an old line soldier; he wouldn't buck Roebling, no matter how his thoughts moved, personally.

There was only one good facet to being taken to the Fort; Marissa, at least, would be safe. Now, if there was only a way he could escape to help Kinter and the others. If he could just get his hands on a gun and break away.

Roebling and Jaffick, finished with their discussion, moved back to the main body of waiting horsemen. The guerrilla chief indicated Stanbuck with a wave of his hand.

"Major, just thinking, the ranchers hereabouts are not going to take kindly to your stepping in on their problems.

90

Rustling is a matter for law here in the valley, not the military. I'd suggest you turn the prisoners over to me. I'll call the ranchers together for a trial and we'll take care of them in our own way."

Dave Stanbuck, instantly alarmed, glanced quickly at Roebling. If the officer accepted the outlaw's suggestion, he and Marissa were as good as dead.

Roebling nodded. He was only too glad to rid himself of the troublesome pair. His hurried acceptance of the offer proved that. He said, "You're right, sir. It is no military matter. Sergeant, release the prisoners to Mr. Jaffick's custody."

Bayes moved back a few steps. He took up the reins held by Marissa and Stanbuck and prodded his horse forward. He handed over the leathers to the guerrilla.

Stanbuck faced Roebling. "This is murder, Major. You are aware of that, I'm sure. Just as soon as you are out of sight, these men will kill us."

"I think not," the officer said stiffly. "You will have a fair trial. I believe I have Mr. Jaffick's word on that." He lifted his glance to the outlaw leader.

Jaffick said, "You got my word, Major. All according to the law."

"You think his word means anything?" Stanbuck demanded. Sweat stood out on his brow in large beads of desperation. He was fighting for his life—Marissa's life and he well knew it. "You can't do this, Major!"

"Sergeant!" Roebling barked, ignoring Stanbuck. "Make ready to move out."

"Do one thing decent, Major," Stanbuck said. "At least take Miss McCarey with you to the fort. She doesn't deserve to fall into the hands of men like these—"

Jack Hazen pushed up beside Stanbuck, a hard grin on his dark face. He took the leather strips from Jaffick's fingers. "Cut the bleatin', cowboy. It'll do you no good," he said.

Roebling turned away, touching his horse lightly with blunted spurs. "I shall expect you and your herd by noon tomorrow," he called over his shoulders to Jaffick. He touched the brim of his hat. "All right, Sergeant. Move out!"

"For—ward!"

Stanbuck heard Roebling's shouted command and the quick thud of hoofs as the horses broke into a trot. He did not trouble to look up and watch the troopers ride out.

Chapter 16

MARISSA WATCHED the soldiers trot off. From the grim set of Dave Stanbuck's jaw, she realized that the hope he held for their lives, and those of the others on the Ridge, went with them. He had tried to make the officer in charge listen, to allow him to prove all he claimed was true, but the major had preferred to believe the outlaw, this red-faced guerrilla they called the Butcher. She had never heard of him in Maryland. But she was aware of guerrillas and knew what they could expect at their hands.

Turley Jaffick and those who rode with him were no different. They had already demonstrated their lust for murder in the way they had taken over Mangus Valley. She trembled slightly, thinking of that. And at once she took control of herself. *I am not afraid,* she murmured. *For Dave's sake, I won't be afraid.* But she was; mortally, fearfully afraid of what lay ahead.

Why were they just sitting there? What were they waiting for?

She glanced around, looking at each of the outlaws briefly; the leader, Jaffick, the one who had eyes like a snake, Jack Hazen, the five other tough-looking men. All watched the soldiers, now off in the distance. She understood then what the delay meant; the outlaws were waiting for the officer and his blue-clad cavalrymen to get out of sight.

That brought her attention quickly to Dave Stanbuck. He was looking at her, his lean face quiet, his deep-set, gray eyes troubled beneath their dark shelf of brow. She tried to smile, to reassure him of her courage, but it wasn't very convincing. He was worried for her, she knew. And somehow that made her feel better. To know that she did matter to him, after all, was some compensation for what they must meet.

If only Jaffick would let them stay together! As long as Dave was at her side, she wouldn't care so much. Let Jaffick, the ruthless Butcher, do what he would. But if they were separated—she wasn't sure she could stand it alone.

She wished she had known Dave longer. Only a day! It was incredible! How could you meet a man, fall completely in love with him and be willing to die at his side, all in one day? Love, she always thought, was different from that. It was a long, gradual process of building up and growing until it reached a high plane. Then you capped it off with marriage. How was it possible for her to be so wholly in love with Dave Stanbuck in so short a time?

And his feelings for her had changed, too, she thought. At the start he had not wanted her with him, had preferred to go it alone. Only Tom Kinter's insistence had placed her at his side. But as the hours had worn on and the dangers had presented themselves and somehow were overcome, he seemed to change. He had said nothing, done nothing out of the ordinary that would lead her to believe he had altered in his attitude toward her, yet she believed it had come to pass. Perhaps she read it in his eyes, in the way he looked at her, or maybe it was just hope, just wishful thinking on her part. She wished she understood him better.

"Ain't they far enough away, Turley?"

Jack Hazen's drawling voice cut through the quiet. The guerrilla leader took his eyes from the now distant dust cloud that marked Roebling and his men.

"Give them plenty of time, Jack," he said.

She saw his attention stop upon Dave Stanbuck, then swing to herself. She watched him wheel, ride in nearer, his thick body slack in the saddle. He was an enigma, this Turley Jaffick. His round, florid face was almost cheerful, his manner of talking casual to the point of friendliness. But beneath it all one sensed a hard, steel core.

He halted before Stanbuck. "You did a right smart amount of talking, mister. You got anything else you'd like to say, better say it now."

"I've had my say," Stanbuck replied. "It got me nowhere."

"Pays to talk to the right man," the guerrilla said.

At once Dave spoke up. "Then, speaking as man to man, how about letting Miss McCarey here go? She can still catch up with Roebling. I got a pretty fair idea what you intend to do with me but there's no cause for you to harm her. She's just a visitor to this country."

Jaffick shook his head. "She's got a mouth. And she can talk. Learned a long time ago a man was a fool to leave any loose ends hanging."

Marissa trembled at the bloodless, cold statement. She saw Jaffick's pale eyes switch from Dave to her and break with faint interest.

"What's so fancy about the woman, anyway? You been carrying on like she was something special." The outlaw paused and looked more closely. "Well, now, that is a pretty piece of merchandise! Hadn't paid no mind to her up until now. Guess I was just thinking she was another one of them horse-faced, baggy-tailed females a man finds in this country. Damned if she isn't a genuine bows-and-lace kind of gal!"

Marissa felt a cold chill sweep through her as his hard, devouring eyes raked her hungrily. From the corner of her eye she saw Dave Stanbuck stiffen and grow taut in the saddle.

"Leave her alone, Jaffick," he said in a low voice.

The guerrilla ignored the warning. "That's about the sportiest pair of britches I ever saw. Step down, girl. Let me have a good look at you."

Stanbuck surged forward suddenly, trying to place himself between Jaffick and Marissa. She saw one of the riders strike out with his hand and smash Dave across the face. Another, his pistol out, jammed the barrel into the rancher's side.

"Set tight, cowboy," the one with the gun said.

Marissa, fearing more harm would come to Dave, climbed down from her horse. Her eyes were upon him. Blood trickled from one corner of his mouth where the outlaw's clenched fist had cut his lip. She could see the wild fury in his eyes and held her breath, fearing he would make some move to protect her and get himself immediately killed.

Jaffick's voice said, "Yes, sir, real nice. Honey, how'd you like to go to Mexico with me? Give you everything you want; fancy clothes, Mexicans to wait on you, hand and foot, plenty of money. Show you a real fine time!"

Marissa gripped her courage. "I'll die first!"

Jaffick threw back his head and laughed. "By hokey, she's got spirit, too! Man couldn't ask for more than that, looks and spirit. It's Mexico for you, girl, soon as I can wind up this business."

Marissa, fear a choking hand about her throat, shook her head violently. "No! You can't make me. I'll never go with you!"

Jaffick said, "We'll see. Lots worse things could happen to you, like being turned over to my boys for a spell."

One of the outlaws behind her laughed. "Now, that's sure a real good thought!"

"But that's not for you, not for a quality gal. Expect you're smart enough to see what's good for you."

Something the guerrilla chief had said earlier apparently had stuck in Jack Hazen's mind. He said. "You got some kind of deal cooked up with that bluebelly major?"

Jaffick pulled his attention from her. "Roebling?"

"Yeh, Roebling. Heard you say something about paying him off."

"Oh, that. He gets five thousand cut for his part."

"Five thousand!" the gunman echoed. "What the hell for?"

"Because I said so, and I'm running this outfit. And so's he'd fix it up to where we could get paid in cash. I got no time to fool around with vouchers."

"Five thousand is a lot of money for that," Hazen grumbled. "Seems to me you're a mite generous."

"Worth a lot to collect in cash," Jaffick said. He came back to Marissa. "Climb back aboard that bay girl. Time we were getting started."

Dave Stanbuck drove his heels into his horse, lunging for the outlaw chief. His face was a livid mask of hate and fury, his eyes like spots of fire. A gun blasted with deafening effect. The bullet missed, triggered by the man who had been at his flank. Marissa saw Dave reach out for Jaffick, his clawing fingers aimed for the man's throat. Jack Hazen, galvanized into action, surged in, pistol out and raised above his head. He brought it down in a swift, bluish arc. Marissa saw Dave's long body quiver, then fold forward in the saddle.

The hammer on Hazen's fancy pistol came back with a

loud clacking noise. He leveled it at Stanbuck's crumpled shape. Horror flooded through Marissa. She screamed, a high, piercing sound that split the hot, morning air.

"Not here!" Jaffick snapped, throwing an angry glance at the gunman. "That fool shot of Keno's is liable to bring Roebling and his soldiers back, as it is! You want them to find him laying here, shot in the head?"

Hazen holstered his gun. He reached down and took the reins to Stanbuck's bay in his hand. "I'll take him over into the brakes. Find a deep arroyo. That suit you?"

"Suit me fine," Jaffick said coldly. He turned back to Marissa. "Get on that horse, girl. Won't say it again."

Marissa fought to keep her courage from deserting her entirely. She was witnessing the last moments of Dave Stanbuck's life, she was certain. And of hers. There could be no way out for either of them. But the need to stay alive, to keep Dave alive for a little longer, in the vague hope that something might turn up, possessed her.

"I'll go with you," she said boldly, facing Jaffick, "if you let Dave go, if you won't hurt him anymore. He can't do you any harm now. Let him go and I promise I won't give you any trouble."

The outlaw studied her in amused silence. Then, "You're quite a woman, pink britches. I'm mighty proud I come across you."

Hazen's question was quick, sharp. "You sure don't figure to do what she wants?"

Jaffick shook his head. "Nope, not me. Stanbuck's the last man I want running loose. He's still got blood in his eye for me over that Grant stunt I pulled. And now with me taking his woman—no, sir! Besides he knows too much about what's been going on around here."

"If you kill him, you'll have to kill me, too!" Marissa declared. "I won't go with you!"

Jaffick, without looking around, said, "All right, Keno. Looks like you'd better lend a hand here."

Marissa felt the arm of the outlaw go about her, lift her easily and place her on the saddle. She reached for the reins automatically, having a desperate notion to flee. The outlaw anticipated her thoughts. He gathered up the leathers and handed them to Jaffick.

"Better hang on to these, Turl. Some rawhide in my saddle-bags. I'll tie her hands."

"Not too tight, now," the guerilla cautioned with mock solicitude. "Don't scratch up the merchandise none."

Marissa felt the last vestige of hope run slowly from her. It was useless to fight any longer. Hopeless. Turley Jaffick had the upper hand and there was no escaping him. She turned for a final look at Dave Stanbuck. He still lay forward on his saddle. A dark rivulet of blood traced down across his forehead from beneath his hat brim. A shiver racked her body and a great emptiness settled over her. *Good-bye, Dave.* She murmured the words silently. She wished again she had known him longer, had met him earlier in her life.

She felt rough hands take her wrists, clamp them together. A narrow strip of pliant leather went swiftly about them, binding them firmly, but not too tightly, to the saddle horn.

"Ain't hurtin' you none, am I, sister?"

She looked down into the dark, bewhiskered face of the man they had called Keno. He gave her a yellow, broken-toothed grin. His foul breath slapped at her and, sickened, she turned away without answering him.

"Harper," Jaffick was saying, "you and Vince take that blasting powder and ride on back to the mountain. Get that job done and over with. Then bring the rest of the boys and meet us at the herd."

One of the outlaws said, "Where'll the herd be?"

Jaffick said nothing for a moment and then spat in disgust. "All you need do is look this way. That dust cloud will be the herd. Think you can find it?"

"Sure, Turley, sure," the man muttered, chastened.

Jack Hazen took up the reins to Stanbuck's bay and started to pull off, heading for the rough badlands a short distance away. "Want me to join you there, too?"

"We'll be riding slow," the outlaw said. "You can catch up with us."

Hazen said, "Good enough," and moved on.

Marissa felt Jaffick's glance upon her. "All set, girl?"

She made no answer. Fear had left her now. There was only resignation to what lay before her and a stubborn determination never to yield. Jaffick would never take her to Mexico. Not alive, anyway.

Chapter 17

DAVE STANBUCK slowly came back to his senses as the deliberate pace of his horse shot shock waves of pain through his head with each solid footfall. It was like some powerful demon standing over him, smashing an iron mallet against his skull with measured regularity.

He gave no sign of consciousness. Trained in the hard, brutal school of experience always to be certain of conditions at such moments, he hung there on the back of the long-legged bay and suffered silently the excruciating pain while his brain cleared and he became aware of his exact situation.

Someone was behind him. He could tell by sound it was only one horse, walking not far back of the bay. He let his head sink lower until his eyes could see beyond the bay's rising and falling hip. The maniac with the mallet slogged mercilessly at him with this effort but he saw what he had looked for—a flash of brilliant yellow. The rider with him was Jack Hazen.

He wondered where Jaffick and the others were, what had happened to them. His heart leaped and thudded to an abrupt halt when he remembered that Marissa would be with them, helpless in the hands of the guerrilla leader. He fought to control the wild panic that gripped him at that thought and cursed himself silently for letting it happen. He had to do something, he thought grimly. He could not leave her to Jaffick's sadistic diversions.

Far off to the right he saw two horsemen riding toward Mangus Mountain. He gave them a few moments close consideration, deciding, finally, that Jaffick had dispatched them to aid the outlaws already on the mountain. He recalled the cans of blasting powder that had been purloined from his storehouse and guessed the pair were taking the explosive to their fellow outlaws where it would be used to finish off Kinter and the others who were yet alive.

He had no illusions as to what lay ahead for himself. He could tell from the gradually roughening ground that they were heading into the arroyo-gashed, brush-and rock-studded wasteland of the brakes. There Jack Hazen would simply kill him, would put a bullet through his head and get him out of the way. Then the gunman would rejoin Jaffick and the others. He tipped his head upward an inch or two, looking forward. They were only a few scant yards from the first stand of thick, screening brush. Hazen likely would stop there. He would not trouble to go far.

He stirred in the saddle, made it appear he was just recovering his battered faculties. He sat up slowly. Small needles pricked at his scalp. Hazen, a man of no nerves and wholly given to impulses, might suddenly decide he had ridden a sufficient distance, draw his weapon and send a stream of bullets tearing into his back.

He waited out the terrible moments. There were no sounds from Hazen, no sharp click of a gun hammer; only the muted tunk-a-tunk of the horses walking over the sandy ground and the occasional clink of a metal shoe against rock. Stanbuck straightened up with deliberate slowness. He lifted his hand and explored the back of his skull gingerly. It was damp, sticky from blood, and the hair was matted.

"Won't bother you much longer, cowboy," Hazen drawled with dry humor.

Stanbuck twisted about. He was making each move carefully, fighting for time while his brain worked at a feverish intensity seeking some way out, some escape from the promise of death, now only moments away. He stared at Hazen. The gunman was slumped lazily in the saddle, white hat pushed forward over his eyes to shade them from the strong sunlight. Both hands were crossed on the horn. He had not drawn either of his guns, knowing Stanbuck was unarmed and could offer no resistance.

"Where we headed?" Stanbuck asked, knowing well the answer. To death, to the finish of all things.

Hazen said, "First deep arroyo we come to. That will be the end of the road for you, cowboy."

"Why go to all the trouble?" Stanbuck wondered. "Why not back there on the flats?"

"Some idea of Jaffick's. Afraid the soldiers might come back and find you and start asking questions."

Stanbuck turned back and looked around. They were in a maze of rock and greasewood and cactus. Ahead another ten yards, he saw the beginning of a deep wash, an arroyo such as the gunman sought. That would be where they would halt. Dave's eyes swept the country hurriedly, seeing again only the heat-blasted growth, the blistered, cracked rocks that made up the badlands. His attention caught on the sharp, black-tipped needlepoints of a yucca; Spanish bayonet, they called it in the valley. Sudden hope flared through him. He had forgotten! He glanced down to the rifle scabbard slung from his saddle. He was not entirely unarmed! Now—if he could get near enough to Hazen . . .

He halted the bay at the edge of the wash and started to ride down. Immediately Hazen's voice lashed out at him.

"Keep going! I'll tell you when to stop."

Stanbuck nodded silently. The gunman had pulled one of his pistols and now held it in his hand, ready for instant use. Stanbuck put his attention back onto the bay, urging him off the low embankment and down into the sandy arroyo. The floor was soft and the bay's hoofs sank quickly into the glittering, hot particles of gypsum. A huge jackrabbit scuttled from beneath a clump of thornbush and raced off in long bounds.

"Reckon you're wishing you had legs like that old jack," Hazen taunted, prodding his own mount down into the arroyo.

Stanbuck shrugged. "Man was meant to be a rabbit, guess he'd have legs like a rabbit."

"Which, like I said, you could sure use right now."

"Not much point in running," Dave replied. "Haven't met the man yet who could outrun a bullet."

"But you could sure try," Hazen suggested, evidently hopeful of some sport in the coming minutes.

"Not me," Stanbuck said. "No use in it."

"All right, that's far enough," Hazen said, abruptly impatient. "Get down off that horse. Don't think Dougherty would like me bringing back his saddle and horse all messed up with blood."

Stanbuck drew in the bay. Sudden tension and pressure was upon him and he felt his nerves begin to tighten, key up and become fiddle-string taut. To break the terrible breathlessness of the moment he sat perfectly still in the saddle, allowing his gaze to reach out across the torn and ragged landscape, to the steel blue of the heavens above him. He felt the hard-core drill of the sun against his back and the thought passed through him that he might be experiencing it for the last time in his life, that he could be taking his final look at the world in which he lived.

"Come on, come on," Hazen's surly voice drove at him. "Get down. Want to get this over with."

Stanbuck shifted his weight to his left foot and stepped from the bay. His mind was moving with lightning speed now as he sought to put into operation his one, desperate plan for survival. He kept the big horse turned broadside, between himself and the gunman. Hazen watched him with a sullen patience from a distance of twenty feet or less. He still held the pistol he had drawn earlier. He cocked it, the tall hammer coming back making its loud snap in the heat-laden quiet of the arroyo.

Both feet firmly on the ground, his hands yet on the saddle, he faced Hazen. "You heading down into Mexico with Jaffick?"

The gunman's gaze was a steady, pushing force. Stanbuck allowed his hands to slide imperceptibly down the hot leather of the saddle skirt, the right angling toward the rifle scabbard.

Hazen said, "Maybe. What's it to you?"

"Worrying about the girl. Hate to think of her with Jaffick."

"She's his," Hazen said, bluntly. "He took a big shine to her. Now, slap that horse on the rump, get him out of the way."

Stanbuck's long fingers slid into the scabbard, closed about the improvised spear he had earlier in the day fashioned and placed there. He took a firm grip on it, his hand as near center of the shaft as possible. It was his one chance—and it would be his only one.

"Hurry it up!" Hazen said, impatient with Stanbuck's dilatory movements. "Get that damned horse out of there!"

Stanbuck nodded. He pulled back a half-step and slapped the bay smartly. The animal, startled, lunged away. Stanbuck's fingers closed over the shaft of his spear. It came out smoothly from its leather sheath. He spun and dropped to a half-crouch, keeping the bay's bulk between himself and the gunman as

101

long as possible. He came to the end of a full, pivoting turn. The knife blade glittered brightly in the sunlight. He hurled it straight at Hazen with every ounce of strength in his body.

Hazen yelled in surprise. His gun exploded as the knife drove into his breast and stuck there, vibrating gently. The bullet from his pistol sang off into the morning sky.

The gunman wrenched the spear from his body. He came off his shying horse in a stumbling, near fall. He brought his pistol up for a second shot. Stanbuck, moving with the speed of lightning, lunged for him. They collided in an explosion of dust. The gun crashed again, and again the bullet was wide of its intended mark. They went over in a tangled, struggling heap, Hazen striving to bring his weapon into play a third time, Stanbuck trying to tear it from his grasp.

They rolled over and over on the hot, sandy floor of the arroyo locked together; they crashed against a clump of tough, resisting mesquite. They reversed, rolling into the needles of a cactus. Hazen yelled in pain and heaved wildly upward as he sought to throw Stanbuck's weight from his body. He was sucking deep for breath, the drag of his efforts loud and rasping.

Stanbuck felt the gunman's strength start to fade. His corded muscles began to soften, to go slack. He seized the pistol by its barrel and tore it from Hazen's stiffening fingers. He tossed it to one side, then reached for the second gun, still in its holster. It came easily into his hand. He jerked away from the gunman's prostrate form and sprang to his feet while sweat poured off his streaked face and down his body.

His legs trembled from the excitement and tremendous effort he had expended. The wound in his scalp had reopened and he could feel the warmer, slower trickle of blood along his hairline. He watched Jack Hazen narrowly. The gunman lay sprawled on his back, arms and legs flung wide. An irregular blotch of red marked the front of his yellow shirt where the knife had driven into his body.

Hazen's eyes were open but a film was gathering over them, a hard sort of glaze. His lips were drawn back into an ugly grimace. They moved faintly, as if he were endeavoring to speak. Abruptly his mouth sagged and his body went limp.

Stanbuck remained motionless for a full minute, remembering those frightful days and nights of the war, living again the horrors and terrors of it, experiencing anew that dull, empty sickness that always came with the killing of another man—any man. He thought he had left it all behind, back in the valleys of Virginia, in the muggy swamps of Mississippi, on the pine-clad hills of Georgia. But here it was again, now a part of the new and peaceful life he had hoped to carve for himself in this land so far removed from those grim and bitter scenes.

There was no escape from it, ever, he thought, and turned wearily to the gunman. He dropped to his knees and examined the man briefly to assure himself he was dead. He had not considered the knife would be so lethal but it had penetrated deeply. He must have hurled it with terrific force.

Immediately, he removed the heavily scrolled leather gun belt and holsters from the man's waist and drew it about his own. He pulled the bright-yellow Mexican shirt from Hazen's body and put it on over his own. The crusting stain on the front presented a problem. He solved it by covering it with the outlaw's large bandana, allowing it to hang from one of the shirt's wide pockets. He then exchanged his hat for the white one worn by the gunman.

He took time to reload the pistol Hazen had tried to use on him and slipped both weapons back into their holsters. That done, he caught up the gunman's horse and swung to the saddle. The bay had trotted off down the arroyo a short distance. He had no difficulty in approaching him and gathering up the reins. Leading the animal behind, he rode out of the wash and gained the higher ground.

He threw a quick, searching glance out across the rolling plains. The men headed back for Mangus Mountain were almost out of sight. Marissa, Jaffick, and his three other riders were directly ahead, a little more than a mile due north.

His long lips pulled down into a grim smile. Time was running out for him at both hands. He would have to move, and move fast, if he expected to save both Marissa and the people on Petticoat Ridge. Immediately he started in pursuit of Jaffick and his party. It was a matter of first things first.

Chapter 18

MARISSA AND THE OUTLAWS were traveling at an easy pace. Far beyond them Dave Stanbuck could see the dust cloud over the herd bulging larger in the clear sky and concluded Jaffick was pointing for it. The guerilla would be riding to have his look at the cattle, to check and assure himself all was being done according to plan. Turley Jaffick was that sort of man; he led his wild bunch with an iron hand and driving will but he never really trusted any of them to do a job.

Stanbuck's passage was not fast. The bay he had previously ridden did not lead well and continuously held back and jerked at the reins. Stanbuck had an urge to forget him, to drop the leathers and let him fend for himself but he abandoned that thought. As Jack Hazen, one of the outlaw band, he knew he would be expected to bring in the bay; to release him might evoke suspicions in Turley Jaffick and some of his men.

Even at so slow a pace, an hour later found him within a hundred yards of Marissa and the guerillas. He approached with hat well forward on his head, ostensibly shading his eyes, as Hazen had been inclined to do. He sought to conceal his face as much as possible, fearing recognition too quickly. For Marissa's sake he knew he must be almost upon the party before they could be allowed to realize his actual identity.

The first casual inspection passed. Jack Hazen's bright Mexican shirt, his broad-brimmed, white hat and the sorrel horse he rode, made that possible. Watching carefully, he saw one of the outlaws half-turn in his saddle, rake him with a slow glance and swing back. He said something to Jaffick who also

104

twisted about and had his look. Neither apparently saw anything amiss and continued on without further indication of interest.

Stanbuck was near enough now to see Marissa clearly. She rode in the center of the four men, sitting forward on her saddle, shoulders sloped and dejected. Her hands were crossed upon the horn, apparently bound there in some way since she held her arms in a stiff, fixed manner before her. If true, this would present a minor problem. She would have a difficult time managing her horse, particularly if he, unguided, was one to run with the herd. But he would face that emergency when it arose.

Fifty yards. The outlaw who rode the outside of the group, a five-abreast line, threw a glance over his shoulder. Again the yellow shirt and white hat of the dead gunman mustered inspection. Stanbuck watched the outlaw resume his position. This, most likely, was the last time he would be able to maintain the deception. Any nearer now and he certainly would be recognized. He studied the group, trying to come up with some sort of attack that would not endanger the girl.

He had Hazen's two guns. That placed him at a strong advantage. But he was reluctant to use the left-hand weapon. He was accustomed to shooting with the right, and with Marissa somewhere in the center of the melee that was bound to ensue when he struck, he could afford to take no chances on hitting her with a poorly directed, awkward shot. The left-hand gun had better be for show only, for reserve.

Twenty-five yards.

Dave Stanbuck released the reins of the bay and allowed him to trot along behind the sorrel. He drew Hazen's pistols, fancy, silver-plated, bone-handled weapons that fit snugly into the palms of his hands. They were beautiful guns, perfectly balanced and smooth as window glass to the touch. He could hear the voice of Turley Jaffick droning on in that half-humorous, overweening way of his. He was speaking to Marissa. Stanbuck watched her shake her head stubbornly, steadily refusing something.

Fifteen yards.

A man with a straight-forward, direct marching mind, Dave Stanbuck could think of no devious way to cope with the moment of attack other than one of headlong approach. He set himself, drew back the hammers on his two weapons and drove spurs into Hazen's sorrel. The big horse leaped forward.

"Hold up!" he shouted. "Marissa—get out of the way!"

The sorrel, bearing down upon the others at a plunging run, sought to veer aside. He stiffened his legs and almost slid into the startled outlaws. Marissa, no less surprised, reacted instantly. She drove her horse forward, flogging him with her knees. She was out of the suddenly milling and confused party of riders in a matter of seconds, wheeling in a tight circle designed to bring her in behind Stanbuck and eventually to his side.

The outlaw on the edge of the wheeling horses dragged at his gun, brought it up in a metallic blur. Stanbuck knocked him from the saddle with a single bullet that struck dead center. Turley Jaffick was shouting, filling the air with curses and commands. Another outlaw pulled off to one side and began to shoot rapidly. Stanbuck heard the drone of bullets. He looked around, worried about Marissa. She could easily get in the line of fire. She had halted a short distance behind him and was struggling with the cord that bound her wrists to the saddle horn.

"Pull out! Get out of the way!"

She did not seem to hear him and, fearing one of the shots, passing so close to him, would carry on by and strike her, Stanbuck drove the frantic sorrel he rode farther to the left.

"Box him in!" Jaffick's voice was a shrill cry on the air. "Get him in a cross fire. Bill—over here, to your right!"

The guerrilla leader was a wheeling, spinning, dodging shadow in the aroused haze of dust. Stanbuck sought to get the outlaw in his sights but the man was wary, never affording him an opportunity. He emptied his gun at the nearest man, missing completely because of the plunging horses, and exchanged that weapon for the fully loaded one in his left hand. He threw a glance at Marissa. They must get out, and at once. The outlaws would soon have him lined up in a cross fire he could not hope to survive.

Marissa still struggled with her bonds. He snapped a shot at the outlaw called Bill, saw him pull away as the bullet grazed his arm. He jerked the sorrel sharply to the right, back to the left, dodging and weaving to keep the guerrillas from getting an easy target.

Bill, directed by Jaffick to come in on the opposite flank, opened up at that moment. From the depths of the boiling dust, Jaffick once more began to shout orders.

"Now—close in on him! Keep up that shooting! Blast him off that horse!"

Stanbuck threw a bullet at the nearest rider, Bill, he thought it was. He snapped a second at the other outlaw on the opposite side. He wheeled tightly. There was no holding his position now. He started for Marissa, shouting at her to turn, to ride for the brakes. She still fought the stubborn cord about her wrists, apparently making no progress in freeing herself. Behind her, the bay Stanbuck had ridden earlier had halted, confused by the furious engagement.

Hazen's sorrel legged it toward her, Stanbuck, both weapons now empty, thrust one into its holster and began to press cartridges from the belt loops. The shouts of Jaffick and the other men were beyond him now, but they were not far. In only brief seconds they would burst through the wall of yellow dust and be after them.

"We've got to get out of here!" he yelled at the girl. "Head back for the brakes!"

In that next fragment of time he felt the sorrel wilt between his knees. The big horse's head snapped down. His legs folded. Stanbuck kicked his feet free of the stirrups and launched himself straight out. He hit the ground in a massive boil of dust as the triumphant shouts of Jaffick and his men went up. He landed on his feet, went over in a long roll, and came back upright.

He wheeled, feeding fresh shells into the cylinder of his gun as he did. Flipping the loading gate closed with his thumb, he snapped a quick shot at the nearest oncoming outlaw. It proved to be Jaffick—and the bullet was near. The guerrilla leader yelled, hauled in sharply, and for several moments there was a spinning tangle of men and mounts as the three outlaws came together.

Stanbuck flung a glance at Marissa. She had not ridden on, as he had directed. Instead she was coming toward him, leading the other bay horse. He rushed to meet her, seeing she had finally freed her hands. He snatched the reins from her fingers and grinnd up at her strained, taut face. Then he vaulted into the saddle, twisted half about and drove another bullet at Jaffick and the others.

"The brakes—get started for it—"

Marissa spun her mount around. He ranged up beside her on his nervously prancing bay and together they headed back across the valley for the safety of the badlands. He looked over his shoulder. Jaffick and his two men were already in pursuit. They were not far behind and riding hard.

"Keep low!" he warned the girl.

He voiced his warning and began to reload his weapon again. Hazen's belt was heavy with cartridges. He had no ammunition worries. He filled the first gun completely, letting the bay run free with no hand on the reins. He replaced that weapon in its holster and loaded the other. Finished, he glanced again to the outlaws. He leveled his pistol, firing two quick shots at them. Immediately they broke apart, fanned out, with Jaffick staying in the center position.

They began to shoot and the now familiar drone of bullets once more reached Stanbuck's ears. He pulled farther to his right, away from Marissa. He saw her turn to him, features pale and set. She began to cut toward him, to close the gap. He shook his head.

"Keep going—straight! Get into the brakes. I'll meet you there!"

She nodded her understanding and rushed on. She was crouched low over the long, reaching bay and she rode well. Tom Kinter had been right when he said she was a good horsewoman.

He took four more shots at the onracing outlaws, then reloaded, keeping the second weapon in reserve for emergencies. His horse was running smooth and easy beneath him, seeming to know that his destination was the rough and rugged depths of the badlands and thus requiring no guiding hand on the leathers. They thundered on.

Stanbuck, reloaded and ready, continued to shoot. The man to his right, seeing Marissa's course split off, altered his own. Immediately Stanbuck concentrated on him, ignored Jaffick and the other rider. The outlaw, finding himself a specific target, lost interest in the girl and began to drift back to his original position with the others.

Stanbuck glanced ahead anxiously. The edge of the brakes was still some distance away. The horses were beginning to tire. The bay he rode had begun to labor a bit, his nostrils flaring as he felt the need for wind. Marissa's mount would be no better off. He glanced at the outlaws. They had not gained, had merely held their own.

He reached down and patted the sweaty neck of the bay.

Another mile, perhaps two, and they would be within the shelter of the brushy arroyos. He hoped the big horse had enough left in him to make it.

Jaffick and his men ceased their firing. Dave wondered what that meant. The guerrilla chief would not be giving up. Such was not his nature. It came to him then, a moment later. The pursuit was simply devolving into a hunt. They would follow Marissa and himself into the brakes and there, doggedly, begin to stalk them.

It was a typical Jaffick procedure. Get on a man's tail and never get off until you've run him into the ground. But Turley Jaffick guessed wrong this time, Dave thought with satisfaction. Jaffick was dealing with no greenhorn at such tactics. He had received a few well-learned lessons in guerrilla warfare himself. He welcomed the opportunity for matching wits with the Butcher. It would be much better than trading wild shots from the backs of hard-running horses—and a lot safer for Marissa.

Marissa reached the edge of the brakes a long minute before him, due to the curving formation of the land. He swung to the left immediately after the bay plunged off the embankment and was down on the sandy bottom of the broad wash. He saw Marissa. She had pulled to a halt behind a long, low pile of sun-bleached rocks. He made his way quickly through the tangle of brush and pulled in beside her. Before he could dismount, she leaned over, threw her arms about his neck and kissed him thankfully.

"Oh, Dave!" she sobbed, giving way for the first time. "I thought I would never see you again! I thought they had killed you!"

For a long minute they sat there. Stanbuck felt the need for her rise and flood through him, knew for a brief period of time what it was like to have the bitter loneliness swept aside; and then he was back to the present, to reality. He took her gently by the shoulders, pushed her away. She stared at him, wonderingly, pain filling her eyes.

"We haven't much time," he murmured in a low voice. "We've got to get away from this bunch and make it to the Ridge."

She nodded her head woodenly.

"We'll lay low here for a bit—"

"By God, they're down in there somewhere!" Turley Jaffick's

109

voice broke in suddenly from somewhere off to their right. "Maybe they run a piece but they won't be going fast—not in all that brush and rock. The two of you get after them."

"You aim to come with us?"

Jaffick said, "Nope, reckon you two can handle it from here on. Time I was getting back to that herd."

"What about that girl? You still figure to take her with you to Mexico."

"Forget her," Jaffick said at once. "Plenty of women in Mexico. You take care of her just like you do Stanbuck. All I want to hear from you when you get back is that there's nobody running around in here that's alive to talk."

Chapter 19

STANBUCK LIFTED HIS FINGER to his lips, cautioning Marissa to be silent, to remain where she was. He dismounted, working his way silently around the upthrust of rock. Removing Hazen's broad-brimmed hat, he peered through the brush toward the edge of the arroyo.

The two outlaws were there. Turley Jaffick had swung about and already was riding back into the valley. Bill and the other outlaw, partially visible, were staring off into the brakes. Stanbuck considered the advisability of drawing his guns, broaching them then and there. Since it was some distance to where they paused and he could get no clear, unimpaired look at them, he decided against it. Besides, it would take time, more than he could afford to spare. The memory of the two outlaws riding for Petticoat Ridge with the blasting powder, and what it unquestionably meant for those trapped there, prodded him with relentless urgency.

"Which way you reckon they went, Bill?"

"Saw the girl cut down right about here. Most likely he joined her somewheres close and they then lit out east, toward the fort. That's where they'll be wantin' to go."

"Could've holed up. Might be smart for us to do the same thing, just sort of set tight until we hear or see somethin'."

"No time for that," Bill answered. "Turley'll be lookin' for us back. Up to us to roust them out, if they've holed up."

"Ain't so sure Turley gives a dang whether we come back or not."

There was a long silence. Then, "Now, what you meanin' by that, Curry?"

"I ain't so sure but what he'd just as soon see us all layin' out there, buzzard meat. Don't bother him none when one of us gets it. You hear him say one word about bein' sorry for Keno or Jack? Or anybody else? It sure don't mean nothin' to him when a man gets a bullet in his brisket."

"War does that to a man, I reckon. Makes him sort of used to dyin'."

Stanbuck waited out the dragging moments, conscious of the critical passage of time. Sweat stood out on his forehead in great beads. *Why don't they move on?*

"Come on, let's get started."

"Which way?"

"Could split up," Bill suggested.

Curry said, "That ain't smart at all! That there Stanbuck is mighty handy with a gun. He plugged old Keno plumb center. And Jack Hazen was good with an iron, too. Nope, I figure best thing is to stick together. Four eyes is better'n two. Besides, we can cover more ground. If they're hidin' out, we'll have a better chance of flushin' them up."

"All right with me," Bill said. "Let's start."

Stanbuck waited, listening for more words. He heard nothing and he decided that the pair, at last, must have ridden on. A minute later he saw them break down into the arroyo, a hundred yards or so below where he stood, and head toward the east. He took a deep breath of relief, turned and hurried back to where Marissa waited.

She had dismounted when he arrived and was standing near the end of the rocks. She looked up, unsmiling, as he halted before her. She was striving to mask the hurt lying deep in her eyes. Having no knowledge of his reasons for rejecting her, she could not entirely cover it over. He looked away, unable to face her directly.

"They've gone. I've got to get to the Ridge." His glance came around to her then. "I know you're all in. Maybe it would be better if you waited here. If you stay hidden in the brush, they won't find you now."

She ignored his suggestion. "You think there's still a chance we can get there in time?"

He said, "I've—we've got to! We can't let those people up there be murdered. Have you heard any explosions coming from that direction?"

She said, "No, why?"

He reached for the reins of her horse and drew her mount in. "There's no time to talk," he said, helping her to the saddle, "but those black cans Jaffick's men had with them were blasting powder. I've got an idea they plan to use it on the Ridge."

She shivered visibly. But she said nothing. She took up the reins and they moved off into the withering heat, their horses traveling at no more than a fast walk in the loose sand. The sun had reached its overhead peak and now began its slow descent toward the western horizon. Thirst was making its need felt upon Stanbuck and the girl, as was hunger. But weariness was more apparent. Yet she said nothing, voiced no complaint, and Stanbuck's heart went out to her. For her sake he hoped it would soon be over with. He did not see how she could stand much more.

Down in the depths of the brake, the heat was intense, more so than on the higher plains of the valley. No breath of air stirred, no breeze, however faint, slipped in from the distant green hills and slopes. It was like being trapped in a gigantic cauldron, with hell's own fires banked above, below, and all about them.

They halted two hours later near an oversize juniper which offered a filigreed smattering of shade. They could not afford the time, Stanbuck knew, but the horses, in such heat, must have rest. They dismounted, sharing the small area with the hot, tired bays which stood, heads down, badly in need of water and relief from the driving sun.

Stanbuck, wary and taking no chances, stationed himself in the tree, selecting a fork that raised him slightly above

112'

ground level and afforded him a fair view of their back trail. He was exposed to the sunlight in such position but he ignored the discomfort. He trusted little in the good fortune that had sent the two outlaws, Bill and Curry, into opposite direction. Soon they would become convinced of their error and turn back. He could not allow Marissa and himself to be taken unaware at this late moment.

"Dave, could there have been an explosion and we didn't hear it?" she asked, after a time.

"Possible," he said, soberly. "Could have happened while all that shooting was going on. Things were pretty wild there for a few minutes."

She made no comment on that but remained silent, occupied with her own thoughts.

"There's still a good chance," he said, hoping to cheer her some, but she only shook her head.

They waited out ten minutes in the breathlessly hot shade of the juniper and then rode on. Marissa was ahead, Stanbuck electing to bring up the rear in the interests of safety. They came finally to the end of the brake and from that point on could see the foot of Mangus Mountain. The area fronting the trail's entrance was too distant to be definite in the wavering heat haze but he could see no horses there. Marissa noted this also and turned to him, her dark eyes filled with dread and anxiety. Had the outlaws completed their job and gone?

"Don't worry about that too much," he said. "Could be they've put their horses in the brush, out of the sun. Or maybe they couldn't round them up, after we drove them off."

In his own mind he would have preferred to see signs of the animals. It would have been proof positive that the outlaws were still there and would have heightened the possibility that Tom Kinter and the others still held out on the Ridge. He did not close his thoughts one way or another; it was still too soon to tell.

Shortly after that they topped out a low knoll and Stanbuck halted long enough to examine the land behind them for a final time. There was nothing to be seen but the seething landscape lying beneath the pitiless sun. He could find no indications that Bill and Curry were anywhere within the immediate country. But Dave Stanbuck would not permit himself to accept that. The blazing heat played tricks on a man's eyes. The outlaws were out there, somewhere; he just couldn't see them.

He swung wide as they drew near the mountain, dropping off to their left in order that they might approach from the blind side. They worked in from the south, making their way through a thick cover of brush that masked their movements completely. They came onto a small spring and there were compelled to pause, unable to restrain the near frantic horses. Allowing them a few swallows and ignoring their own needs, they continued on.

The bays were not so nervous after that and moved at a quiet walk. They came to a dense stand of briar and there Stanbuck halted. It would be dangerous to proceed further on horse. They were just below the entrance to the trail, he judged. They dismounted and tethered the horses.

In the deep quiet of the afternoon, they made their way through the brush and rock. Stanbuck, gun in hand, ready for any eventuality, walked a step ahead of the girl. Suddenly they broke into a clearing. Tom Kinter's carriage, minus its horses, stood in the center. He pulled up short, Marissa at his elbow.

"What does it mean—" she began.

He shook his head and cautioned her to silence. He pointed off to their right. A hundred yards distant, where the open plains of the valley began, a half-dozen men were gathered. Beyond them several more could be seen as they worked at rounding up their scattered horses.

Chapter 20

HOPE LIFTED WITHIN HIM. Perhaps the outlaws had not yet begun their assault on Petticoat Ridge and all was still well with Charlie Pierce and Tom Kinter and his party. There was one way to be certain. He dropped to a crouch, motioning for Marissa to do likewise. Keeping low, they moved across the clearing and drew nearer to the trail's opening. Lifting his head cautiously, Stanbuck peered through the brush. A lone guard stood at the entrance.

He felt a great wave of relief sweep through him. The outlaws had not carried out their plans for the Ridge yet, otherwise there would be no need for the sentry. Apparently they had deemed it wise to first recover their scattered horses and for that purpose they had appropriated the span that had been hitched to Tom Kinter's carriage and had drafted the two outlaws Turley Jaffick had dispatched later.

Stanbuck turned and smiled at Marissa. "Looks like we're in time," he said, and watched her eyes go soft with thankfulness.

He swung his attention back to the outlaws. They had recaptured several of the horses, about half the total; four men were engaged in running down, roping and bringing in the others. As he watched them, a plan quickly took shape in his mind. But he would have to act immediately. The outlaw's attention would not be drawn to that different point for much longer. Indeed, those who had recovered their mounts might decide to return to the trail at any moment. Only idle interest was holding them where they were.

He came about and touched Marissa lightly on the arm. Still keeping down, they worked their way toward the mouth of the trail that led up the mountain—in the direction of the lone sentry.

"We move fast enough, maybe we can get Kinter and the rest off the Ridge before Jaffick's bunch gets back," he explained. "Be touch-and-go for a spell but it's our only chance. There's a dozen of them. They hit us all at one time, we'll never be able to stand them off."

"What do we do?" she asked, without hesitation.

"Go up the trail, bring your uncle and the others back down. Get them off the Ridge and away from here before Jaffick's bunch realizes what's happened."

"The guard—"

He nodded. "That's the first problem. Stay close to me."

They crept in nearer to the sentry, moving now on hands and knees. Staying to the thick brush, progressing with extreme caution so as to rattle no dry branches, displace no loose gravel, they crawled to within a scant ten feet of the man. Then only open ground separated them from the outlaw. He stood, turned partly away, watching the activities at the edge of the valley. He wore a pistol at his hip and a rifle was cradled in his arms.

Stanbuck studied the area about the man. It would be difficult, practically impossible in fact, to approach him unseen. There was no sheltering brush through which he could work his way, no rocks behind which he might hide. His one chance was to rush the man, overpower him before he knew what was happening. That would be dangerous, Stanbuck realized. Not so much for himself, but in the resulting struggle the outlaw might cry out or his rifle might accidently discharge, either of which would bring the remaining guerrillas down upon them immediately.

He glanced toward the valley. Another horse had been captured. Only three were yet free. Time was moving by swiftly. As it were, they would be cutting it perilously thin.

Marissa understood the problem. With motions she suggested a plan; she would drop back, present herself to the guard from an opposite point. Stanbuck, at that moment, could then strike from behind. He considered the idea for a bit, reluctant to allow her to expose herself in such a way. But there was no great danger, he saw. He would be close at hand at all times.

He nodded his agreement. "Keep as much out of sight of the others as you can," he whispered. "If one of them just happens to look around and sees either one of us, we're in trouble."

She smiled, indicated she understood and crawled off through the scrub oak and other low growth. Stanbuck immediately wormed his way in closer to the guard, seeking the nearest possible position from which to act, once Marissa showed herself.

He lay quietly in the brush, still a good ten feet from the sentry, and rode out the hot, tense moments. He could no longer see the men as they worked with the horses, since the ragged weeds were above his head and he dared not risk rising to his knees. He could hear their shouts, however, their laughing and jeering as a thrown loop dropped short of its mark or a rider fell or one of the elusive, stubborn horses slipped through a trap that was thought to be a certainty.

He saw the shoulders of the guard stiffen abruptly. Some-

116

thing had caught his attention. Stanbuck drew his legs up beneath him, preparing to spring. The sentry remained tense for a few moments, then relaxed.

Marissa's voice said: "My horse threw me. I wonder if you could lend me——"

Stanbuck launched himself from the brush in a long, silent arc. This was the big risk, he well knew. If one of the outlaws at the edge of the valley happened to be looking in their direction at that precise moment, his plan was a failure.

The guard had lowered his rifle, was in the act of leaning it against a nearby rocky ledge when Stanbuck's full weight struck him from behind. The impact of collision drove him solidly into the unyielding surface of the wall. Breath exploded from his crushed lungs in a gusty whistle. His head rapped the stone sharply and he collapsed beneath Stanbuck without a sound.

Stanbuck pulled himself away quickly. He seized the outlaw by the hair and peered into his face closely. He was out cold and likely would remain so for some time.

"Up the trail!" he said to Marissa. "Better sing out so th will know who you are."

Marissa hurried to the opening, then paused. "What about you?"

"I'll be right behind you. First got to make this guard look like he's still on the job."

He pulled the outlaw about to a sitting position and propped him against the rock with his rifle. His head persisted in dropping forward but there was no help for that. At a distance he would appear to be carrying out his assigned duties as a sentry and that was all Stanbuck could wish for.

He wheeled then and ducked into the brushy opening of the pathway. Ahead and above he could hear Marissa climbing rapidly, could hear her calling to Tom Kinter and, after a few moments, caught the rancher's reply. He reached the top almost at the same time as she. They pulled themselves onto the ledge, both breathing heavily. Stanbuck, on his knees, crawled to the rim. He flung a glance toward the valley. The outlaws were almost finished.

He drew back, facing Kinter and Ollie Dennis. "No time to spare," he said in clipped words, "if we're going to get off here alive. They'll be coming in a few minutes."

He handed one of his pistols to Kinter. "You go ahead. Take

Marissa and your wife." He swiveled his attention to Ollie. "You take Mrs. McCarey. I'll bring Pierce. Everybody fast and quiet now!"

Kinter was already hurrying to the mouth of the trail, urging his wife to follow. Mattie Kinter held back, her glance on her wounded sister. When she saw Ollie lift the stricken woman in his arms, she turned and ran to where her husband and Marissa waited.

Stanbuck kneeled beside Pierce. The old puncher was dozing. His eyes came open as Stanbuck gathered up his slight body. He grinned weakly.

"You made it, eh?"

"Maybe," Dave replied, grimly. "We're still not out of the woods yet."

Ollie was already on the trail, slipping and sliding as he fought to maintain his footing on the steep grade. Further along, Stanbuck could see Marissa. Kinter and his wife were ahead of her, out of sight beyond the first sharp turn. He dropped into the passageway, Pierce moaning faintly from the pain the solid jar evoked.

They descended as rapidly as possible, both Stanbuck and Ollie Dennis, now red-eyed and cold sober and anxious to please, taking considerable punishment as they sought to prevent their suffering charges from incurring more pain and injury.

Marissa had halted the others at the foot of the trail and was awaiting Stanbuck. The unconscious guard had slipped sideways, resting now at a peculiar, drunken angle, head against the rock. Stanbuck threw a hurried look at the girl.

"They still there?"

She nodded. "Caught the last horse. Think they're about ready to start back."

"We'll make a run for it," he said. "Head for the carriage. You give the word when it's clear, Marissa."

The girl turned her attention again to the outlaws. She watched them for a moment and then, evidently choosing the instant when there was no possibility of any of the men seeing them, she said, "Now!"

They broke from the brushy shelter of the trail and raced for the cover of the oak shrubbery. It took only brief seconds but to Dave Stanbuck it seemed like endless minutes before they reached the shelter and plunged into its depth. He did not permit them to halt then, although the weight of Pierce in his arms had sucked him dry of breath during the short sprint and one glance at Ollie told him he was no better off.

"Get to your rig," he said. "They won't be long in finding out what's happened."

"There's no horses," Tom Kinter said. "They took mine when they went after their own. Carriage won't be much use to us—"

"We've got two horses," Stanbuck said. "There's no harness. We'll have to rig up something with ropes."

They reached the vehicle and placed the two injured members of the party on the seats, along with Mattie Kinter whose job was to keep them as comfortable as possible and prevent their falling out.

They did not wait to bring the horses but put their strength to the carriage and rolled it to where the two bays were tethered. Stanbuck and Kinter immediately set about rigging up an improvised harness with rope that would enable the horses to draw the vehicle. It was a crude arrangement and there were no reins for the driver, which necessitated that the team be led. But they could move out and that was all Dave Stanbuck hoped for.

"Got to get as far away from here as possible," he said. "Head straight on, swing around the brakes, there's a small grove there. You can hide in it until dark. Ollie," he added, picking up an empty canteen which lay on the floor of the rig. "Fill this at that spring, just on ahead. Ought to make everybody feel a little better."

Marissa was watching him, a frown on her face. "What are you going to do?"

"Hang along behind, give you a chance to reach that grove. That bunch with the horses aren't the only ones we've got to watch for. There's Curry and Bill—"

"No need to look for us, mister," Curry's drawling voice cut in from the edge of the clearing. "We done found you instead."

Stanbuck saw the two ride further into the open, their eyes upon him. From the tail of his eye, he saw Tom Kinter, unnoticed by the two outlaws, whirl about. The hush of the afternoon erupted with gunfire, two rapid shots. Curry and Bill stiffened in their saddles, doubled forward and fell heavily.

119

Stanbuck had tried to cry out, to stay the rancher, but he was too slow. The reports would now bring the remainder of the outlaws on the run—but it was too late to regret that now.

"In the carriage, quick!" he shouted. "Ollie, see if you can get that team going."

"I can sure do that!" the cowboy replied and vaulted onto one of the bays. He drove his heels into the animal's flanks and set it lunging forward in the rope traces. The other horse shied, sought to pull away but Ollie caught at its bridle and yanked it into line.

Stanbuck wheeled. Marissa was not in the carriage. "Go with the others!" he ordered. "Hurry!"

She shook her head, then ran to where the horses of the two dead outlaws, Curry and Bill, waited. She gathered in the reins, leading the animals back to him. "I'll stay with you," she stated in a firm voice.

They swung to the saddle. He rode in close to her. Seizing the bridle of her mount, he pulled it around to face the disappearing carriage.

"You go with them!" he repeated his command and, reaching back, slapped the horse soundly on the rump.

The startled animal leaped forward and set out after the rig. Stanbuck whirled about, facing the direction of the trail. It was his job now to draw the outlaws off and give Tom Kinter and the others time to escape.

Chapter 21

THEY WERE NOT LONG IN COMING.

They rode in easily, quietly. Their guns were drawn and ready. They emerged from the deep shadows of the brush like silent, vengeful phantoms, saw the crumpled figures of Curry and Bill lying dead on the forest floor, and halted.

"That's what them two shots was," one of them said, after a time.

Stanbuck braced himself in the saddle. He had already chosen his course of flight; a short clearing no wider than the length of a buckboard in which he would expose himself for a brief moment, and then a narrow pathway through the dense brush down which he would flee. They would be able to hear but there would be little opportunity for them to see him.

"Over here!" he suddenly yelled and drove his heels into the flanks of his mount.

The horse bolted across the opening and plunged into the thick shrubbery. A spatter of gunfire ripped through the quiet and Stanbuck heard the business-like *clip-clip* of bullets cutting through the brush. But the outlaws were shooting blind, far to his right.

He heard them get underway behind him. Keeping low over the saddle, he pointed the buckskin for the brakes, the safest area he could think of that was nearby. They raced on through the brush and trees, the pursuing outlaws setting up a steady drumming sound as they came on fast and hard.

They came to the end of the brush and reached the lower, rougher area of the badlands. He sent the buckskin off the bank in a long jump. The little horse stumbled and went to his knees. He came up quickly and rushed on, shaking his head violently, the whites of his eyes showing plain. They ducked behind a tall stand of osage orange, swerved sharp right into a deep cluster of tamarack and halted.

"Some of you get down in there!" a voice behind Stanbuck shouted. "Rest of you stay up here with me. Watch close, now! Don't override him."

Stanbuck heard the grunt of several horses as they came down onto the floor of the wash, caught the squeak of leather as the riders fought to hold their seats. He held the buckskin in close, hoping he would make no sound, waiting out the time it would take the outlaws to draw abreast. He was too far to the side to hear them go by but he judged by the passage of time and, finally, when he was convinced they were beyond him, he cut the buckskin around in a wide circle and came back to a point near where he had first entered the brake.

There he dismounted well within another screening growth of tamarack. He would remain there until he was certain Jaffick's men were deep in the rough country before he returned to the grove, to the plains and—

His thoughts came to a full stop. *Before he did what?* Marissa and Tom Kinter and Pierce and the others were safe now. That was over and done with. His responsibility to them had ended. What came next? Turley Jaffick. Now he was free to settle with him. Now he could set forth and hunt the man down, take his revenge. The old bitterness and hatred awakened within him, beginning to boil anew. There was nothing to hinder him now, no one to stand in his way.

The faint footfall of an approaching horse drew him up sharply. He moved away from the buckskin, instinctively drawing his gun. The rider was walking his mount slowly. Another of Jaffick's outlaws, most likely. It could be the guard he had knocked out at the mouth of the trail, unable to join his companions at the start but now recovered and taking up the chase.

Stanbuck glanced down to the weapon in his hand. It would be wiser not to shoot, to use it as a club. He doubted if the rest of Jaffick's men were far enough away yet to not hear a gunshot. He tried to guess where the rider would first make an appearance and set himself to act accordingly.

It was Marissa.

He stepped from the concealing tamarack. She saw him and a glad cry escaped her lips. She leaped from the saddle, rushed to him and threw her arms about him.

"Oh, Dave! I was afraid something had happened to you! I heard all that shooting—"

He held her close. "You shouldn't have come back. You should have stayed with the others, where you will be safe."

"I don't want to be safe—unless it's with you!" she cried. "Can't you understand that, Dave? I don't want it any other way."

He shook his head, pushing her gently away. "It's no good, Marissa."

"Why? I know you love me, just as I love you. It's something you can't hide. Don't you want me?"

"Want you?" he echoed in a despairing voice. "Almost from the first moment I saw you, I've wanted you. And I've fought against it because I know it's not right."

"Why would you do—"

"Because I'm on borrowed time. I've got a bullet in my body that can kill me any minute. Fact is, the doctors once told me I should be dead—only I'm not. But there's no telling when it will happen. That's why I can't let the way I feel about you get out of hand. There's no future in it, for either of us. I've got nothing to offer you, not even a half a life."

For a long moment she stared at him and then suddenly she was back in his arm. "Oh, men are such blind fools! You think that makes any difference? It doesn't count at all. All that matters is that we love each other, that we can be together, even if it is for just a little while."

"For a little while," he echoed. "That's what it would be, Marissa; only a little while."

"For five minutes—five years, or for all time; it doesn't make any difference."

He took her by the shoulders, his face solemn. "Then I promise this, Marissa, however long it is, you'll not regret a minute of it. We'll cram a full lifetime into what days we have left together."

"Days will never count," she said softly, "as long as we are with each other."

He took up the reins of her horse and they walked back into the tamarack where the buckskin stood. "Best we hide out here for a spell," he said, "then I've got one more job to do.

That done, we can start thinking and planning for the future."

"One more job?" she repeated.

"One more," he said. "Turley Jaffick."

She stared at him wonderingly. "You mean you want to hunt him down—kill him?"

He nodded. "It's something I have to do."

"But why? Just because of what he's done here in the valley? The law, or the army, will make him answer for that."

"That's only part of it," he said, and told her then of Mississippi and Grant and of what had happened to him. He did not speak of the tortuous hours and days and months that followed but she sensed their existence and her eyes were soft when she answered.

"I can understand many things about you now, Dave. The reasons you were the sort of man you were. But you must remember that is all in the past, that a new life has opened up for you now. Jaffick and what he did no longer matter. That has all been wiped clean, like a schoolboy's slate."

"Only Jaffick dead will wipe out the past," he replied.

"Your killing him will just deepen the hate and bitterness in you!" she cried, placing both her hands on his chest. "You must realize that! It will always be in your mind—what he did to you and how you revenged yourself. It will be a dark memory, like a shadow that never goes away."

He shook his head wearily. "I hoped you would understand. There are some things a man must do if he is to live at peace with himself."

"You'll find no peace in murder," she said quickly, "no matter what the reason for it. And as for my understanding, I know only that you are overlooking the most important part of it all. You are free of the past if only you would accept it. You have won despite Turley Jaffick and what he did to you."

He lifted his glance to her, not grasping her words or her reasoning.

"Once he took from you all the things you thought counted; your place in the army, your friends. He made you an outcast, sent you into disgrace. Luck or fate or whatever you want to call it sent him into this valley and you met again. And you've beaten him for you've made new friends, cut a place and a new life in this country for yourself. The very man you felt ruined you has remade you, given you a second chance. And you want to throw it all away by reopening the past!"

For a long time he stared out beyond her into the wild and broken world of the desolate brake. He shook his head slowly, wearily. "The past was never closed, Marissa," he said, at length, "only forgotten for awhile. We had better go. I'll ride back to the carriage with you."

She moved away from him, to her horse, saying nothing. When she was in the saddle and he also was mounted, she said, "I know the way. No need for you to come."

Nevertheless, he followed her out of the wash, up onto the high ground. When they reached that level, she stopped, turning to face him. She started to speak. Her words cut off as she looked beyond him toward the valley. He turned quickly, following her gaze.

A squad of soldiers approached them at a steady gallop.

Chapter 22

THERE WAS NO POINT IN FLIGHT. They remained where they were, half in, half out of a clump of oak brush. Stanbuck watched the cavalrymen narrowly and after a time he saw the officer in the lead was not Roebling but a young lieutenant. The rotund features of the sergeant were familiar; Bayes.

The half-dozen riders drew up before them and halted. The lieutenant saluted, touching the brim of his hat to Marissa.

"Afternoon. I'm Lieutenant Brady. From Fort Quinton. You are Mr. Stanbuck and Miss McCarey, I take it?"

Stanbuck said, "You take it right, Lieutenant. What's on your mind?"

"A man you know right well, I understand from the sergeant here. Turley Jaffick. By any chance have you seen him —in the last two or three hours, I mean?"

Stanbuck shook his head. "We haven't seen him. I supposed he would be at the Fort at this time, completing the sale of the cattle he stole."

"He was there, all right," Brady said, "only he slipped through our fingers. Are the people he had trapped on that mountain there safe?"

Stanbuck shifted his weight in the saddle. Something had taken place he knew nothing of. "They are," he said. "What's this all about, Lieutenant?"

Brady grinned. "Guess you wouldn't know, at that. The colonel got suspicious of Roebling and the deal he was pushing through. All that cash money and the like. Then there were a few things Sergeant Bayes here said when we questioned him. It all added up to quite a mess. The colonel had Roebling placed under arrest and we set up a trap for Jaffick and his bunch when they brought in that herd of cattle."

"Only Jaffick got away," Stanbuck finished, his voice bitter. All the time worn hatred washed through him once again; Jaffick—the Butcher—the man with the charmed life. He always got away. He never was forced to pay.

"Picked up some of his bunch down the way a piece, sent them on with the rest of the platoon to the Fort. Jaffick wasn't with them. We figure he's out here somewhere, however. We know he rode this way."

The army had bungled again. Just as it had done once before when he was involved. And it would happen again if they were fortunate enough to stumble upon Jaffick. It was useless to leave it to them, as he had already concluded. If anyone was to bring Turley Jaffick to account, it was he.

"Doubt if you'll find him around here," he said then. "You might have a look at the mountain. He could take it in mind to hole up on the Ridge."

Lieutenant Brady saluted again. "Obliged, Mr. Stanbuck. We'll do that. If you see any signs of him, I'd appreciate your sending for us. Good day, ma'am."

They wheeled off in a churning of dust and sound. Dave and Marissa watched them in silence until they rounded an outthrust of brush and rock. She turned to him.

"Why did you send them to the mountain. He wouldn't go there. He knows that once on it there's no way off."

He nodded. "I wanted them out of the way. You see, now it is up to me. If Jaffick's to be brought down, it will have to be me that does it."

Her face was stilled. "That's not really so. It's just that you are making yourself believe it's true. The army will take care of Jaffick, if you will only let them. It's not necessary that you risk your life—and our future—in taking it upon yourself."

He said, "Talk like this gets us nowhere, Marissa. Go back to the Kinters. When its over and done with I'll come to you—"

"If you do come back," she broke in, quietly.

"—And we can pick up where we left off, or end it right there," he finished, ignoring her interruption. "You will have had time to think matters over."

"I need no time to think over and realize what killing Turley Jaffick will do to you," she said. "But if there is no stopping you, no making you see it, then I've done all I could. Good-bye, Dave."

"Yeh—good-bye, Dave," the sardonic voice of Jaffick sliced through the hush, coming from the tamaracks in the brake. He had slipped in unheard, unseen.

A wild surge of rage flashed through Dave Stanbuck. He reacted instantly. He threw himself forward onto the off side of his horse, drawing as he moved. He fired as he came under the animal's neck, twice, in rapid succession. He saw Jaffick's body jolt from the second bullet; saw the red flood of stain that appeared at his left shoulder. He struck the ground, ready for a third, more accurate shot at the outlaw. Jaffick, badly off balance, was striving to bring his pistol around and level it. His face was blanched, torn with a terrible fear; his eyes spread wide as they looked upon the certainty of death. He was, at the moment, helpless. Stanbuck had only to press the trigger of his weapon and it would be finished.

Then the memory of that cold, wet morning in the swamps of Mississippi would be erased, the long, cruel hours that had followed would be avenged, and the old score would be settled. He stared at Turley Jaffick, at the red-maned, evil countenance of the man they called the Butcher. The fury within him began to subside. A feeling of sickness, of revul-

127

sion swept suddenly through him. Marissa was right. Nothing could ever completely wipe out that which had gone before; only time and friends and happiness could heal over it, thrust it deep into the background. Killing would serve only to keep it alive.

"Drop that gun," he said then, and moved away from his horse.

Jaffick took a step forward, staggering a bit. "Kill me!" he cried. "You best finish the job or I'll live to come—"

"You'll live just long enough to hang," Stanbuck said coldly. "Now, drop that pistol or do I put a bullet in your other arm?"

Jaffick glared at him for a moment. The weapon slipped from his fingers and fell to the ground. "I'll never hang," he muttered. "I'm a soldier—a firing squad, maybe, but I won't hang."

"You're an outlaw," Stanbuck replied, "and you'll be treated as such. Maybe you were a soldier once but, like a lot of other things, that, too, is in the past. Now you're just an outlaw and you'll die like one, at the end of a rope. The army, for us both, is a long way behind us."

He moved forward to where Jaffick's pistol lay and kicked it far off into the brush. He turned then to the girl. She was smiling and her pride shone through her eyes.

"Marissa, ride for that lieutenant. Tell him we've got his man."